Anthony Hope

The God in the Car

Anthony Hope

The God in the Car

ISBN/EAN: 9783337031404

Printed in Europe, USA, Canada, Australia, Japan

Cover: Foto ©Andreas Hilbeck / pixelio.de

More available books at **www.hansebooks.com**

THE GOD IN THE CAR

A NOVEL

BY

ANTHONY HOPE

AUTHOR OF THE PRISONER OF ZENDA, ETC.

NEW YORK
D. APPLETON AND COMPANY
1894

CONTENTS.

THE GOD IN THE CAR.

CHAPTER I.

AN INSOLENT MEMORY.

"I'm so blind," said Miss Ferrars plaintively. "Where are my glasses?"

"What do you want to see?" asked Lord Seming-ham.

"The man in the corner, talking to Mr. Loring."

"Oh, you won't know him even with the glasses. He's the sort of man you must be introduced to three times before there's any chance of a permanent impression."

"You seem to recognise him."

"I know him in business. We are, or rather are going to be, fellow-directors of a company."

"Oh, then I shall see you in the dock together some day."

"What touching faith in the public prosecutor! Does nothing shake your optimism?"

"Perhaps your witticisms."

"Peace, peace!"

"Well, who is he?"

"He was once," observed Lord Semingham, as though stating a curious fact, "in a Government. His name is Foster Belford, and he is still asked to the State Concerts."

"I knew I knew him! Why, Harry Dennison thinks great things of him!"

"It is possible."

"And he, not to be behindhand in politeness, thinks greater of Maggie Dennison."

"His task is the easier."

"And you and he are going to have the effrontery to ask shareholders to trust their money to you?"

"Oh, it isn't us; it's Ruston."

"Mr. Ruston? I've heard of him."

"You very rarely admit that about anybody."

"Moreover, I've met him."

"He's quite coming to the front, of late, I know."

"Is there any positive harm in being in the fashion? I like now and then to talk to the people one is obliged to talk about."

"Go on," said Lord Semingham, urbanely.

"But, my dear Lord Semingham——"

"Hush! Keep the truth from me, like a kind woman. Ah! here comes Tom Loring—— How are you, Loring? Where's Dennison?"

" At the House.   I ought to be there, too."

" Why, of course.   The place of a private secretary is by the side of——"

" His chief's wife.   We all know that," interposed Adela Ferrars.

" When you grow old, you'll be sorry for all the wicked things you've said," observed Loring.

" Well, there'll be nothing else to do.   Where are you going, Lord Semingham ? "

" Home."

" Why ? "

" Because I've done my duty.   Oh, but here's Dennison, and I want a word with him."

Lord Semingham passed on, leaving the other two together.

" Has Harry Dennison been speaking to-day ? " asked Miss Ferrars.

" Well, he had something prepared."

" He had something ! You know you write them." Mr. Loring frowned.

" Yes, and I know we aren't allowed to say so," pursued Adela.

" It's neither just nor kind to Dennison."

Miss Ferrars looked at him, her brows slightly raised.

" And you are both just and kind, really," he added.

" And you, Mr. Loring, are a wonderful man.

You're not ashamed to be serious! Oh, yes, I've annoyed—you're quite right. I was—whatever I was—on the ninth of last March, and I think I'm too old to be lectured."

Tom Loring laughed, and, an instant later, Adela followed suit.

"I suppose it was horrid of me," she said. "Can't we turn it round and consider it as a compliment to you?"

Tom looked doubtful, but, before he could answer, Adela cried:

"Oh, here's Evan Haselden, and—yes—it's Mr. Ruston with him?"

As the two men entered, Mrs. Dennison rose from her chair. She was a tall woman; her years fell one or two short of thirty. She was not a beauty, but her broad brow and expressive features, joined to a certain subdued dignity of manner and much grace of movement, made her conspicuous among the women in her drawing-room. Young Evan Haselden seemed to appreciate her, for he bowed his glossy curly head, and shook hands in a way that almost turned the greeting into a deferentially distant caress. Mrs. Dennison acknowledged his hinted homage with a bright smile, and turned to Ruston.

"At last!" she said, with another smile. "The first time after—how many years?"

"Eight, I believe," he answered.

"Oh, you're terribly definite. And what have you been doing with yourself?"

He shrugged his square shoulders, and she did not press her question, but let her eyes wander over him.

"Well?" he asked.

"Oh—improved. And I?"

Suddenly Ruston laughed.

"Last time we met," he said, "you swore you'd never speak to me again."

"I'd quite forgotten my fearful threat."

He looked straight in her face for a moment, as he asked—

"And the cause of it?"

Mrs. Dennison coloured.

"Yes, quite," she answered; and conscious that her words carried no conviction to him, she added hastily, "Go and speak to Harry. There he is."

Ruston obeyed her, and being left for a moment alone, she sat down on the chair placed ready near the door for her short intervals of rest. There was a slight pucker on her brow. The sight of Ruston and his question stirred in her thoughts, which were never long dormant, and which his coming woke into sudden activity. She had not anticipated that he would venture to recall to her that incident—at least, not at once—in the first instant of meeting, at such a time and such a place. But as he had, she found herself yielding to the reminiscence he induced. Forgotten

the cause of her anger with him? For the first two
or three years of her married life, she would have
answered, "Yes, I have forgotten it." Then had
come a period when now and again it recurred to her,
not for his sake or its own, but as a summary of her
stifled feeling; and during that period she had resolutely struggled not to remember it. Of late that
struggle had ceased, and the thing lay a perpetual
background to her thoughts: when there was nothing
else to think about, when the stage of her mind was
empty of moving figures, it snatched at the chance
of prominence, and thus became a recurrent consciousness from which her interests and her occupa-
tions could not permanently rescue her. For example, here she was thinking of it in the very midst of
her party. Yet this persistence of memory seemed
impertinent, unreasonable, almost insolent. For, as
she told herself, finding it necessary to tell herself
more and more often, her husband was still all that
he had been when he had won her heart—good-look-
ing, good-tempered, infinitely kind and devoted.
When she married she had triumphed confidently in
these qualities; and the unanimous cry of surprised
congratulations at the match she was making had
confirmed her own joy and exultation in it. It had
been a great match; and yet, beyond all question, also
a love match.

But now the chorus of wondering applause was

forgotten, and there remained only the one voice which had been raised to break the harmony of approbation—a voice that nobody, herself least of all, had listened to then. How should it be listened to? It came from a nobody—a young man of no account, whose opinion none cared to ask; whose judgment, had it been worth anything in itself, lay under suspicion of being biassed by jealousy. Willie Ruston had never declared himself her suitor; yet (she clung hard to this) he would not have said what he did had not the chagrin of a defeated rival inspired him; and a defeated rival, as everybody knows, will say anything. Certainly she had been right not to listen, and was wrong to remember. To this she had often made up her mind, and to this she returned now as she sat watching her husband and Willie Ruston, forgetful of all the chattering crowd beside.

As to what it was she resolved not to remember, and did remember, it was just one sentence—his only comment on the news of her engagement, his only hint of any opinion or feeling about it. It was short, sharp, decisive, and, as his judgments were, even in the days when he, alone of all the world, held them of any moment, absolutely confident; it was also, she had felt on hearing it, utterly untrue, unjust, and ungenerous. It had rung out like a pistol-shot, "Maggie, you're marrying a fool," and then a snap of tight-fitting lips, a glance of scornful eyes, and a quick, unhesitating stride away that hardly waited for a contemptuous smile at her angry cry, "I'll never speak to you again." She had been in a fury of wrath—she had a power of wrath—that a plain, awkward, penniless, and obscure youth—one whom she sometimes disliked for his arrogance, and sometimes derided for his self-confidence—should dare to say such a thing about her Harry, whom she was so proud to love, and so proud to have won. It was indeed an insolent memory that flung the thing again and again in her teeth.

The party began to melt away. The first good-bye roused Mrs. Dennison from her enveloping reverie. Lady Valentine, from whom it came, lingered for a gush of voluble confidences about the charm of the house, and the people, and the smart little band that played softly in an alcove, and what not; her daughter stood by, learning, it is to be hoped, how it is meet to behave in society, and scanning Evan Haselden's trim figure with wary, critical glances, alert to turn aside if he should glance her way. Mrs. Dennison returned the ball of civility, and, released by several more departures, joined Adela Ferrars. Adela stood facing Haselden and Tom Loring, who were arm-in-arm. At the other end of the room Harry Dennison and Ruston were still in conversation.

"These *men*, Maggie," began Adela—and it seemed a mere caprice of pronunciation, that the word did

not shape itself into " monkeys "—" are the absurdest
creatures. They say I'm not fit to take part in poli-
tics! And why?"

Mrs. Dennison shook her head, and smiled.

" Because, if you please, I'm too emotional. Emotional, indeed! And I can't generalise! Oh, couldn't
I generalise about men!"

" Women can never say ' No,' " observed Evan
Haselden, not in the least as if he were repeating a
commonplace.

" You'll find you're wrong when you grow up,"
retorted Adela.

" I doubt that," said Mrs. Dennison, with the
kindest of smiles.

" Maggie, you spoil the boy. Isn't it enough that
he should have gone straight from the fourth form—
where, I suppose, he learnt to generalise——"

" At any rate, not to be emotional," murmured
Loring.

" Into Parliament, without having his head turned
by——"

" You'd better go, Evan," suggested Loring in a
warning tone.

" I shall go too," announced Adela.

" I'm walking your way," said Evan, who seemed
to bear no malice.

" How delightful!"

" You don't object?"

" Not the least.   I'm driving."

" A mere schoolboy score ! "

" How stupid of me ! You haven't had time to forget them."

" Oh, take her away," said Mrs. Dennison, and they disappeared in a fire of retorts, happy, or happy enough for happy people, and probably Evan drove with the lady after all.

Mrs. Dennison walked towards where her husband and Ruston sat on a sofa in talk.

" What are you two conspiring about ? " she asked.

" Ruston had something to say to me about business."

" What, already ? "

" Oh, we've met in the city, Mrs. Dennison," explained Ruston, with a confidential nod to Harry.

" And that was the object of your appearance here to-day ? I was flattering my party, it seems."

" No. I didn't expect to find your husband. I thought he would be at the House."

" Ah, Harry, how did the speech go ? "

" Oh, really pretty well, I think," answered Harry Dennison, with a contented air. " I got nearly half through before we were counted out."

A very faint smile showed on his wife's face.

" So you were counted out ? " she asked.

" Yes, or I shouldn't be here."

"You see, I am acquitted, Mrs. Dennison. Only an accident brought him here."

"An accident impossible to foresee," she acquiesced, with the slightest trace of bitterness—so slight that her husband did not notice it.

Ruston rose.

"Well, you'd better talk to Semingham about it," he remarked to Harry Dennison; "he's one of us, you know."

"Yes, I will. And I'll just get you that pamphlet of mine; you can put it in your pocket."

He ran out of the room to fetch what he promised. Mrs. Dennison, still faintly smiling, held out her hand to Ruston.

"It's been very pleasant to see you again," she said graciously. "I hope it won't be eight years before our next meeting."

"Oh, no; you see I'm floating now."

"Floating?" she repeated, with a smile of enquiry.

"Yes; on the surface. I've been in the depths till very lately, and there one meets no good society."

"Ah! You've had a struggle?"

"Yes," he answered, laughing; "you may call it a bit of a struggle."

She looked at him with grave curious eyes.

"And you are not married?" she asked abruptly.

"No, I'm glad to say."

"Why glad, Mr. Ruston? Some people like being married."

"Oh, I don't claim to be above it, Mrs. Dennison," he answered with a laugh, "but a wife would have been a great hindrance to me all these years."

There was a simple and *bona fide* air about his statement; it was not raillery; and Mrs. Dennison laughed in her turn.

"Oh, how like you!" she murmured.

Mr. Ruston, with a passing gleam of surprise at her merriment, bade her a very unemotional farewell, and left her. She sat down and waited idly for her husband's return. Presently he came in. He had caught Ruston in the hall, delivered his pamphlet, and was whistling cheerfully. He took a chair near his wife.

"Rum chap that!" he said. "But he's got a good deal of stuff in him;" and he resumed his lively tune.

The tune annoyed Mrs. Dennison. To suffer whistling without visible offence was one of her daily trials. Harry's emotions and reflections were prone to express themselves through that medium.

"I didn't do half-badly, to-day," said Harry, breaking off again. "Old Tom had got it all splendidly in shape for me—by Jove, I don't know what I should do without Tom—and I think I put it pretty well. But, of course, it's a subject that doesn't catch on with everybody."

It was the dullest subject in the world; it was also, in all likelihood, one of the most unimportant; and dull subjects are so seldom unimportant that the perversity of the combination moved Maggie Dennison to a wondering pity. She rose and came behind the chair where her husband sat. Leaning over the back, she rested her elbows on his shoulders, and lightly clasped her hands round his neck. He stopped his whistle, which had grown soft and contented, laughed, and kissed one of the encircling hands, and she, bending lower, kissed him on the forehead as he turned his face up to look at her.

"You poor dear old thing!" she said with a smile and a sigh.

CHAPTER II.

THE COINING OF A NICKNAME.

WHEN it was no later than the middle of June,
Adela Ferrars, having her reputation to maintain,
ventured to sum up the season. It was, she said, a
Ruston-cum-Violetta season. Violetta's doings and
unexampled triumphs have, perhaps luckily, no place
here; her dancing was higher and her songs more
surpassing in another dimension than those of any
performer who had hitherto won the smiles of society; and young men who are getting on in life still
talk about her. Ruston's fame was less widespread,
but his appearance was an undeniable fact of the
year. When a man, the first five years of whose adult
life have been spent on a stool in a coal merchant's
office, and the second five somewhere (an absolutely
vague somewhere) in Southern or Central Africa,
comes before the public, offering in one closed hand a
new empire, or, to avoid all exaggeration, at least a
province, asking with the other opened hand for three
million pounds, the public is bound to afford him

the tribute of some curiosity. When he enlists in his scheme men of eminence like Mr. Foster Belford, of rank like Lord Semingham, of great financial resources like Dennison Sons & Company, he becomes one whom it is expedient to bid to dinner and examine with scrutinising enquiry. He may have a bag of gold for you ; or you may enjoy the pleasure of exploding his *prestige ;* at least, you are timely and up-to-date, and none can say that your house is a den of fogies, or yourself, in the language made to express these things (for how otherwise should they get themselves expressed ?) on other than "the inner rail."

It chanced that Miss Ferrars arrived early at the Seminghams, and she talked with her host on the hearth-rug, while Lady Semingham was elaborately surveying her small but comely person in a mirror at the other end of the long room. Lord Semingham was rather short and rather stout; he hardly looked as if his ancestors had fought at Hastings—perhaps they had not, though the peerage said they had. He wore close-cut black whiskers, and the blue of his jowl witnessed a suppressed beard of great vitality. His single eye-glass reflected answering twinkles to Adela's *pince-nez,* and his mouth was puckered at the world's constant entertainment ; men said that he found his wife alone a sufficient and inexhaustible amusement.

"The Heathers are coming," he said, "and Lady Val and Marjory, and young Haselden, and Ruston."

"*Toujours* Ruston," murmured Adela.

"And one or two more. What's wrong with Ruston? There is, my dear Adela, no attitude more offensive than that of indifference to what the common herd finds interesting."

"He's a fright," said Adela. "You'd spike yourself on that bristly beard of his."

"If you happened to be near enough, you mean? —a danger my sex and our national habits render remote. Bessie!"

Lady Semingham came towards them, with one last craning look at her own back as she turned. She always left the neighbourhood of a mirror with regret.

"Well?" she asked with a patient little sigh.

"Adela is abusing your friend Ruston."

"He's not my friend, Alfred. What's the matter, Adela?"

"I don't think I like him. He's hard."

"He's got a demon, you see," said Semingham. "For that matter we all have, but his is a whopper."

"Oh, what's my demon?" cried Adela. Is not oneself always the most interesting subject?

"Yours? Cleverness; he goads you into saying things one can't see the meaning of."

"Thanks! And yours?"

"Grinning—so I grin at your things, though I don't understand 'em."

"And Bessie's?"

"Oh, forgive me. Leave us a quiet home."

"And now, Mr. Ruston's?"

"His is——"

But the door opened, and the guests, all arriving in a heap, just twenty minutes late, flooded the room and drowned the topic. Another five minutes passed, and people had begun furtively to count heads and wonder whom they were waiting for, when Evan Haselden was announced. Hot on his heels came Ruston, and the party was completed.

Mr. Otto Heather took Adela Ferrars in to dinner. Her heart sank as he offered his arm. She had been heard to call him the silliest man in Europe; on the other hand, his wife, and some half-dozen people besides, thought him the cleverest in London.

"That man," he said, swallowing his soup and nodding his head towards Ruston, "personifies all the hideous tendencies of the age—its brutality, its commercialism, its selfishness, its——"

Miss Ferrars looked across the table. Ruston was seated at Lady Semingham's left hand, and she was prattling to him in her sweet indistinct little voice. Nothing in his appearance warranted Heather's outburst, unless it were a sort of alert and almost defiant readiness, smacking of a challenge to catch him napping.

"I'm not a mediævalist myself," she observed, and prepared to endure the penalty of an *exposé* of Heather's theories. During its progress, she peered—for her near sight was no affectation—now and again at the occasion of her sufferings. She had heard a good deal about him—something from her host, something from Harry Dennison, more from the paragraphists who had scented their prey, and gathered from the four quarters of heaven (or wherever they dwelt) upon him. She knew about the coal merchant's office, the impatient flight from it, and the rush over the seas; there were stories of real naked want, where a bed and shelter bounded for the moment all a life's aspirations. She summed him up as a buccaneer modernised; and one does not expect buccaneers to be amiable, while culture in them would be an incongruity. It was, on the whole, not very surprising, she thought, that few people liked William Roger Ruston—nor that many believed in him.

"Don't you agree with me?" asked Heather.

"Not in the least," said Adela at random.

The odds that he had been saying something foolish were very large.

"I thought you were such friends!" exclaimed Heather in surprise.

" Well, to confess, I was thinking of something else. Who do you mean?"

" Why, Mrs. Dennison. I was saying that her calm queenly manner——"

" Good gracious, Mr. Heather, don't call women ' queenly.' You're like — what is it? — a ' dime novel.' "

If this comparison were meant to relieve her from the genius' conversation for the rest of dinner, it was admirably conceived. He turned his shoulder on her in undisguised dudgeon.

" And how's the great scheme ?" asked somebody of Ruston.

" We hope to get the money," he said, turning for a moment from his hostess. " And if we do that, we're all right."

" Everything's going on very well," called Semingham from the foot of the table. " They've killed a missionary."

" How dreadful ! " lisped his wife.

" Regrettable in itself, but the first step towards empire," explained Semingham with a smile.

" It's to stop things of that kind that we are going there," Mr. Belford pronounced ; the speech was evidently meant to be repeated, and to rank as authoritative.

" Of course," chuckled Semingham.

If he had been a shopman, he could not have

resisted showing his customers how the adulteration was done.

In spite of herself—for she strongly objected to being one of an admiring crowd, and liked a personal *cachet* on her emotions—Adela felt pleasure when, after dinner, Ruston came straight to her and, displacing Evan Haselden, sat down by her side. He assumed the position with a business-like air, as though he meant to stay. She often, indeed habitually, had two or three men round her, but to-night none contested Ruston's exclusive possession; she fancied that the business-like air had something to do with it. She had been taken possession of, she said to herself, with a little impatience and yet a little pleasure also.

" You know everybody here, I suppose?" he asked. His tone cast a doubt on the value of the knowledge.

" It's my tenth season," said Adela, with a laugh. " I stopped counting them once, but there comes a time when one has to begin again."

He looked at her—critically, she thought—as he said,

" The ravages of time no longer to be ignored?"

" Well, the exaggerations of friends to be checked. Yes, I suppose I know most of——"

She paused for a word.

" The gang," he suggested, leaning back and crossing his legs.

" Yes, we are a gang, and all on one chain. You're a recent captive, though."

" Yes," he assented, " it's pretty new to me. A year ago I hadn't a dress coat."

" The gods are giving you a second youth then."

" Well, I take it. I don't know that I have much to thank the gods for."

" They've been mostly against you, haven't they? However, what does that matter, if you beat them ? "

He did not disdain her compliment, but neither did he accept it. He ignored it, and Adela, who paid very few compliments, was amused and vexed.

" Perhaps," she added, " you think your victory still incomplete ? "

This gained no better attention. Mr. Ruston seemed to be following his own thoughts.

" It must be a curious thing," he remarked, " to be born to a place like Semingham's."

" And to use it—or not to use it—like Lord Semingham ? "

" Yes, I was thinking of that," he admitted.

" To be eminent requires some self-deception, doesn't it ? Without that, it would seem too absurd. I think Lord Semingham is overweighted with humour." She paused and then—to show that she was not in awe of him—she added,—" Now, I should say, you have very little."

"Very little, indeed, I should think," he agreed composedly.

"You're the only man I ever heard admit that of himself; we all say it of one another."

"I know what I have and haven't got pretty well."

Adela was beginning to be more sure that she disliked him, but the topic had its interest for her and she went on,

"Now I like to think I've got everything."

To her annoyance, the topic seemed to lose interest for him, just in proportion as it gained interest for her. In fact, Mr. Ruston did not apparently care to talk about what she liked or didn't like.

"Who's that pretty girl over there," he asked, " talking to young Haselden ? "

"Marjory Valentine," said Adela curtly.

"Oh! I think I should like to talk to her."

" "Pray, don't let me prevent you," said Adela in very distant tones.

The man seemed to have no manners.

Mr. Ruston said nothing, but gave a short laugh. Adela was not accustomed to be laughed at openly. Yet she felt defenceless; this pachydermatous animal would be impervious to the pricks of her rapier.

" You're amused ? " she asked sharply.

" Why were you in such a hurry to take offence? I didn't say I wanted to go and talk to her now."

" It sounded like it."

"Oh, well, I'm very sorry," he conceded, still smiling, and obviously thinking her very absurd.

She rose from her seat.

"Please do, though. She'll be going soon, and you mayn't get another chance."

"Well, I will then," he answered simply, accompanying the remark with a nod of approval for her sensible reminder. And he went at once.

She saw him touch Haselden on the shoulder, and make the young man present him to Marjory. Ruston sat down and Haselden drifted, aimless and forlorn, on a solitary passage along the length of the room.

Adela joined Lady Semingham.

"That's a dreadful man, Bessie," she said; "he's a regular Juggernaut."

She disturbed Lady Semingham in a moment of happiness; everybody had been provided with conversation, and the hostess could sit in peaceful silence, looking, and knowing that she looked, very dainty and pretty; she liked that much better than talking.

"Who's what, dear?" she murmured.

"That man—Mr. Ruston. I say he's a Juggernaut. If you're in the way, he just walks over you—and sometimes when you're not: for fun, I suppose."

"Alfred says he's very clever," observed Lady Semingham, in a tone that evaded any personal responsibility for the truth of the statement.

"Well, I dislike him very much," declared Adela.

"We won't have him again when you're coming, dear," promised her friend soothingly.

Adela looked at her, hesitated, opened her fan, shut it again, and smiled.

"Oh, I didn't mean that, Bessie," she said with half a laugh. "Do, please."

"But if you dislike him——"

"Why, my dear, doesn't one hate half the men one likes meeting—and all the women!"

Lady Semingham smiled amiably. She did not care to think out what that meant; it was Adela's way, just as it was her husband's way to laugh at many things that seemed to her to afford no opening for mirth. But Adela was not to escape. Semingham himself appeared suddenly at her elbow, and observed,

"That's either nonsense or a truism, you know."

"Neither," said Adela with spirit; but her defence was interrupted by Evan Haselden.

"I'm going," said he, and he looked out of temper. "I've got another place to go to. And anyhow——"

"Well?"

"I'd like to be somewhere where that chap Ruston isn't for a little while."

Adela glanced across. Ruston was still talking to Marjory Valentine.

"What can he find to say to her?" thought Adela.

"What the deuce she finds to talk about to that fellow, I can't think," pursued Evan, and he flung off to bid Lady Semingham good-night.

Adela caught her host's eye and laughed. Lord Semingham's eyes twinkled.

"It's a big province," he observed, "so there may be room for him—out there."

"I," said Adela, with an air of affected modesty, "have ventured, subject to your criticism, to dub him Juggernaut."

"H'm," said Semingham, "it's a little obvious, but not so bad for you."

CHAPTER III.

NEXT door to Mrs. Dennison's large house in Curzon Street there lived, in a small house, a friend of hers, a certain Mrs. Cormack. She was a Frenchwoman, who had been married to an Englishman, and was now his most resigned widow. She did not pretend to herself, or to anybody else, that Mr. Cormack's death had been a pure misfortune, and by virtue of her past trials—perhaps, also, of her nationality—she was keenly awake to the seamy side of matrimony. She would rhapsodise on the joys of an ideal marriage, with a skilful hint of its rarity, and condemn transgressors with a charitable reservation for insupportable miseries. She was, she said, very romantic. Tom Loring, however (whose evidence was tainted by an intense dislike of her), declared that *affaires du cœur* interested her only when one at least of the parties was lawfully bound to a third person; when both were thus trammelled, the situation was ideal. But the loves of those who were in a position to marry one

"

another, and had no particular reason for not following that legitimate path to happiness, seemed to her
(still according to Tom) dull, uninspiring—all, in fact,
that there was possible of English and stupid. She
hardly (Tom would go on, warming to his subject)
believed in them at all, and she was in the habit of regarding wedlock merely as a condition precedent to
its own violent dissolution. Whether this unhappy
mode of looking at the matter were due to her own
peculiarities, or to those of the late Mr. Cormack,
or to those of her nation, Tom did not pretend to
say; he confined himself to denouncing it freely,
and to telling Mrs. Dennison that her next-door
neighbour was in all respects a most undesirable acquaintance; at which outbursts Mrs. Dennison would
smile.

Mrs. Dennison, coming out on to the balcony to
see if her carriage were in sight down the street,
found her friend close to her elbow. Their balconies
adjoined, and friendship had led to a little gate being
substituted for the usual dwarf-wall of division. Tom
Loring erected the gate into an allegory of direful
portent. Mrs. Cormack passed through it, and laid
an affectionate grasp on Maggie Dennison's arm.

"You're starting early," she remarked.

"I'm going a long way—right up to Hampstead.
I've promised Harry to call on some people there."

"Ah! Who?"

"Their name's Carlin. He knows Mr. Carlin in business. Mr. Carlin's a friend of Mr. Ruston's."

"Oh, of Ruston's? I like that Ruston. He is interesting—inspiring."

"Is he?" said Mrs. Dennison, buttoning her glove. "You'd better marry him, Berthe."

"Marry him? No, indeed. I think he would beat one."

"Is that being inspiring? I'm glad Harry's not inspiring."

"Oh, you know what I mean. He's a man who——"

Mrs. Cormack threw up her arms as though praying for the inspired word. Mrs. Dennison did not wait for it.

"There's the carriage. Good-bye, dear," she said.

Mrs. Dennison started with a smile on her face. Berthe was so funny; she was like a page out of a French novel. She loved anything not quite respectable, and peopled the world with heroes of loose morals and overpowering wills. She adored a dominating mind and lived in the discovery of affinities. What nonsense it all was—so very remote from the satisfactory humdrum of real life. One kept house, and gave dinners, and made the children happy, and was fond of one's husband, and life passed most——Here Mrs. Dennison suddenly yawned, and fell to hoping that the Carlins would not be oppressively

dull. She had been bored all day long; the children
had been fretful, and poor Harry was hurt and in low
spirits because of a cruel caricature in a comic paper,
and Tom Loring had scolded her for laughing at the
caricature (it hit Harry off so exactly), and nobody
had come to see her, except a wretch who had once
been her kitchenmaid, and had come to terrible grief,
and wanted to be taken back, and of course couldn't
be, and had to be sent away in tears with a sovereign,
and the tears were no use and the sovereign not much.

The Carlins fortunately proved tolerably interesting in their own way. Carlin was about fifty-five—
an acute man of business, it seemed, and possessed by
an unwavering confidence in the abilities of Willie
Ruston. Mrs. Carlin was ten or fifteen years younger
than her husband—a homely little woman, with a
swarm of children. Mrs. Dennison wondered how
they all fitted into the small house, but was told that
it was larger by two good rooms than their old dwelling in the country town, whence Willie had summoned them to take a hand in his schemes. Willie
had not insisted on the coal business being altogether
abandoned—as Mrs. Carlin said, with a touch of
timidity, it was well to have something to fall back
upon—but he required most of Carlin's time now, and
the added work made residence in London a necessity.
In spite of Mr. Carlin's air of hard-headedness, and
his wife's prudent recognition of the business aspect

3

of life, they neither of them seemed to have a will of their own. Willie—as they both called him—was the Providence, and the mixture of reverence and familiarity presented her old acquaintance in a new light to Maggie Dennison. Even the children prattled about "Willie," and their mother's rebukes made "Mr. Ruston" no more than a strange and transitory effort. Mrs. Dennison wondered what there was in the man—consulting her own recollections of him in hope of enlightenment.

"He takes such broad views," said Carlin, and seemed to find this characteristic the sufficient justification for his faith.

"I used to know him very well, you know," remarked Mrs. Dennison, anxious to reach a more friendly footing, and realising that to connect herself with Ruston offered the best chance of it. "I daresay he's spoken of me—of Maggie Sherwood?"

They thought not, though Willie had been in Carlin's employ at the time when he and Mrs. Dennison parted. She was even able, by comparison of dates, to identify the holiday in which that scene had occurred and that sentence been spoken; but he had never mentioned her name. She very much doubted whether he had even thought of her. The fool and the fool's wife had both been dismissed from his mind. She frowned impatiently. Why should it be anything to her if they had?

There was a commotion among the children, starting from one who was perched on the window-sill. Ruston himself was walking up to the door, dressed in a light suit and a straw hat. After the greetings, while all were busy getting him tea, he turned to Mrs. Dennison.

"This is very kind of you," he said in an under-tone.   .

"My husband wished me to come," she replied.

He seemed in good spirits. He laughed, as he answered,

"Well, I didn't suppose you came to please me."

"You spoke as if you did," said she, still trying to resent his tone, which she thought a better guide to the truth than his easy disclaimer.

"Why, you never did anything to please me!"

"Did you ever ask me?" she retorted.

He glanced at her for a moment, as he began to answer,

"Well, now, I don't believe I ever did; but I——"

Mrs. Carlin interposed with a proffered cup of tea, and he broke off.

"Thanks, Mrs. Carlin. I say, Carlin, it's going first-rate. Your husband's help's simply invaluable, Mrs. Dennison."

"Harry?" she said, in a tone that she regretted a moment later, for there was a passing gleam in Ruston's eye before he answered gravely,

"His firm carries great weight. Well, we're all in it here, sink or swim; aren't we, Carlin?"

Carlin nodded emphatically, and his wife gave an anxious little sigh.

"And what's to be the end of it?" asked Mrs. Dennison.

"Ten per cent," said Carlin, with conviction. He could not have spoken with more utter satisfaction of the millennium.

"The end?" echoed Ruston. "Oh, I don't know."

"At least he won't say," said Carlin admiringly.

Mrs. Dennison rose to go, engaging the Carlins to dine with her—an invitation accepted with some nervousness, until the extension of it to Ruston gave them a wing to come under. Ruston, with that directness of his that shamed mere dexterity and superseded tact, bade Carlin stay where he was, and himself escorted the visitor to her carriage. Half-way down the garden walk she looked up at him and remarked,

"I expect you're the end."

His eyes had been wandering, but they came back sharply to hers.

"Then don't tell anybody," said he lightly.

She did not know whether what he said amounted to a confession or were merely a jest. The next moment he was off at a tangent.

"I like your friend Miss Ferrars. She says a lot of sharp things, and now and then something sensible."

"Now and then! Poor Adela!"

"Well, she doesn't often try. Besides, she's handsome."

"Oh, you've found time to notice that?"

"I notice that first," said Mr. Ruston.

They were at the carriage-door.

"I'm not dressed properly, so I mustn't drive with you," he said.

"Supposing that was the only reason," she replied, smiling, "would it stop you?"

"Certainly."

"Why?"

"Because of other fools."

"I'll take you as far as Regent's Park. The other fools are on the other side of that."

"I'll chance so far," and, waving his hand vaguely towards the house, he got in. It did not seem to occur to him that there was any want of ceremony in his farewell to the Carlins.

"I suppose," she said, "you think most of us fools?"

"I've been learning to think it less and to show it less still."

"You're not much changed, though."

"I've had some of my corners chipped off by collision with other hard substances."

"Thank you for that 'other'!" cried Mrs. Dennison, with a little laugh. "They must have been very hard ones."

" I didn't say that they weren't a little bit injured too."

"Poor things! I should think so."

"I have my human side."

"Generally the other side, isn't it?" she asked with a merry glance. The talk had suddenly become very pleasant. He laughed, and stopped the carriage. A sigh escaped from Mrs. Dennison.

"Next time," he said, "we'll talk about you, or Miss Ferrars, or that little Miss Marjory Valentine, not about me. Good-bye," and he was gone before she could say a word to him.

But it was natural that she should think a little about him. She had not, she said to herself with a weary smile, too many interesting things to think about, and she began to find him decidedly interesting; in which fact again she found a certain strangeness and some material for reflection, because she recollected very well that as a girl she had not found him very attractive. Perhaps she demanded then more colouring of romance than he had infused into their intercourse; she had indeed suspected ·him of suppressed romance, but the suppression had been very thorough, betraying itself only doubtfully here and there, as in his judgment of her accepted suitor.

Moreover, let his feelings then have been what they
might, he was not, she felt sure, the man to cherish a
fruitless love for eight or nine years, or to suffer any
resurrection of expired emotions on a renewed encounter with an old flame. He buried his dead too
deep for that; if they were in the way, she could
fancy him sometimes shovelling the earth over them
and stamping it down without looking too curiously
whether life were actually extinct or only flickering
towards its extinction; if it were not quite gone at
the beginning of the gravedigger's work, it would be
at the end, and the result was the same. Nor did she
suppose that ghosts gibbered or clanked in the orderly trim mansions of his brain. In fact, she was
to him a more or less pleasant acquaintance, sand-
wiched in his mind between Adela Ferrars and Marjory Valentine—with something attractive about her,
though she might lack the sparkle of the one and had
been robbed of the other's youthful freshness. This
was the conclusion which she called upon herself to
draw as she drove back from Hampstead—the plain
and sensible conclusion. Yet, as she reached Curzon
Street, there was a smile on her face; and the conclusion was hardly such as to make her smile—unless indeed she had added to it the reflection that it is ill
judging of things till they are finished. Her acquaintance with Willie Ruston was not ended yet.

"Maggie, Maggie!" cried her husband through

the open door of his study as she passed up-stairs. "Great news! We're to go ahead. We settled it at the meeting this morning."

Harry Dennison was in exuberant spirits. The great company was on the verge of actual existence. From the chrysalis of its syndicate stage it was to issue a bright butterfly.

"And Ruston was most complimentary to our house. He said he could never have carried it through without us. He's in high feather."

Mrs. Dennison listened to more details, thinking, as her husband talked, that Ruston's cheerful mood was fully explained, but wondering that he had not himself thought it worth while to explain to her the cause of it a little more fully. With that achievement fresh in his hand, he had been content to hold his peace. Did he think her not worth telling?

With a cloud on her brow and her smile eclipsed, she passed on to the drawing-room. The window was open and she saw Tom Loring's back in the balcony. Then she heard her friend Mrs. Cormack's rather shrill voice.

"Not say such things?" the voice cried, and Mrs. Dennison could picture the whirl of expostulatory hands that accompanied the question. "But why not?"

Tom's voice answered in the careful tones of a

man who is trying not to lose his temper, or, anyhow, to conceal the loss.

"Well, apart from anything else, suppose Dennison heard you? It wouldn't be over-pleasant for him."

Mrs. Dennison stood still, slowly peeling off her gloves.

"Oh, the poor man! I would not like to hurt him. I will be silent. Oh, he does his very best! But you can't help it."

Mrs. Dennison stepped a yard nearer the window.

"Help what?" asked Tom in the deepest exasperation, no longer to be hidden.

"Why, what must happen? It must be that the true man——"

A smile flickered over Maggie Dennison's face. How like Berthe! But whence came this topic?

"Nonsense, I tell you!" cried Tom with a stamp of his foot.

And at the sound Mrs. Dennison smiled again, and drew yet nearer to the window.

"Oh, it's always nonsense what I say! Well, we shall see, Mr. Loring," and Mrs. Cormack tripped in through her window, and wrote in her diary—she kept a diary full of reflections—that Englishmen were all stupid. She had written that before, but the deep truth bore repetition.

Tom went in too, and found himself face to face

with Mrs. Dennison. Bright spots of colour glowed on her cheeks; had she answered the question of the origin of the topic? Tom blushed and looked furtively at her.

"So the great scheme is launched," she remarked, "and Mr. Ruston triumphs!"

Tom's manner betrayed intense relief, but he was still perturbed.

"We're having a precious lot of Ruston," he observed, leaning against the mantelpiece and putting his hands in his pockets.

"*I* like him," said Maggie Dennison.

"Those are the orders, are they?" asked Tom with a rather wry smile.

"Yes," she answered, smiling at Tom's smile. It amused her when he put her manner into words.

"Then we all like him," said Tom, and, feeling quite secure now, he added, "Mrs. Cormack said we should, which is rather against him."

"Oh, Berthe's a silly woman. Never mind her. Harry likes him too."

"Lucky for Ruston he does. Your husband's a useful friend. I fancy most of Ruston's friends are of the useful variety."

"And why shouldn't we be useful to him?"

"On the contrary, it seems our destiny," grumbled Tom, whose destiny appeared not to please him.

CHAPTER IV.

TWO YOUNG GENTLEMEN.

LADY VALENTINE was the widow of a baronet of good family and respectable means; the one was to be continued and the other absorbed by her son, young Sir Walter, now an Oxford undergraduate and just turned twenty-one years of age. Lady Valentine had a jointure, and Marjory a pretty face. The remaining family assets were a country-house of moderate dimensions in the neighbourhood of Maidenhead, and a small flat in Cromwell Road. Lady Valentine deplored the rise of the plutocracy, and had sometimes secretly hoped that a plutocrat would marry her daughter. In other respects she was an honest and unaffected woman.

Young Sir Walter, however, had his own views for his sister, and young Sir Walter, when he surveyed the position which the laws and customs of the realm gave him, was naturally led to suppose that his opinion had some importance. He was hardly responsible for the error, and very probably Mr. Ruston would have been better advised had his bearing towards the young man not indicated so very plainly that the error was an error. But in the course of the visits to Cromwell Road, which Ruston found time to pay in the intervals of floating the Omofaga Company—and he was a man who found time for many things—this impression of his made itself tolerably evident, and, consequently, Sir Walter entertained grave doubts whether Ruston were a gentleman. And, if a fellow is not a gentleman, what, he asked, do brains and all the rest of it go for? Moreover, how did the chap live? To which queries Marjory answered that " Oxford boys " were very silly—a remark which embittered, without in the least elucidating, the question.

Almost everybody has one disciple who looks up to him as master and mentor, and, ill as he was suited to such a post, Evan Haselden filled it for Walter Valentine. Evan had been in his fourth year when Walter was a freshman, and the reverence engendered in those days had been intensified when Evan had become, first, secretary to a minister and then, as he showed diligence and aptitude, a member of Parliament. Evan was a strong Tory, but payment of members had an unholy attraction for him; this indication of his circumstances may suffice. Men thought him a promising youth, women called him a nice boy, and young Sir Walter held him for a statesman and a man of the world.

Seeing that what Sir Walter wanted was an unfavourable opinion of Ruston, he could not have done better than consult his respected friend. Juggernaut—Adela Ferrars was pleased with the nickname, and it began to be repeated—had been crushing Evan in one or two little ways lately, and he did it with an unconsciousness that increased the brutality. Besides displacing him from the position he wished to occupy at more than one social gathering, Ruston, being in the Lobby of the House one day (perhaps on Omofaga business), had likened the pretty (it was his epithet) young member, as he sped with a glass of water to his party leader, to Ganymede in a frock-coat—a description, Evan felt, injurious to a serious politician.

"A gentleman?" he said, in reply to young Sir Walter's inquiry. "Well, everybody's a gentleman now, so I suppose Ruston is."

"I call him an unmannerly brute," observed Walter, "and I can't think why mother and Marjory are so civil to him."

Evan shook his head mournfully.

"You meet the fellow everywhere," he sighed.

"Such an ugly mug as he's got too," pursued young Sir Walter. "But Marjory says it's full of character."

"Character! I should think so. Enough to hang him on sight," said Evan bitterly.

"He's been a lot to our place. Marjory seems to

like him. I say, Haselden, do you remember what you spoke of after dinner at the Savoy the other day?"

Evan nodded, looking rather embarrassed; indeed he blushed, and little as he liked doing that, it became him very well.

"Did you mean it? Because, you know, I should like it awfully."

"Thanks, Val, old man. Oh, rather, I meant it."

Young Sir Walter lowered his voice and looked cautiously round—they were in the club smoking-room.

"Because I thought, you know, that you were rather—you know—Adela Ferrars?"

"Nothing in that, only *pour passer le temps*," Evan assured him with that superb man-of-the-world-liness.

It was a pity that Adela could not hear him. But there was more to follow.

"The truth is," resumed Evan—and, of course, I rely on your discretion, Val—I thought there might be a—an obstacle."

Young Sir Walter looked knowing.

"When you were good enough to suggest what you did—about your sister—I doubted for a moment how such a thing would be received by—well, at a certain house."

"Oh!"

" I shouldn't wonder if you could guess."

" N—no, I don't think so."

" Well, it doesn't matter where."

" Oh, but I say, you might as well tell me. Hang it, I've learnt to hold my tongue."

" You hadn't noticed it? That's all right. I'm glad to hear it," said Evan, whose satisfaction was not conspicuous in his tone.

" I'm so little in town, you see," said Walter tactfully.

" Well—for heaven's sake, don't let it go any farther—Curzon Street."

" What! Of course! Mrs.——"

" All right, yes. But I've made up my mind. I shall drop all that. Best, isn't it?"

Walter nodded a sagacious assent.

" There was never anything in it, really," said Evan, and he was not displeased with his friend's incredulous expression. It is a great luxury to speak the truth and yet not be believed.

" Now, what you propose," continued Evan, " is most—but, I say, Val, what does she think?"

" She likes you—and you'll have all my influence," said the Head of the Family in a tone of importance.

" But how do you know she likes me?" insisted Evan, whose off-hand air gave place to a manner betraying some trepidation.

" I don't know for certain, of course. And, I say,

Haselden, I believe mother's got an idea in her head about that fellow Ruston."

"The devil! That brute! Oh, hang it, Val, she can't—your sister, I mean—I tell you what, I shan't play the fool any longer."

Sir Walter cordially approved of increased activity, and the two young gentlemen, having settled one lady's future and disposed of the claims of two others to their complete satisfaction, betook themselves to recreation.

Evan was not, however, of opinion that anything in the conversation above recorded, imposed upon him the obligation of avoiding entirely Mrs. Dennison's society. On the contrary, he took an early opportunity of going to see her. His attitude towards her was one of considerably greater deference than Sir Walter understood it to be, and he had a high idea of the value of her assistance. And he did not propose to deny himself such savour of sentiment as the lady would allow; and she generally allowed a little. He intended to say nothing about Ruston, but as it happened that Mrs. Dennison's wishes set in an opposing direction, he had not been long in the drawing room at Curzon Street before he found himself again with the name of his enemy on his lips. He spoke with refreshing frankness and an engaging confidence in his hostess' sympathy. Mrs. Dennison had no difficulty in seeing that he had a special reason for his bitterness.

"Is it only because he called you Ganymede? And it's a very good name for you, Mr. Haselden."

To be compared to Ganymede in private by a lady and in public by a scoffer, are things very different. Evan smiled complacently.

"There's more than that, isn't there?" asked Mrs. Dennison.

Evan admitted that there was more, and, in obedience to some skilful guidance, he revealed what there was more—what beyond mere offended dignity—between himself and Mr. Ruston. He had to complain of no lack of interest on the part of his listener. Mrs. Dennison questioned him closely as to his grounds for anticipating Ruston's rivalry. The idea was evidently quite new to her; and Evan was glad to detect her reluctance to accept it—she must think as he did about Willie Ruston. The tangible evidence appeared on examination reassuringly small, and Evan, by a strange conversion, found himself driven to defend his apprehensions by insisting on just that power of attraction in his foe which he had begun by denying altogether. But that, Mrs. Dennison objected, only showed, even if it existed, that Marjory might like Ruston, not that Ruston would return her liking. On the whole Mrs. Dennison comforted him, and, dismissing Ruston from the discussion, said with a smile,

"So you're thinking of settling down already, are you?"

"I say, Mrs. Dennison, you've always been awfully good to me; I wonder if you'd help me in this?"

"How could I help you?"

"Oh, lots of ways. Well, for instance, old Lady Valentine doesn't ask me there often. You see, I haven't got any money."

"Poor boy! Of course you haven't. Nice young men never have any money."

"So I don't get many chances of seeing her."

"And I might arrange meetings for you? That's how I could help? Now, why should I help?"

Evan was encouraged by this last question, put in his friend's doubtfully-serious doubtfully-playful manner.

"It needn't," he said, in a tone rather more timid than young Sir Walter would have expected, "make any difference to our friendship, need it? If it meant that——"

The sentence was left in expressive incompleteness.

Mrs. Dennison wanted to laugh; but why should she hurt his feelings? He was a pleasant boy, and, in spite of his vanity, really a clever one. He had been a little spoilt; that was all. She turned her laugh in another direction.

"Berthe Cormack would tell you that it would be sure to intensify it," she said. "Seriously, I shan't hate you for marrying, and I don't suppose Marjory will hate me."

"Then" (Mrs. Dennison had to smile at that little word), "you'll help me?"

"Perhaps," said Mrs. Dennison, allowing her smile to become manifest.

"You won't be against me?"

"Perhaps not."

"Good-bye," said Evan, pressing her hand.

He had enjoyed himself very much, and Mrs. Dennison was glad that she had been good-natured, and had not laughed.

"Good-bye, and I hope you'll be very happy, if you succeed. And—Evan—don't kill Mr. Ruston!"

The laugh came at last, but he was out of the door in time, and Mrs. Dennison had no leisure to enjoy it fully, for, the moment her visitor was gone, Mr. Belford and Lord Semingham were announced. They came together, seeking Harry Dennison. There was a "little hitch" of some sort in the affairs of the Omofaga Company—nothing of consequence, said Mr. Belford reassuringly. Mrs. Dennison explained that Harry Dennison had gone off to call on Mr. Ruston.

"Oh, then he knows by now," said Semingham in a tone of relief.

"And it'll be all right," added Belford contentedly.

"Mr. Belford," said Mrs. Dennison, "I'm living in an atmosphere of Omofaga. I eat it, and drink it, and wear it, and breathe it. And, what in the end, is it?"

“Ask Ruston,” interposed Semingham.

“I did; but I don’t think he told me.”

“But surely, my dear Mrs. Dennison, your husband takes you into his confidence?” suggested Mr. Belford.

Mrs. Dennison smiled, as she replied,

“Oh, yes, I know what you’re doing. But I want to know why you’re doing it. I don’t believe you’ll ever get anything out of it, you know.”

“Oh, directors always get something,” protested Semingham. “Penal servitude sometimes, but always something.”

“I’ve never had such implicit faith in any undertaking in my life,” asserted Mr. Belford. “And I know that your husband shares my views. It’s bound to be the greatest success of the day. Ah, here’s Dennison!”

Harry came in wiping his brow. Belford rushed to him, and drew him to the window, button-holing him with decision. Lord Semingham smiled lazily and pulled his whisker.

“Don’t you want to hear the news?” Mrs. Dennison asked.

“No! He’s been to Ruston.”

Mrs. Dennison looked at him for an instant with something rather like scorn in her eye. Lord Semingham laughed.

“I’m not quite as bad as that, really,” he said.

"And the others?" she asked, leaning forward and taking care that her voice did not reach the other pair.

"He turns Belford round his fingers."

"And Mr. Carlin?"

"In his pocket."

Mrs. Dennison cast a glance towards the window.

"Don't go on," implored Semingham, half-seriously.

"And my husband?" she asked in a still lower voice.

Lord Semingham·protested with a gesture against such cross-examination.

"Surely it's a good thing for me to know?" she said.

"Well—a great influence."

"Thank you."

There was a pause for an instant. Then she rose with a laugh and rang the bell for tea.

"I hope he won't ruin us all," she said.

"I've got Bessie's settlement," observed Lord Semingham; and he added after a moment's pause, "What's the matter? I thought you were a thorough-going believer."

"I'm a woman," she answered. "If I were a man——"

"You'd be the prophet, not the disciple, eh?"

She looked at him, and then across to the couple by the window.

"To do Belford justice," remarked Semingham, reading her glance, "he never admits that he isn't a great man—though surely he must know it."

"Is it better to know it, or not to know it?" she asked, restlessly fingering the teapot and cups which had been placed before her. "I sometimes think that if you resolutely refuse to know it, you can alter it."

Belford's name had been the only name mentioned in the conversation; yet Semingham knew that she was not thinking of Belford nor of him.

"I knew it about myself very soon," he said. "It makes a man better to know it, Mrs. Dennison."

"Oh, yes—better," she answered impatiently.

The two men came and joined them. Belford accepted a cup of tea, and, as he took it, he said to Harry, continuing their conversation,

"Of course, I know his value; but, after all, we must judge for ourselves."

"Of course," acquiesced Harry, handing him bread-and-butter.

"We are the masters," pursued Belford.

Mrs. Dennison glanced at him, and a smile so full of meaning—of meaning which it was as well Mr. Belford should not see—appeared on her face, that Lord Semingham deftly interposed his person between them, and said, with apparent seriousness,

"Oh, he mustn't think he can do just what he likes with us."

"I am entirely of your opinion," said Belford, with a weighty nod.

After tea, Lord Semingham walked slowly back to his own house. He had a trick of stopping still, when he fell into thought, and he was motionless on the pavement of Piccadilly more than once on his way home. The last time he paused for nearly three minutes, till an acquaintance, passing by, clapped him on the back, and inquired what occupied his mind.

"I was thinking," said Semingham, laying his forefinger on his friend's arm, "that if you take what a clever man really is, and add to it what a clever woman who is interested in him thinks he is, you get a most astonishing person."

The friend stared. The speculation seemed hardly pressing enough to excuse a man for blocking the pavement of Piccadilly.

"If, on the other hand," pursued Semingham, "you take what an ordinary man isn't, and add all that a clever woman thinks he isn't, you get——"

"Hadn't we better go on, old fellow?" asked the friend.

"No, I think we'd better not," said Semingham, starting to walk again.

CHAPTER V.

A TELEGRAM TO FRANKFORT.

THE success of Lady Valentine's Saturday to
Monday party at Maidenhead was spoilt by the un-
scrupulous, or (if the charitable view be possible) the
muddle-headed conduct of certain eminent African
chiefs—so small is the world, so strong the chain of
gold (or shares) that binds it together. The party
was marred by Willie Ruston's absence; and he was
away because he had to go to Frankfort, and he had
to go to Frankfort because of that little hitch in the
affairs of the Omofaga. The hitch was, in truth, a
somewhat grave one, and it occurred, most annoying-
ly, immediately after a gathering, marked by uncommon enthusiasm and composed of highly influential
persons, had set the impress of approval on the
scheme. On the following morning, it was asserted
that the said African chiefs, from whom Ruston and
his friends derived their title to Omofaga, had acted
in a manner that belied the character for honesty and
simplicity in commercial matters (existing side by side

with intense savagery and cruelty in social and political life) that Mr. Foster Belford had attributed to
them at the great meeting. They had, it was said,
sold Omofaga several times over in small parcels, and
twice, at least, *en bloc*—once to the Syndicate (from
whom the Company was acquiring it) and once to an
association of German capitalists. The writer of the
article, who said that he knew the chiefs well, went so
far as to maintain that any person provided with a
few guns and a dozen or so bottles of ardent spirits
could return from Omofaga with a portmanteau full
of treaties, and this facility in obtaining the article
could not, in accordance with the law of supply and
demand, do other than gravely affect the value of it.
Willie Ruston was inclined to make light of this disclos-
ure; indeed, he attributed it to a desire—natural but
unprincipled—on the part of certain persons to obtain
Omofaga shares at less than their high intrinsic value;
he called it a " bear dodge " and sundry other oppro-
brious names, and snapped his fingers at all possible
treaties in the world except his own. Once let him
set his foot in Omofaga, and short would be the shrift
of rival claims, supposing them to exist at all! But
the great house of Dennison, Sons & Company, could
not go on in this happy-go-lucky fashion—so the
senior partner emphatically told Harry Dennison—
they were already, in his opinion, deep enough in this
affair; if they were to go any deeper, this matter of

the association of German capitalists must be inquired into. The house had not only its money, but its credit and reputation to look after; it could not touch any doubtful business, nor could it be left with a block of Omofagas on its hands. In effect they were trusting too much to this Mr. Ruston, for he, and he alone, was their security in the matter. Not another step would the house move till the German capitalists were dissolved into thin air. So Willie Ruston packed his portmanteau—likely enough the very one that had carried the treaties away from Omofaga—and went to Frankfort to track the German capitalists to their lair. Meanwhile, the issue of the Omofaga was postponed, and Mr. Carlin was set a-telegraphing to Africa.

Thus it also happened that, contrary to her fixed intention, Lady Valentine was left with a bedroom to spare, and with no just or producible reason whatever for refusing her son's request that Evan Haselden might occupy it. This, perhaps, should, in the view of all true lovers, be regarded as an item on the credit side of the African chiefs' account, though in the hostess' eyes it aggravated their offence. Adela Ferrars, Mr. Foster Belford and Tom Loring, who positively blessed the African chiefs, were the remaining guests.

All parties cannot be successful, and, if truth be told, this of Lady Valentine's was no conspicuous triumph. Belford and Loring quarrelled about Omofaga, for Loring feared (he used that word) that there might be a good deal in the German treaties, and Belford was loud-mouthed in declaring there could be nothing. Marjory and her brother had a " row " because Marjory, on the Saturday afternoon, would not go out in the Canadian canoe with Evan, but insisted on taking a walk with Mr. Belford and hearing all about Omofaga. Finally, Adela and Tom Loring had a rather serious dissension because—well, just because Tom was so intolerably stupid and narrow-minded and rude. That was Adela's own account of it, given in her own words, which seems pretty good authority.

The unfortunate discussion began with an expression of opinion from Tom. They were lounging very comfortably down stream in a broad-bottomed boat. It was a fine still evening and a lovely sunset. It was then most wanton of Tom—even although he couched his remark in a speciously general form—to say,

" I wonder at fellows who spend their life worming money out of other people for wild-cat schemes instead of taking to some honest trade."

There was a pause. Then Adela fitted her glasses on her nose, and observed, with a careful imitation of Tom's forms of expression,

" I wonder at fellows who drift through life in

subordinate positions without the—the *spunk*—to try and do anything for themselves."

"Women have no idea of honesty."

"Men are such jealous creatures."

"I'm not jealous of him," Tom blurted out.

"Of who?" asked Adela.

She was keeping the cooler of the pair.

"Confound those beastly flies," said Tom, peevishly. There was a fly or two about, but Adela smiled in a superior way. "I suppose I've some right to express an opinion," continued Tom. "You know what I feel about the Dennisons, and—well, it's not only the Dennisons."

"Oh! the Valentines?"

"Blow the Valentines!" said Tom, very ungratefully, inasmuch as he sat in their boat and had eaten their bread.

He bent over his sculls, and Adela looked at him with a doubtful little smile. She thought Tom Loring, on the whole, the best man she knew, the truest and loyalest; but, these qualities are not everything, and it seemed as if he meant to be secretary to Harry Dennison all his life. Of course he had no money, there was that excuse; but to some men want of money is a reason, not for doing nothing, but for attempting everything; it had struck Willie Ruston in that light. Therefore she was at times angry with Tom —and all the more angry the more she admired him.

"You do me the honour to be anxious on my account?" she asked very stiffly.

"He asked me how much money you had the other day."

"Oh, you're insufferable; you really are. Do you always tell women that men care only for their money?"

"It's not a bad thing to tell them when it's true."

"I call this the very vulgarest dispute I was ever entrapped into."

"It's not my fault. It's—— Hullo!"

His attention was arrested by Lady Valentine's footman, who stood on the bank, calling "Mr Loring, sir," and holding up a telegram.

"Thank goodness, we're interrupted," said Adela. "Row ashore, Mr. Loring."

Loring obeyed, and took his despatch. It was from Harry Dennison, and he read it aloud.

"Can you come up? News from Frankfort."

"I must go," said Tom.

"Oh, yes. If you're not there, Mr. Ruston will do something dreadful, won't he? I should like to come too. News from Frankfort would be more interesting than views from Mr. Belford."

They parted without any approach towards a reconciliation. Tom was hopelessly sulky, Adela persistently flippant. The shadow of Omofaga lay heavy on Lady Valentine's party, and still shrouded Tom Loring on his way to town.

The important despatch from Frankfort had come in cipher, and when Tom arrived in Curzon Street, he found Mr. Carlin, who had been sent for to read it, just leaving the house. The men nodded to one another, and Carlin hastily exclaimed,

"You must reassure Dennison! You can do it!" and leapt into a hansom.

Tom smiled. If the progress of Omofaga depended on encouragement from him, Omofaga would remain in primitive barbarism, though missionaries fell thick as the leaves in autumn.

Harry Dennison was walking up and down the library; his hair was roughened and his appearance indicative of much unrest; his wife sat in an armchair, looking at him and listening to Lord Semingham, who, poising a cigarette between his fingers, was putting, or trying to put, a meaning to Ruston's message.

"Position critical. Must act at once. Will you give me a free hand? If not, wire how far I may go."

That was how it ran when faithfully interpreted by Mr. Carlin.

"You see," observed Lord Semingham, "it's clearly a matter of money."

Tom nodded.

"Of course it is," said he; "it's not likely to be a question of anything else."

"Therefore the Germans have something worth paying for," continued Semingham.

"Well," amended Tom, "something Ruston thinks it worth his while to pay for, anyhow."

"That is to say they have treaties touching, or purporting to touch, Omofaga."

"And," added Harry Dennison, who did not lack a certain business shrewdness, "probably their Government behind them to some extent."

Tom flung himself into a chair.

"The thing's monstrous," he pronounced. "Semingham and you, Dennison, are, besides himself—and he's got nothing—the only people responsible up to now. And he asks you to give him an unlimited credit without giving you a word of information! It's the coolest thing I ever heard of in all my life."

"Of course he means the Company to pay in the end," Semingham reminded the hostile critic.

"Time enough to talk of the Company when we see it," retorted Tom, with an aggressive scepticism.

"Position critical! Hum. I suppose their treaties must be worth something," pursued Semingham. "Dennison, I can't be drained dry over this job."

Harry Dennison shook his head in a puzzled fashion.

"Carlin says it's all right," he remarked.

"Of course he does!" exclaimed Tom impatiently. "Two and two make five for him if Ruston says they do."

"Well, Tom, what's your advice?" asked Semingham.

"You must tell him to do nothing till he's seen you, or at least sent you full details of the position."

The two men nodded. Mrs. Dennison rose from her chair, walked to the window, and stood looking out.

"Loring just confirms what I thought," said Semingham.

"He says he must act at once," Harry reminded them; he was still wavering, and, as he spoke, he glanced uneasily at his wife; but there was nothing to show that she even heard the conversation.

"Oh, he hates referring to anybody," said Tom. "He's to have a free hand, and you're to pay the bill. That's his programme, and a very pretty one it is—for him."

Tom's *animus* was apparent, and Lord Semingham laughed gently.

"Still, you're right in substance," he conceded when the laugh was ended, and as he spoke he drew a sheet of notepaper towards him and took up a pen.

" We'd better settle just what to say," he observed. " Carlin will be back in half an hour, and we promised to have it ready for him. What you suggest seems all right, Loring."

Tom nodded. Harry Dennison stood stock still for an instant and then said, with a sigh,

" I suppose so. He'll be furious—and I hope to God we shan't lose the whole thing."

Lord Semingham's pen-point was in actual touch with the paper before him, when Mrs. Dennison suddenly turned round and faced them. She rested one hand on the window-sash, and held the other up in a gesture which demanded attention.

" Are you really going to back out now ? " she asked in a very quiet voice, but with an intonation of contempt that made all the three men raise their heads with the jerk of startled surprise. Lord Semingham checked the movement of his pen, and leant back in his chair, looking at her. Her face was a little flushed and she was breathing quickly.

" My dear," said Harry Dennison very apologetically, " do you think you quite understand——? "

But Tom Loring's patience was exhausted. His interview with Adela left him little reserve of toleration ; and the discovery of another and even worse case of Rustomania utterly overpowered his discretion.

" Mrs. Dennison," he said, " wants us to deliver ourselves, bound hand and foot, to this fellow."

5

“Well, and if I do?” she demanded, turning on him. “Can’t you even follow, when you’ve found a man who can lead?”

And then, conscious perhaps of having been goaded to an excess of warmth by Tom’s open scorn, she turned her face away.

“Lead, yes! Lead us to ruin!” exclaimed Tom.

“You won’t be ruined, anyhow,” she retorted quickly, facing round on him again, reckless in her anger how she might wound him.

“Tom’s anxious for us, Maggie,” her husband reminded her, and he laid his hand on Tom Loring’s shoulder.

Tom’s excitement was not to be soothed.

“Why are we all to be his instruments?” he demanded angrily.

“I should be proud to be,” she said haughtily.

Her husband smiled in an uneasy effort after nonchalance, and Lord Semingham shot a quick glance at her out of his observant eyes.

“I should be proud of a friend like you if I were Ruston,” he said gently, hoping to smooth matters a little.

Mrs. Dennison ignored his attempt.

“Can’t you see?” she asked. “Can’t you see that he’s a man to—to do things? It’s enough for us if we can help him.”

She had forgotten her embarrassment; she spoke

half in contempt, half in entreaty, wholly in an earnest urgency, that made her unconscious of any strangeness in her zeal. Harry looked uncomfortable. Semingham with a sigh blew a cloud of smoke from his cigarette.

Tom Loring sat silent. He stretched out his legs to their full length, rested the nape of his neck on the chair-back, and stared up at the ceiling. His attitude eloquently and most rudely asserted folly—almost lunacy—in Mrs. Dennison. She noticed it and her eyes flashed, but she did not speak to him. She looked at Semingham and surprised an expression in his eyes that made her drop her own for an instant; she knew very well what he was thinking—what a man like him would think. But she recovered herself and met his glance boldly. ·

Harry Dennison sat down and slowly rubbed his brow with his handkerchief. Lord Semingham took up the pen and balanced it between his fingers. There was silence in the room for full three minutes. Then came a loud knock at the hall door.

" It's Carlin," said Harry Dennison.

No one else spoke, and for another moment there was silence. The steps of the butler and the visitor were already audible in the hall when Lord Semingham, with his own shrug and his own smile, as though nothing in the world were worth so much dispute or so much bitterness, said to Dennison,

"Hang it! Shall we chance it, Harry?"

Mrs. Dennison made one swift step forward towards him, her face all alight; but she stopped before she reached the table and turned to her husband. At the moment Carlin was announced. He entered with a rush of eagerness. Tom Loring did not move. Semingham wrote on his paper,—

"Use your discretion, but make every effort to keep down expenses. Wire progress."

"Will that do?" he asked, handing the paper to Harry Dennison and leaning back with a smile on his face; and, though he handed the paper to Harry, he looked at Mrs. Dennison.

Mrs. Dennison was standing by her husband now, her arm through his. As he read she read also. Then she took the paper from his yielding hand and came and bent over the table, shoulder to shoulder with Lord Semingham. Taking the pen from his fingers, she dipped it in the ink, and with a firm dash she erased all save the first three words of the message. This done, she looked round into Semingham's face with a smile of triumph.

"Well, it'll be cheap to send, anyhow," said he.

He got up and motioned Carlin to take his place.

Mrs. Dennison walked back to the window, and he followed her there. They heard Carlin's cry of delight, and Harry Dennison beginning to make excuses and trying to find business reasons for what had been done. Suddenly Tom Loring leapt to his feet and strode swiftly out of the room, slamming the door behind him. Mrs. Dennison heard the sound with a smile of content. She seemed to have no misgivings and no regrets.

" Really," said Lord Semingham, sticking his eyeglass in his eye and regarding her closely, " you ought to be the Queen of Omofaga."

With her slim fingers she began to drum gently on the window-pane.

" I think there's a king already," she said, looking out into the street.

" Oh, yes, a king," he answered with a laugh.

Mrs. Dennison looked round. He did not stop laughing, and presently she laughed just a little herself.

" Oh, of course, it's always that in a woman, isn't it ? " she asked sarcastically.

" Generally," he answered, unashamed.

She grew grave, and looked in his face almost—so it seemed to him—as though she sought there an answer to something that puzzled her. He gave her none. She sighed and drummed on the window again ; then she turned to him with a sudden bright smile.

" I don't care ; I'm glad I did it," she said defiantly.

CHAPTER VI.

PROBABLY no one is always wrong; at any rate,
Mr. Otto Heather was right now and then, and he
had hit the mark when he accused Willie Ruston of
"commercialism." But he went astray when he concluded, *per saltum*, that the object of his antipathy
was a money-grubbing, profit-snatching, upper-hand-
getting machine, and nothing else in the world.
Probably, again, no one ever was. Ruston had not
only feelings, but also what many people consider a
later development—a conscience. And, whatever the
springs on which his conscience moved, it acted as a
restraint upon him. Both his feelings and his conscience would have told him that it would not do for
him to delude his friends or the public with a scheme
which was a fraud. He would have delivered this
inner verdict in calm and temperate terms; it would
have been accompanied by no disgust, no remorse, no
revulsion at the idea having made its way into his
mind; it was just that, on the whole, such a thing

wouldn't do. The vagueness of the phrase faithfully embodied the spirit of the decision, for whether it wouldn't do, because it was in itself unseemly, or merely because, if found out, it would look unseemly, was precisely one of those curious points with which Mr. Ruston's practical intellect declined to trouble itself. If Omofaga had been a fraud, then Ruston would have whistled it down the wind. But Omofaga was no fraud—in his hands at least no fraud. For, while he believed in Omofaga to a certain extent, Willie Ruston believed in himself to an indefinite, perhaps an infinite, extent. He thought Omofaga a fair security for anyone's money, but himself a superb one. Omofaga without him—or other people's Omofagas—might be a promising speculation; add him, and Omafaga became a certainty. It will be seen, then, that Mr. Heather's inspiration had soon failed—unless, that is, machines can see visions and dream dreams, and melt down hard facts in crucibles heated to seven times in the fires of imagination. But a man may do all this, and yet not be the passive victim of his dreams and imaginings. The old buccaneers—and Adela Ferrars had thought Ruston a buccaneer modernised—dreamt, but they sailed and fought too; and they sailed and fought and won because they dreamt. And if many of their dreams were tinted with the gleam of gold, they were none the less powerful and alluring for that.

Ruston had laid the whole position before Baron von Geltschmidt of Frankfort, with—as it seemed—the utmost candour. He and his friends were not deeply committed in the matter; there was, as yet, only a small syndicate; of course they had paid something for their rights, but, as the Baron knew (and Willie's tone emphasised the fact that he must know) the actual sums paid out of pocket in these cases were not of staggering magnitude; no company was formed yet; none would be, unless all went smoothly. If the Baron and his friends were sure of their ground, and preferred to go on—why, he and his friends were not eager to commit themselves to a long and arduous contest. There must, he supposed, be a give-and-take between them.

"It looks," he said, "as far as I can judge, as if either we should have to buy you out, or you would have to buy us out."

"Perhaps," suggested the Baron, blinking lazily behind his gold spectacles, "we could get rid of you without buying you out."

"Oh, if you drove us to it, by refusing to treat, we should have a shot at that too, of course," laughed Willie Ruston, swallowing a glass of white wine. The Baron had asked him to discuss the matter over luncheon.

"It seems to me," observed the Baron, lighting a cigar, "that people are rather cold about speculations just now."

"I should think so; but this is not a speculation; it's a certainty."

"Why do you tell me that, when you want to get rid of me?"

"Because you won't believe it. Wasn't that Bismarck's way?"

"You are not Bismarck—and a certainty is what the public thinks one."

"Is that philosophy or finance?" asked Ruston, laughing again.

The Baron, who had in his day loved both the subjects referred to, drank a glass of wine and chuckled as he delivered himself of the following doctrine:

"What the public thinks a certainty, is a certainty for the public—that would be philosophy, eh?"

"I believe so. I never read much, and your extract doesn't raise my idea of its value."

"But what the public thinks a certainty, is a certainty—for the promotors—that is finance. You see the difference is simple."

"And the distinction luminous. This, Baron, seems to be the age of finance."

"Ah, well, there are still honest men," said the Baron, with the optimism of age.

"Yes, I'm one—and you're another."

"I'm much obliged. You've been in Omofaga?"

" Oh, yes. And you haven't, Baron."

" Friends of mine have."

" Yes. They came just after I left."

The Baron knew that this statement was true. As his study of Willie Ruston progressed, he became inclined to think that it might be important. Mere right (so far as such a thing could be given by prior treaties) was not of much moment; but right and Ruston together might be formidable. Now the Baron (and his friends were friends much in the way, *mutatis mutandis*, that Mr. Wagg and Mr. Wenham were friends of the Marquis of Steyne, and may therefore drop out of consideration) was old and rich, and, by consequence, at a great disadvantage with a man who was young and poor.

" I don't see the bearing of that," he observed, having paused for a moment to consider all its bearings.

" It means that you can't have Omofaga," said Willie Ruston. " You were too late, you see."

The Baron smoked and drank and laughed.

" You're a young fool, my boy—or something quite different," said he, laying a hand on his companion's arm. Then he asked suddenly, " What about Dennisons ? "

" They're behind me if——"

" Well ? "

" If you're not in front of me."

“But if I am, my son?” asked the Baron, almost caressingly.

“Then I leave for Omofaga by the next boat.”

“Eh! And for what?”

“Never mind what. You’ll find out when you come.”

The Baron sighed and tugged his beard.

“You English!” said he. “Your Government won’t help you.”

“Damn my Government.”

“You English!” said the Baron again, his tone struggling between admiration and a sort of oppression, while his face wore the look a man has who sees another push in front of him in a crowd, and wonders how the fellow works his way through.

There was a long pause. Ruston lit his pipe, and, crossing his arms on his breast, blinked at the sun; the Baron puffed away, shooting a glance now and then at his young friend, then he asked,

“Well, my boy, what do you offer?”

“Shares,” answered Ruston composedly.

The Baron laughed. The impudence of the offer pleased him.

“Yes, shares, of course. And besides?”

Willie Ruston turned to him.

“I shan’t haggle,” he announced. “I’ll make you one offer, Baron, and it’s an uncommon handsome offer for a trunk of waste paper.”

"What's the offer?" asked the Baron, smiling with rich subdued mirth.

"Fifty thousand down, and the same in shares fully paid."

"Not enough, my son."

"All right," and Mr. Ruston rose. "Much obliged for your hospitality, Baron," he added, holding out his hand.

"Where are you going?" asked the Baron.

"Omofaga—_viá_ London."

The Baron caught him by the arm, and whispered in his ear,

"There's not so much in it, first and last."

"Oh, isn't there? Then why don't you take the offer?"

"Is it your money?"

"It's good money. Come, Baron, you've always liked the safe side," and Willie smiled down upon his host.

The Baron positively started. This young man stood over him and told him calmly, face-to-face, the secret of his life. It was true. How he had envied men of real nerve, of faith, of daring!, But he had always liked the safe side. Hence he was very rich— and a rather weary old man.

Two days later, Willie Ruston took a cab from Lord Semingham's, and drove to Curzon Street. He arrived at twelve o'clock in the morning. Harry Dennison had gone to a Committee at the House. The butler had just told him so, when a voice cried from within,

" Is it you, Mr. Ruston ? "

Mrs. Dennison was standing in the hall. He went in, and followed her into the library.

" Well ? " she asked, standing by the table, and wasting no time in formal greetings.

" Oh, it's all right," said he.

" You got my telegram ? "

" Your telegram, Mrs. Dennison ? " said he with a smile.

" I mean—the telegram," she corrected herself, smiling in her turn.

" Oh, yes," said Ruston, and he took a step towards her. " I've seen Lord Semingham," he added.

" Yes ? And these horrid Germans are out of the way ? "

" Yes ; and Semingham is letting his shooting this year."

She laughed, and glanced at him as she asked,

" Then it cost a great deal ? "

" Fifty thousand ! "

" Oh, then we can't take Lord Semingham's shooting, or anybody else's. Poor Harry ! "

" He doesn't know yet ? "

" Aren't you almost afraid to tell him, Mr. Ruston ? "

"Aren't you, Mrs. Dennison?"

He smiled as he asked, and Mrs. Dennison lifted her eyes to his, and let them dwell there.

"Why did you do it?" he asked.

"Will the money be lost?"

"Oh, I hope not; but money's always uncertain."

"The thing's not uncertain?"

"No; the thing's certain now."

She sat down with a sigh of satisfaction, and passed her hand over her broad brow.

"Why did you do it?" Ruston repeated; and she laughed nervously.

"I hate going back," she said, twisting her hands in her lap.

He had asked her the question which she had been asking herself without response.

He sat down opposite her, flinging his soft cloth hat—for he had not been home since his arrival in London—on the table.

"What a bad hat!" said Mrs. Dennison, touching it with the end of a forefinger.

"It's done a journey through Omofaga."

"Ah!" she laughed gently. "Dear old hat!"

"Thanks to you, it'll do another soon."

Mrs. Dennison sat up straight in her chair.

"You hope——?" she began.

"To be on my way in six months," he answered in solid satisfaction.

"And for long?"

"It must take time."

"What must?"

"My work there."

She rose and walked to the window, as she had when she was about to send the telegram. Now also she was breathing quickly, and the flush, once so rare on her cheeks, was there again.

"And we," she said in a low voice, looking out of the window, "shall just hear of you once a year?"

"We shall have regular mails in no time," said he. "Once a year, indeed! Once a month, Mrs. Dennison!"

With a curious laugh, she dashed the blind-tassel against the window. It was not for the sake of hearing of her that he wanted the mails. With a sudden impulse she crossed the room and stood opposite him.

"Do you care *that*," she asked, snapping her fingers, "for any soul alive? You're delighted to leave us all and go to Omofaga!"

Willie Ruston seemed not to hear; he was mentally organizing the mail service from Omofaga.

"I beg pardon?" he said, after a perceptible pause.

"Oh!" cried Maggie Dennison, and at last her tone caught his attention.

He looked up with a wrinkle of surprise on his brow.

"Why," said he, "I believe you're angry about something. You look just as you did on—on the memorable occasion."

"Oh, we aren't all Carlins!" she exclaimed, carried away by her feelings.

The least she had expected from him was grateful thanks; a homage tinged with admiration was, in truth, no more than her due; if she had been an ugly dull woman, yet she had done him a great service, and she was not an ugly dull woman. But then neither was she Omofaga.

"If everybody was as good a fellow as old Carlin——" began Willie Ruston.

"If everybody was as useful and docile, you mean; as good a tool for you——"

At last it was too plain to be missed.

"Hullo!" he exclaimed. "What are you pitching into me for, Mrs. Dennison?"

His words were ordinary enough, but at last he was looking at her, and the mails of Omofaga were for a moment forgotten.

"I wish I'd never made them send the wretched telegram," she flashed out passionately. "Much thanks I get!"

"You shall have a statue in the chief street of the chief town of——"

"How dare you! I'm not a girl to be chaffed."

The tears were standing in her eyes, as she threw

herself back in a chair. Willie Ruston got up and stood by her.

"You'll be proud of that telegram some day," he said, rather as though he felt bound to pay her a compliment.

"Oh, you think that now?" she said, unconvinced of his sincerity.

"Yes. Though was it very difficult?" he asked with a sudden change of tone most depreciatory of her exploit.

She glanced at him and smiled joyfully. She liked the depreciation better than the compliment.

"Not a bit," she whispered, "for me."

He laughed slightly, and shut his lips close again. He began to understand Mrs. Dennison better.

"Still, though it was easy for you, it was precious valuable to me," he observed.

"And how you hate being obliged to me, don't you?"

He perceived that she understood him a little, but he smiled again as he asked,

"Oh, but what made you do it, you know?"

"You mean you did? Mr. Ruston, I should like to see you at work in Omofaga."

"Oh, a very humdrum business," said he, with a shrug.

"You'll have soldiers?"

"We shall call 'em police," he corrected, smiling.

"Yes; but they keep everybody down, and—and do as you order?"

"If not, I shall ask 'em why."

"And the natives?"

"Civilise 'em."

"You—you'll be governor?"

"Oh, dear, no.   Local administrator."

She laughed in his face; and a grim smile from him seemed to justify her.

"I'm glad I sent the telegram," she half-whispered, lying back in the chair and looking up at him.   "I shall have had something to do with all that, shan't I?   Do you want any more money?"

"Look here," said Willie Ruston, "Omofaga's mine.   I'll find you another place, if you like, when I've put this job through."

A luxury of pleasure rippled through her laugh. She darted out her hand and caught his.

"No.   I like Omofaga too!" she said, and as she said it, the door suddenly opened, and in walked Tom Loring—that is to say—in Tom Loring was about to walk; but when he saw what he did see, he stood still for a moment, and then, without a single word, either of greeting or apology, he turned his back, walked out again, and shut the door behind him.   His entrance and exit were so quick and sudden, that Mrs. Dennison had hardly dropped Willie Ruston's hand before

he was gone; she had certainly not dropped it before
he came.

Willie Ruston sat down squarely in a chair. Mrs.
Dennison's hot mood had been suddenly cooled. She
would not ask him to go, but she glanced at the hat
that had been through Omofaga. He detected her.

"I shall stay ten minutes," he observed.

She understood and nodded assent. Very little
was said during the ten minutes. Mrs. Dennison
seemed tired; her eyes dropped towards the ground,
and she reclined in her chair. Ruston was frowning
and thrumming at intervals on the table. But presently his brow cleared and he smiled. Mrs. Dennison
saw him from under her drooping lids.

"Well?" she asked in a petulant tone.

"I believe you were going to fight me for Omofaga."

"I don't know what I was doing."

"Is that fellow a fool?"

"He's a much better man than you'll ever be, Mr.
Ruston. Really you might go now."

"All right, I will. I'm going down to the city to
see your husband and Carlin."

"I'm afraid I've wasted your time."

She spoke with a bitterness which seemed impossible to miss. But he appeared to miss it.

"Oh, not a bit, really," he assured her anxiously.
"Good-bye," he added, holding out his hand.

"Good-bye. I've shaken hands once."

He waited a moment to see if she would speak again, but she said nothing. So he left her.

As he called a hansom, Mrs. Cormack was leaning over her balcony. She took a little jewelled watch out of her pocket and looked at it.

"An hour and a quarter!" she cried. "And I know the poor man isn't at home!"

CHAPTER VII.

AN ATTEMPT TO STOP THE WHEELS.

Miss Adela Ferrars lived in Queen's Gate, in
company with her aunt, Mrs. Topham. Mrs. Topham's husband had been the younger son of a peer
of ancient descent; and a practised observer might
almost have detected the fact in her manner, for she
took her station in this life as seriously as her position
in the next, and, in virtue of it, assumed a responsibility for the morals of her inferiors which betrayed
a considerable confidence in her own. But she was a
good woman, and a widow of the pattern most opposite to that of Mrs. Cormack. She dwelt more
truly in the grave of her husband than in Queen's
Gate, and permitted herself no recreations except
such as may privily creep into religious exercises and
the ministrations of favourite clergymen; and it is
pleasant to think that she was very happy. As may
be supposed, however, Adela (who was a good woman
in quite another way, and therefore less congenial
with her aunt than any mere sinner could have been)

and Mrs. Topham saw very little of one another, and would not have thought of living together unless each had been able to supply what the other wanted. Adela found money for the house, and Mrs. Topham lent the shelter of her name to her niece's unprotected condition. There were separate sitting-rooms for the two ladies, and, if rumour were true (which, after all, it usually is not), a separate staircase for the clergy.

Adela was in her drawing-room one afternoon when Lord Semingham was announced. He appeared to be very warm, and he carried a bundle of papers in his hand. Among the papers there was one of those little smooth white volumes which epitomise so much of the joy and sorrow of this transitory life. He gave himself a shake, as he sat down, and held up the book.

"The car has begun to move," he observed.

"Juggernaut's?"

"Yes; and I have been to see my bankers. I take a trip to the seaside instead of a moor this year, and have let my own pheasant shooting."

He paused and added,

"Dennison has not taken my shooting. They go to the seaside too—with the children."

He paused again and concluded,

"The Omofaga prospectus will be out to-morrow."

Adela laughed.

"Bessie is really quite annoyed," remarked Lord Semingham. "I have seldom seen her so perturbed—but I've sent Ruston to talk to her."

"And why did you do it?" asked Adela.

"I should like to tell you a little history," said he.

And he told her how Mrs. Dennison had sent a telegram to Frankfort. This history was long, for Lord Semingham told it dramatically, as though he enjoyed its quality. Yet Adela made no comment beyond asking,

"And wasn't she right?"

"Oh, for the Empire perhaps—for us, it means trips to the seaside."

He drew his chair a little nearer hers, and dropped his affectation of comic plaintiveness.

"A most disgusting thing has happened in Curzon Street," he said. "Have you heard?"

"No; I've seen nothing of Maggie lately. You've all been buried in Omofaga."

"Hush! No words of ill-omen, please! Well, it's annoyed me immensely I can't think what the foolish fellow means. Tom Loring's going."

"Tom—Loring—going?" she exclaimed with a punctuated pause between every word. "What in the world for?"

"What is the ultimate cause of everything that happens to us now?" he asked, sticking his glass in his eye.

Adela felt as though she were playing at some absurd game of questions and answers, and must make her reply according to the rules.

"Oh, Mr. Ruston!" she said, with a grimace.

Her visitor nodded—as though he had been answered according to the rules.

"Tom broke out in the most extraordinary manner. He said he couldn't stay with Dennison, if Dennison let Ruston lead him by the nose (*ipsissima verba*, my dear Adela), and told Ruston to his face that he came for no good."

"Were you there?"

"Yes. The man seemed to choose the most public opportunity. Did you ever hear such a thing?"

"He's mad about Mr. Ruston. He talked just the same way to me. What did Harry Dennison say?"

"Harry went up to him and took his hand, and shook it, and, you know old Harry's way, tried to smooth it all down, and get them to shake hands. Then Ruston got up and said he'd go and leave them to settle it between Tom and him. Oh, Ruston behaved very well. It was uncommonly awkward for him, you know."

"Yes; and when he'd gone?"

"Harry told Tom that he must keep his engagements; but that, sooner than lose him, he'd go no deeper. That was pretty handsome, I thought, but it didn't suit Tom. 'I can't stay in the house while that fellow comes,' he said."

" While he comes to the house?" cried Adela.

Lord Semingham nodded. " You've hit the point," he seemed to say, and he went on,

" And then they both turned and looked at Maggie Dennison. She'd been sitting there without speaking a single word the whole time. I couldn't go—Harry wouldn't let me—so I got into a corner and looked at the photograph book. I felt rather an ass, between ourselves, you know."

" And what did Maggie say ? "

" Harry was looking as puzzled as an owl, and Tom as obstinate as a toad, and both stared at her. She looked first at Harry, and then at Tom, and smiled in that quiet way of hers. By the way, I never feel that I quite understand——"

" Oh, never mind ! Of course you don't. Go on."

" And then she said, ' What a fuss! I hope that after all this Omofaga business is over Mr. Loring will come back to us.' Pretty straight for Tom, eh? He turned crimson, and walked right out of the room, and she sat down at the piano and began to play some infernal tune, and that soft-hearted old baby, Harry, blew his nose, and damned the draught."

" And he's going ? "

" Yes."

"But," she broke out, "how can he? He's got no money. What'll he live on?"

"Harry offered him as much as he wanted ; but he said he had some savings, and wouldn't take a farthing. He said he'd write for papers, or some such stuff."

"He's been with the Dennisons ever since—oh, years and years! Can't you take him? He'd be awfully useful to you."

"My dear girl, I can't offer charity to Tom Loring," said Semingham, and he added quickly, "No more can you, you know."

"I quarrelled with him desperately a week ago," said she mournfully.

"About Ruston?"

"Oh, yes. About Mr. Ruston, of course."

Lord Semingham whistled gently, and, after a pause, Adela leant forward and asked,

"Do you feel quite comfortable about it?"

"Hang it, no! But I'm too deep in. I hope to heaven the public will swallow it!"

"I didn't mean your wretched Company."

"Oh, you didn't?"

"No; I meant Curzon Street."

"It hardly lies in my mouth to blame Dennison, or his wife either. If they've been foolish, so have I." Adela looked at him as if she thought him profoundly unsatisfactory. He was vaguely conscious of her depreciation, and added, " Ruston's not a rogue, you know."

" No. If I thought he was, I shouldn't be going to take shares in Omofaga."

" You're not?"

" Oh, but I am !"

" Another spinster lady on my conscience! I shall certainly end in the dock!" Lord Semingham took his hat and shook hands. Just as he got to the door, he turned round, and, with an expression of deprecating helplessness, fired a last shot. " Ruston came to see Bessie the other day," he said. " The new mantle she's just invented is to be called—the Omofaga : That is unless she changes it because of the moor. I suggested the *Pis-aller*, but she didn't see it. She never does, you know. Good-bye."

The moment he was gone, Adela put on her hat and drove to Curzon Street. She found Mrs. Dennison alone, and opened fire at once.

" What have you done, Maggie ? " she cried, flinging her gloves on the table and facing her friend with accusing countenance.

Mrs. Dennison was smelling a rose ; she smelt it a little longer, and then replied with another question.

" Why can't men hate quietly ? They must make a fuss. I can go on hating a woman for years and never show it."

" We have the vices of servility," said Adela.

"Harry is a melancholy sight," resumed Mrs. Dennison. "He spends his time looking for the blotting-paper; Tom Loring used to keep it, you know."

Her tone deepened the expression of disapproval on Adela's face.

"I've never been so distressed about anything in my life," said she.

"Oh, my dear, he'll come back." As she spoke, a sudden mischievous smile spread over her face. "You should hear Berthe Cormack on it!" she said.

"I don't want to hear Mrs. Cormack at all. I hate the woman—and I think that I—at any rate—show it."

It surprised Adela to find her friend in such excellent spirits. The air of listlessness, which was apt to mar her manner, and even to some degree her appearance (for to look bored is not becoming), had entirely vanished.

"You don't seem very sorry about poor Mr. Loring," Adela observed.

"Oh, I am; but Mr. Loring can't stop the wheels of the world. And it's his own fault."

Adela sighed. It did not seem of consequence whose fault it was.

"I don't think I care much about the wheels of the world," she said. "How are the children, Maggie?"

“Oh, splendid, and in great glee about the sea-side”—and Mrs. Dennison laughed.

“And about losing Tom Loring?”

“They cried at first.”

“Does anyone ever do anything more than ‘cry at first’?” exclaimed Adela.

“Oh, my dear, don’t be tragical, or cynical, or whatever you are being,” said Maggie pettishly. “Mr. Loring has chosen to be very silly, and there’s an end of it.   Have you seen the prospectus?   Do you know Mr. Ruston brought it to show me before it was submitted to Mr. Belford and the others—the Board, I mean?”

“I think you see quite enough of Mr. Rus-ton,” said Adela, putting up her glass and exam-ining Mrs. Dennison closely.   She spoke coolly, but with a nervous knowledge of her presump-tion.

Mrs. Dennison may have had a taste for diplo-macy and the other arts of government, but she was no diplomatist.   She thought herself gravely wronged by Adela’s suggestion, and burst out an-grily,

“Oh, you’ve been listening to Tom Loring!” and her heightened colour seemed not to agree with the idea that, if Adela had listened, Tom had talked of nothing but Omofaga.   “I don’t mind it from Berthe,” Mrs. Dennison continued, “but from you it’s too bad. I suppose he told you the whole thing? I declare I wasn't dreaming of anything of the kind; I was just excited, and——"

"I haven't seen Mr. Loring," put in Adela as soon as she could.

"Then how do you know——?"

"Lord Semingham told me you quarrelled with Mr. Loring about Omofaga."

"Is that all?"

"Yes. Maggie, was there any more?"

"Do you want to quarrel with me too?"

"I believe Mr. Loring had good reasons."

"You must believe what you like," said Mrs. Dennison, tearing her rose to pieces. "Yes, there was some more."

"What?" asked Adela, expecting to be told to mind her own business.

Mrs. Dennison flung away the rose and began to laugh.

"He found me holding Willie Ruston's hand and telling him I—liked Omofaga! That's all."

"Holding his hand!" exclaimed Adela, justifiably scandalised and hopelessly puzzled. "What did you do that for?"

"I don't know," said Mrs. Dennison. "It happened somehow as we were talking. We got interested, you know."

Adela's next question was also one at which it was

possible to take offence; but she was careless now whether offence were taken or not.

"Are you and the children going to the seaside soon?"

"Oh, yes," rejoined her friend, still smiling. "We shall soon be deep in pails and spades and bathing, and buckets and paddling, and a final charming walk with Harry in the moonlight."

As the sentence went on, the smile became more fixed and less pleasant.

"You ought to be ashamed to talk like that," said Adela.

Mrs. Dennison walked up the room and down again.

"So I am," she said, pausing to look down on Adela, and then resuming her walk.

"I wish to goodness this Omofaga affair—yes, and Mr. Ruston too—had never been invented. It seems to set us all wrong."

"Wrong!" cried Mrs. Dennison. "Oh, yes, if it's wrong to have something one can take a little interest in!"

"You're hopeless to-day, Maggie. I shall go away. What did you take his hand for?"

"Nothing. I tell you I was excited."

"Well, I think he's a man one ought to keep cool with."

"Oh, he's cool enough. He'll keep you cool."

“ But he didn’t——”

“ Oh, don’t—pray don’t ! ” cried Mrs. Dennison.

Adela took her leave ; and, as luck would have it, opened the door just as Tom Loring was walking downstairs with an enormous load of dusty papers in his hands. She pulled the door close behind her hastily, exclaiming,

“ Why, I thought you’d gone ! ”

“ So you’ve heard ? I’m just putting things ship-shape.   I go this evening.”

“ Well, I’m sorry—still, for your sake, I’m glad.”

“ Why ? ”

“ You may do something on your own account now.”

“ I don’t want to do anything,” said Tom obstinately.

“ Come and see me some day. I’ve forgiven you, you know.”

“ So I will.”

“ Mr. Loring, are you going to say good-bye to Maggie ? ”

“ I don’t know. I suppose so.” Then he added, detecting Adela’s unexpressed hope, “ Oh, it’s not a bit of use, you know.”

Adela passed on, and, later, Loring, having finished his work and being about to go, sought out Mrs. Dennison.

“ You’re determined to go, are you ? ” she asked,

with the air of one who surrenders before an inexplicable whim.

"Yes," said Tom. "You know I must go."

"Why?"

"I'm not a saint—nor a rogue; if I were either, I might stay."

"Or even if you were a sensible man," suggested Maggie Dennison.

"Being merely an honest man, I think I'll go. I've tried to put all Harry's things right for him, and to make it as easy for him to get along as I can."

"Can he find his papers and blue-books and things?"

"Oh, yes; and I got abstracts ready on all the things he cares about."

"He'll miss you horribly. Ah, well!"

"I suppose a little; but, really, I think he'll learn to get along——"

Mrs. Dennison interrupted with a laugh.

"Do you know," she asked, "what we remind me of? Why, of a husband and wife separating, and wondering whether the children will miss poor papa— though poor papa insists in going, and mamma is sure he must."

"I never mentioned the children," said Tom angrily.

"I know you didn't."

Tom looked at her for an instant.

"For God's sake," said he, "don't let him see that!"

"Oh, how you twist things!" she cried in impatient protest.

Tom only shook his head. The charge was not sincere.

"Good-bye, Tom," she went on after a pause. "I believe, some day or other, you'll come back—or, at any rate, come and live next door—instead of Berthe Cormack, you know. But I don't know in what state you'll find us."

"I'd just like to tell you one thing, if I may," said Tom, resolutely refusing to meet the softened look in her eyes with any answering friendliness.

"Yes?"

"You've got one of the best fellows in the world for a husband."

"Well, I know that, I suppose, at least, as well as you do."

"That's all. Good-bye."

Without more he left her. She drew the window-curtain aside and watched him get into his cab and be driven away. The house was very still. Her husband was in his place at Westminster, and the children had gone to a party. She went upstairs to the nursery, hoping to find something to criticise; then to Harry's dressing-room, where she filled his pin-cushion with pins and put fresh water to the

flowers in the vase. She could find no other offices of
wife or mother to do, and she presently found herself
looking into Tom's room, which was very bare and
desolate, stripped of the homelike growth of a five
years' tenancy. Her excitement was over; she felt
terribly like a child after a tantrum; she flung open
the window of the room and stood listening to the
noise of the town. It was the noise of happy people,
who had plenty to do; or of happier still, who did
not want to do anything, and thus found content.
She turned away and walked downstairs with a step
as heavy as physical weariness brings with it. It
came as a curious aggravation—light itself, but gain-
ing weight from its surroundings—that, for once in a
way, she had no engagements that evening. All the
tide seemed to be flowing by, leaving her behind high
and dry on the shore. Even the children had their
party, even Harry his toy at Westminster; and Willie
Ruston was working might and main to give a good
start to Omofaga. Only of her had the world no
need—and no heed.

CHAPTER VIII.

HAD Lord Semingham and Harry Dennison taken
an opportunity which many persons would have
thought that they had a right to take, they might
have shifted the burden of the Baron's *douceur* and
of sundry other not trifling expenses on to the shoulders of the public, and enjoyed their moors that year
after all; for at the beginning Omofaga obtained such
a moderate and reasonable "boom" as would have en-
abled them to perform the operation known as "un-
loading" (and literary men must often admire the
terse and condensed expressiveness of "City" meta-
phors) with much profit to themselves. But either
they conceived this course of conduct to be beneath
them, or they were so firm of faith in Mr. Ruston
that they stood to their guns and their shares, and
took their seats at the Board, over which Mr. Foster
Belford magniloquently presided, still possessed of the
strongest personal interest in the success of Omofaga. Lady Semingham, having been made aware

that Omofaga shares were selling at forty shillings a piece, was quite unable to understand why Alfred and Mr. Dennison did not sell all they had, and thereby procure moors or whatever else they wanted. Willie Ruston had to be sent for again, and when he told her that the same shares would shortly be worth five pounds (which he did with the most perfect confidence), she was equally at a loss to see why they were on sale to anybody who chose to pay forty shillings. Ruston, who liked to make everybody a convert to his own point of view, spent the best part of an afternoon conversing with the little lady, but, when he came away, he left her placidly admiring the Omofaga mantle which had just arrived from the milliner's, and promised to create an immense sensation.

"I believe she's all gown," said he despairingly, at the Valentines in the evening. "If you undressed her there'd be no one there."

"Well, there oughtn't to be many people," said young Sir Walter, with a hearty laugh at his boyish joke.

"Walter, how can you!" cried Marjory.

This little conversation, trivial though it be, has its importance, as indicating the very remarkable change which had occurred in young Sir Walter. There at least Ruston had made a notable convert, and he had effected this result by the simple but audacious device of offering to take Sir Walter with him to Omofaga. Sir Walter was dazzled. Between spending another year or two at Oxford *in statu pupillari*, vexed by schools and disciplined by proctors —between being required to be in by twelve at night and unable to visit London without permission—between this unfledged state and the position of a man among the men who were in the vanguard of the empire there rolled a flood; and the flood was mighty enough to sweep away all young Sir Walter's doubts about Mr. Ruston being a gentleman, to obliterate Evan Haselden's sneers, to uproot his influence—in a word, to transform that youthful legislator from a paragon of wisdom and accomplishments into " a good chap, but rather a lot of side on, you know."

Marjory, having learnt from literature that hers was supposed to be the fickle sex, might well open her eyes and begin to feel very sorry indeed for poor Evan Haselden. But she also was under the spell and hailed the sun of glory rising for her brother out of the mists of Omofaga; and if poor Lady Valentine shed some tears before Willie Ruston convinced her of the rare chance it was for her only boy—and a few more after he had so convinced her—why, it would be lucky if these were the only tears lost in the process of developing Omofaga; for it seems that great enterprises must always be watered by the tears of mothers and nourished on the blood of sons. *Sic fortis Etruria crevit.*

One or two other facts may here be chronicled about Omofaga. There were three great meetings: one at the Cannon Street Hotel, purely commercial; another at the Westminster Town Hall, commercial-political; a third at Exeter Hall, commercial-religious. They were all very successful, and, taken together, were considered to cover the ground pretty completely. The most unlike persons and the most disparate views found a point of union in Omofaga. Adela Ferrars put three thousand pounds into it, Lady Valentine a thousand. Mr. Carlin finally disposed of the coal business, and his wife dreamt of the workhouse all night and scolded herself for her lack of faith all the morning. Willie Ruston spoke of being off in five months, and Sir Walter immediately bought a complete up-country outfit.

Suddenly there was a cloud. Omofaga began to be " written down," in the most determined and able manner. The anonymous detractor—in such terms did Mr. Foster Belford refer to the writer—used the columns of a business paper of high standing, and his letters, while preserving a judicial and temperate tone, were uncompromisingly hostile and exceedingly damaging. A large part of Omofaga (he said) had not been explored, indeed, nobody knew exactly what was and what was not Omofaga; let the shareholders get what comfort they could out of that; but, so far as Omofaga had been explored, it had been proved to be barren of all sources of wealth. The writer grudgingly admitted that it might feed a certain head of cattle, though he hastened to add that the flies were fatal all the hot months; but as for gold, or diamonds, or any such things as companies most love, there were none, and if there were, they could not be won, and if they could be won no European could live to win them. It was a timid time on the markets then, and people took fright easily. In a few days any temptation that might have assailed Lord Semingham and Harry Dennison lost its power. Omofagas were far below par, and Lady Semingham was entreating her husband to buy all he could against the hour when they should be worth five pounds a piece, because, as she said, Mr. Ruston was quite sure that they were going to be, and who knew more about it than Mr. Ruston ?

It was just about this time that Tom Loring, who had vanished completely for a week or two, after his departure from Curzon Street, came up out of the depths and called on Adela Ferrars in Queen's Gate; and her first remark showed that she was a person of some perspicacity.

"Isn't this rather small of you?" she asked, putting on her eyeglasses and finding an article which she indicated. "You may not like him, but still——"

"How like a woman!" said Tom Loring in the

tone of a man who expects and, on the whole, welcomes ill-usage. "How did you know it was mine?"

"It's so like that article of Harry Dennison's. I think you might put your name, anyhow."

"Yes, and rob what I say of all weight. Who knows my name?"

Adela felt an impulse to ask him angrily why nobody knew his name, but she inquired instead what he thought he knew about Omofaga. She put this question in a rather offensive tone.

It appeared that Tom Loring knew a great deal about Omofaga, all, in fact, that there was to be learnt from blue-books, consular reports, gazetteers, travels, and other heavy works of a like kind.

"You've been moling in the British Museum," cried Adela accusingly.

Tom admitted it without the least shame.

"I knew this thing was a fraud and the man a fraud, and I determined to show him up if I could," said he.

"It's because you hate him."

"Then it's lucky for the British investor that I do hate him."

"It's not lucky for me," said Adela.

"You don't mean to say you've been——"

"Fool enough? Yes, I have. No, don't quarrel again. It won't ruin me, anyhow. Are the things you say really true?"

Tom replied by another question.

"Do you think I'd write 'em if I didn't believe they were?"

"No, but you might believe they were because you hate him."

Tom seemed put out at this idea. It is not one that generally suggests itself to a man when his own views are in question.

"I admit I began because I hate him," he said, with remarkable candour, after a moment's consideration; "but, by Jove, as I went on I found plenty of justification. Look here, you mustn't tell anyone I'm writing them."

Tom looked a little embarrassed as he made this request.

Adela hesitated for a moment. She did not like the request, either.

"No, I won't," she said at last; and she added, "I'm beginning to think I hate him, too. He's turning me into an hospital."

"What?"

"People he wounds come to me. Old Lady Valentine came and cried because Walter's going to Omofaga; and Evan came and—well, swore because Walter worships Mr. Ruston; and Harry Dennison came and looked bewildered, and—you know—because—oh, because of you, and so on."

"And now I come, don't I?"

“Yes, and now you.”

“And has Mrs. Dennison come?” asked Tom, with a look of disconcerting directness.

“No,” snapped Adela, and she looked at the floor, whereupon Tom diverted his eyes from her and stared at the ceiling.

Presently he searched in his waistcoat pocket and brought out a little note.

“Read that,” he said, a world of disgust in his tone.

“‘I told you so.—B. C.’” read Adela.” Oh, it’s that Cormack woman!” she cried.

“You see what it means? She means I’ve been got rid of in order that——” Tom stopped, and brought his clenched fist down on his opened palm. “If I thought it, I’d shoot the fellow,” he ended.

He looked at her for the answer to his unexpressed question.

Adela turned the pestilential note over and over in her fingers, handling it daintily as though it might stain.

“I don’t think he means it,” she said at last, without trying to blink the truth of Tom’s interpretation.

Tom rose and began to walk about.

“Women beat me,” he broke out. “I don’t understand ’em. How should I? I’m not one of these fellows who catch women’s fancy—thank God!”

“If you continue to dislike the idea, you’ll probably manage to escape the reality," observed Adela, and her tone, for some reason or other—perhaps merely through natural championship of her sex— was rather cold and her manner stiff.

"Oh, some women are all right;" and Adela acknowledged the concession with a satirical bow. "Look here, can't you help?" he burst out. "Tell her what a brute he is."

"Oh, you do not understand women!"

"Well, then, I shall tell Dennison. He won't stand nonsense of that kind."

"You'll deserve horsewhipping if you do," remarked Adela.

"Then what am I to do?"

"Nothing. In fact, Mr. Loring, you have no genius for delicate operations."

"Of course I'm a fool."

Adela played with her *pince-nez* for a minute or two, put it on, looked at him, and then said, with just a touch of unwonted timidity in her voice,

"Anyhow, you happen to be a gentleman."

Poor Tom had been a good deal buffeted of late, and a friendly stroking was a pleasant change. He looked up with a smile, but as he looked up Adela looked away.

"I think I'll stop those articles," said he.

"Yes, do," she cried, a bright smile on her face.

"They've pretty well done their work, too."

“Don’t! Don’t spoil it! But—but don’t you get money for them?”

Tom was in better humour now. He held out his hand with his old friendly smile.

“Oh, wait till I am in the workhouse, and then you shall take me out.”

“I don’t believe I did mean that,” protested Adela.

“You always mean everything that—that the best woman in the world could mean,” and Tom wrung her hand and disappeared.

Adela’s hand was rather crushed and hurt, and for a moment she stood regarding it ruefully.

“I thought he was going to kiss it,” she said. “One of those fellows who take women’s fancy, perhaps, would have! And—and it wouldn’t have hurt so much. Ah, well, I’m very glad he’s going to stop the articles.”

And the articles did stop; and perhaps things might have fallen out worse than that an honest man, driven hard by bitterness, should do a useful thing from a doubtful motive, and having done just enough of it, should repent and sin no more; for unquestionably the articles prevented a great many persons from paying an unduly high price for Omofaga shares. This line of thought seems defensible, but it was not Adela’s. She rejoiced purely that Tom should turn away from the doubtful thing; and if Tom had been a man of greater acuteness, it would have struck him as worthy of note, perhaps even of gratification, that Miss Adela Ferrars should care so much whether he did or did not do doubtful things. But then Miss Ferrars—for it seems useless to keep her secret any longer, the above recorded interview having somewhat impaired its mystery—was an improbably romantic person—such are to be met even at an age beyond twenty-five—and was very naturally ashamed of her weakness. People often are ashamed of being better than their surroundings. Being better they feel better, and feeling better they feel priggish, and then they try not to be better, and happily fail. So Adela was very shamefaced over her ideal, and would as soon have thought of preaching on a platform—of which practice she harboured a most bigoted horror—as of proclaiming the part that love must play in her marriage. The romantic resolve lay snug in its hidden nest, sheltered from cold gusts of ridicule by a thick screen of worldly sayings, and, when she sent away a suitor, of worldly-wise excuses. Thus no one suspected it, not even Tom Loring, although he thought her "the best of women;" a form of praise, by the way, that gave the lady honoured by it less pleasure than less valuable commendation might have done. Why best? Why not most charming? Well, probably because he thought the one and didn't think the other. She was the best; but there was another whose doings and whose peril had robbed Tom Loring of his peace, and made him do the doubtful thing. Why had he done it? Or (and Adela smiled mockingly at this resurrection of the Old Woman), if he did do it, why did he do it for Maggie Dennison? She didn't believe he would ever do a doubtful thing for her. For that she loved him; but perhaps she would have loved him— well, not less—if he did; for how she would forgive him!

After half-an-hour of this kind of thing—it was her own summary of her meditations—she dressed, went out to dinner, sat next Evan Haselden, and said cynical things all the evening; so that, at last Evan told her that she had no more feeling than a mummified Methodist. This was exactly what she wanted.

CHAPTER IX.

AN OPPRESSIVE ATMOSPHERE.

THE Right Honourable Foster Belford, although
not, like Mr. Pitt, famous for " ruining Great Britain
gratis "—perhaps merely from want of the opportunity—had yet not made a fortune out of political life,
and it had suggested a pleasant addition to his means,
when Willie Ruston offered him the chairmanship of
the Omofaga Company, with the promise of a very
comfortable yearly honorarium. He accepted the
post with alacrity, but without undue gratitude, for
he considered himself well worth the price; and the
surprising fact is that he was well worth it. He
bulked large to the physical and mental view. His
colleagues in the Cabinet had taken a year or two to
find out his limits, and the public had not found them
out yet. Therefore he was not exactly a fool. On
the other hand, the limits were certainly there, and so
there was no danger of his developing an inconvenient
greatness. As has been previously hinted, he enjoyed
Harry Dennison's entire confidence; and he could be

relied upon not to understand Lord Semingham's
irreverence. Thus his appointment did good to the
Omofaga as well as to himself, and only the initiated
winked when Willie Ruston hid himself behind this
imposing figure and pulled the strings.

"The best of it is," Ruston remarked to Semingham, "that you and Carlin will have the whole thing
in your own hands when I've gone out. Belford
won't give you any trouble."

"But, my dear fellow, I don't want it all in my
hands. I want to grow rich out of it without any
trouble."

Ruston twisted his cigar in his mouth. The prospect of immediate wealth flowing in from Omofaga was, as Lord Semingham knew very well, not
assured.

"Loring's stopped hammering us," said Ruston;
"thats one thing."

"Oh, you found out he wrote them?"

"Yes; and uncommonly well he did it, confound
him. I wish we could get that fellow. There's a
good deal in him."

"You see," observed Lord Semingham, "he
doesn't like you. I don't know that you went the
right way about to make him."

The remark sounded blunt, but Semingham had
learnt not to waste delicate phrases on Willie Ruston.

"Well, I didn't know he was worth the trouble."

8

“One path to greatness is said to be to make no enemies.”

“A very roundabout one, I should think. I’m going to make a good many enemies in Omofaga.”

Lord Semingham suddenly rose, put on his hat, and left the offices of the Company. Mrs. Dennison had, a little while ago, complained to him that she ate, drank, breathed and wore Omofaga. He had detected the insincerity of her complaint, but he was becoming inclined to echo it in all genuineness on his own account. There were moments when he wondered how and why he had allowed this young man to lead him so far and so deep; moments when a convulsion of Nature, redistributing Africa and blotting out Omofaga, would have left him some thousands of pounds poorer in purse, but appreciably more cheerful in spirit. Perhaps matters would mend when the Local Administrator had departed to his local administration, and only the mild shadow of him which bore the name of Carlin trod the boards of Queen Street, Cheapside. Ruston began to be oppressive. The restless energy and domineering mind of the man wearied Semingham’s indolent and dilettante spirit, and he hailed the end of the season as an excellent excuse for putting himself beyond the reach of his colleague for a few weeks. Yet, the more he quailed, the more he trusted; and when a very great man, holding a very great office, met him in the House of

Lords, and expressed the opinion that when the Company and Mr. Ruston went to Omofaga they would find themselves in a pretty hornets' nest, Lord Semingham only said that he should be sorry for the hornets.

"Don't ask us to fetch your man out for you, that's all," said the very great man.

And for an instant Lord Semingham, still feeling that load upon his shoulders, fancied that it would be far from his heart to prefer such a request. There might be things less just and fitting than that Willie Ruston and those savage tribes of Omofaga should be left to fight out the quarrel by themselves, the civilised world standing aloof. And the dividends—well, of course, there were the dividends, but Lord Semingham had in his haste forgotten them.

"Ah, you don't know Ruston," said he, shaking a forefinger at the great man.

"Don't I? He came every day to my office for a fortnight."

"Wanted something?"

"Yes, he wanted something certainly, or he wouldn't have come, you know."

"Got it, I suppose?" asked Lord Semingham, in a tone curiously indicative of resignation rather than triumph.

"Well, yes; I did, at last, not without hesitation, accede to his request."

Then Lord Semingham, with no apparent excuse, laughed in the face of the great man, left the House (much in the same sudden way as he had left Queen Street, Cheapside), and passed rapidly through the lobbies till he reached Westminster Hall. Here he met a young man, clad to perfection, but looking sad. It was Evan Haselden. With a sigh of relief at meeting no one of heavier metal, Semingham stopped him and began to talk. Evan's melancholy air enveloped his answers in a mist of gloom. Moreover there was a large streak on his hat, where the nap had been rubbed the wrong way; evidently he was in trouble. Presently he seized his friend by the arm, and proposed a walk in the Park.

" But are you paired ? " asked Semingham ; for an important division was to occur that day in the Commons.

" No," said Evan fiercely. " Come along ; " and Lord Semingham went, exclaiming inwardly, " A girl ! "

" I'm the most miserable devil alive," said Evan, as they left the Horse Guards on the right hand.

Semingham put up his eyeglass.

" I've always regarded you as the favourite of fortune," he said. " What's the matter ? "

The matter unfolded itself some half-hour after they had reached the Row and sat down. It came forth with difficulty ; pride obstructed the passage, and something better than pride made the young man diffuse in the telling of his trouble. Lord Semingham grew very grave indeed. Let who would laugh at happy lovers, he had a groan for the unfortunate— a groan with reservations.

"She said she liked me very much, but didn't feel —didn't, you know, look up to me enough, and so on," said poor Evan in puzzled pain. "I—I can't think what's come over her. She used to be quite different. I don't know what she means by talking like that."

Lord Semingham played a tune on his knee with the fingers of one hand. He was waiting.

"Young Val's gone back on me too," moaned Evan, who took the brother's deposal of him hardly more easily than the sister's rejection. Suddenly he brightened up; a smile, but a bitter one, gleamed across his face.

"I think I've put one spoke in his wheel, though," he said.

"Ruston's?" inquired Semingham, still playing his tune.

"Yes. A fortnight ago, old Detchmore" (Lord Detchmore was the very great man before referred to) "asked me if I knew Loring. You know Ruston's been trying to get Detchmore to back him up in making a railway to Omofaga?"

"I didn't know," said Lord Semingham, with an unmoved face.

“ You’re a director, aren’t you ? ”

“ Yes.   Go on, my dear boy.”

“ And Detchmore had seen Loring’s articles. Well, I took Tom to him, and we left him quite decided to have nothing to do with it.   Oh, by Jove, though, I forgot; I suppose you’d be on the other side there, wouldn’t you ? ”

“ I suppose I should, but it doesn’t matter.”

“ Why not ? ”

“ Because I fancy Ruston’s got what he wanted ; ” and Lord Semingham related what he had heard from the Earl of Detchmore.

Evan listened in silence, and, the tale ended, the two lay back in their chairs, and idly looked at the passing carriages.   At last Lord Semingham spoke.

“ He’s going to Omofaga in a few months,” he observed.   “ And, Evan, you don’t mean that he’s your rival at the Valentines’ ? ”

“ I’m not so sure, confound him.   You know how pretty she is.”

Semingham knew that she was pretty; but he also knew that she was poor, and thought that she was, if not too insipid (for he recognised the unusual taste of his own mind), at least too immature to carry Willie Ruston off his feet, and into a love affair that promised no worldly gain.

“ I asked Mrs. Dennison what she thought,” pursued Evan.

“ Oh, you did ? ”

“ But the idea seemed quite a new one to her.
That’s good, you know. I expect she’d have noticed
if he’d shown any signs.”

Lord Semingham thought it very likely.

“ Anyhow,” Evan continued, “ Marjory’s awfully
keen about him.”

“ He’ll be in Omofaga in three or four months,”
Semingham repeated. It was all the consolation he
could offer.

Presently Evan got up and strode away. Lord
Semingham sat on, musing on the strange turmoil the
coming of the man had made in the little corner of
the world he dwelt in. He was reminded of what was
said concerning Lord Byron by another poet. They
all felt Ruston. His intrusion into the circle had
changed all the currents, so that sympathy ran no
longer between old friends, and hearts answered to a
new stimulus. Some he attracted, some he repelled;
none did he leave alone. From great to small his influence ran; from the expulsion of Tom Loring to the
christening of the Omofaga mantle. Semingham had
an acute sense of the absurdity of it all, but he had
seen absurd things happen too often to be much relieved by his intuition. And when absurd things
happen, they have consequences just as other things
have. And the most exasperating fact was the utter
unconsciousness of the disturber. He had no mys-

tery-airs, no graces, no seeming fascinations. He was
relentlessly business-like, unsentimental, downright;
he took it all as a matter of course. He did not pry
for weak spots. He went right on—on and over—
and seemed not to know when he was going over. A
very Juggernaut indeed! Semingham thanked Adela
for teaching him the word.

He was suddenly roused by the merry laughter of
children. Three or four little ones were scampering
along the path in the height of glee. As they came
up, he recognised them. He had seen them once before. They were Carlin's children. Five there were,
he counted now; three ran ahead; two little girls
held each a hand of Willie Ruston's, who was laughing as merrily as his companions. The whole group
knew Semingham, and the eldest child was by his
knees in a moment.

"We've been to the Exhibition," she cried exult-
antly; "and now Willie—Mr. Ruston, I mean—is
taking us to have ices in Bond Street."

"A human devil!" said the astonished man to
himself, as Willie Ruston plumped down beside him,
imploring a brief halt, and earnestly asseverating that
his request was in good faith, and concealed no lurk-
ing desire to evade the ices.

"I met young Haselden as we came along," Ruston observed, wiping his brow.

"Ah! Yes, he's been with me."

The children had wandered a few yards off, and stood impatiently looking at their hero.

"He's had a bit of a facer, I fancy," pursued Willie Ruston. "Heard about it?"

"Something."

"It'll come all right, I should think," said Ruston, in a comfortably careless tone. "He's not a bad fellow, you know, though he's not over-appreciative of me." Lord Semingham found no comment. "I hear you're going to Dieppe next week?" asked Ruston.

"Yes. My wife and Mrs. Dennison have put their heads together, and fixed on that. You know we're economising."

Ruston laughed.

"I suppose you are," he said through his white teeth. The idea seemed to amuse him. "We may meet there. I've promised to run over for a few days if I can."

"The deuce you have!" would have expressed his companion's feelings; but Lord Semingham only said, "Oh, really?"

"All right, I'm coming directly," Ruston cried a moment later to his young friends, and, with a friendly nod, he rose and went on his way. Lord Semingham watched the party till it disappeared through the Park gates, hearing in turn the children's shrill laugh and Willie Ruston's deeper notes. The

effect of the chance meeting was to make his fancies
and his fancied feelings look still more absurd. That
he perceived at once; the devil appeared so very human in such a mood and such surroundings. Yet
that attribute — that most demoniac attribute — of
ubiquity loomed larger and larger. For not even a
foreign land—not even a watering-place of pronounced
frivolity—was to be a refuge. The man was coming
to Dieppe! And on whose bidding? Semingham
had no doubt on whose bidding; and, out of the airy
forms of those absurd fancies, there seemed to rise a
more material shape, a reality, a fabric not com-
pounded wholly of dreams, but mixed of stuff that
had made human comedies and human tragedies since
the world began. Mrs. Dennison had bidden Willie
Ruston to Dieppe. That was Semingham's instant
conclusion; she had bidden him, not merely by a formal invitation, or by a simple acquiescence, but by
the will and determination which possessed her to be
of his mind and in his schemes. And perhaps Evan
Haselden's innocent asking of her views had carried its
weight also. For nearly an hour Semingham sat and
mused. For awhile he thought he would act; but how
should he act? And why? And to what end? Since
what must be must, and in vain do we meddle with fate.
An easy, almost eager, recognition of the inevitable
in the threatened, of the necessary in everything that
demanded effort for its avoidance, had stamped his

life and grown deep into his mind. Wherefore now, faced with possibilities that set his nerves on edge, and wrung his heart for good friends, he found nothing better to do than shrug his shoulders and thank God that his own wife's submission to the man went no deeper than the inside lining of that famous Omofaga mantle, nor his own than the bottom, or near the bottom, of his trousers' pocket.

"Though that, in faith," he exclaimed ruefully, as at last he rose, "is, in this world of ours, pretty deep!"

CHAPTER X.

A LADY'S BIT OF WORK.

THE Dennison children, after a two nights' banishment, had come down to dessert again. They had been in sore disgrace, caused (it was stated to Mrs. Cormack, who had been invited to dine *en famille*) by a grave breach of hospitality and good manners which Madge had led the younger ones—who tried to look plaintively innocent—into committing.

The Carlin children had come to tea, and a great dissension had arisen between the two parties. The Carlins had belauded the generous donor of ices; Madge had taken up the cudgels fiercely on Tom Loring's behalf, and Dora and Alfred had backed her up. Each side proceeded from praise of its own favourite to sneers—by no means covert—at the other's man, and the feud had passed from the stage of words to that of deeds before it was discovered by the superior powers and crushed. On the hosts, of course, the blame had to fall; they were sent to bed, while the guests drove off in triumph, comforted by sweets and shillings. Madge did not think, or pretend to think, that this was justice, and her mother's recital of her crimes to Mrs. Cormack, so far from reducing her to penitence, brought back to her cheeks and eyes the glow they had worn when she slapped (there is no use in blinking facts) Jessie Carlin, and told her that she hated Mr. Ruston. Madge Dennison was like her mother in face and temper. That may have been the reason why Harry Dennison squeezed her hand under the table, and by his tacit aid broke the force of his wife's cold reproofs. But there was perhaps another reason also.

Mrs. Cormack said that she was shocked, and looked very much amused. The little history made up for the bore of having the children brought in. That was a thing she objected to very much; it stopped all rational conversation. But now her curiosity was stirred.

"Why don't you like Mr. Ruston, my child?" she asked Madge.

"I don't dislike him," said Madge, rosy red, and speaking with elaborate slowness. She said it as though it were a lesson she had learnt.

"But why, then," said Mrs. Cormack, whirling her hands, "beat the little Carlin?"

"That was before mamma told me," answered Madge, the two younger ones sitting by, open-mouthed, to hear her explanation.

"Oh, what an obedient child! How I should have liked a little girl like you, darling!"

Madge hated sarcasm, and her feelings towards Mrs. Cormack reflected those of her idol, Tom Loring.

"I don't know what you mean," she said curtly; and then she looked anxiously at her mother.

But Mrs. Dennison was smiling.

"Let her alone, Berthe," she said. "She's been punished. Give her some fruit, Harry."

Harry Dennison piled up the plate eagerly held out to him.

"Who'll give you fruit at Dieppe?" he asked, stroking his daughter's hair.

Mrs. Cormack pricked up her ears.

"Didn't we tell you?" asked Mrs. Dennison. "Harry can't come for a fortnight. That tiresome old Sir George" (Sir George was the senior partner in Dennison, Sons & Company) "is down with the gout, and Harry's got to stay in town. But I'll give Madge fruit—if she's good."

"Papa gives it me anyhow," said Madge, who preferred unconditional benefits.

Harry laughed dolefully. He had been looking forward to a holiday with his children. Their uninterrupted society would have easily consoled him for the loss of the moor.

"It's an awful bore," he said; "but there's no

help for it. Sir George can't put a foot to the ground."

"Anyhow," suggested Mrs. Cormack, "you will be able to help Mr. Ruston with the Omofaga."

"Papa," broke out Madge, her face bright with a really happy idea, which must, she thought, meet with general acceptance, "since you can't come, why shouldn't Tom?"

Mrs. Cormack grew more amused. Oh, it was quite worth while to have the children! They were so good at saying things one couldn't say oneself; and then one could watch the effect. In an impulse of gratitude, she slid a banana on to Madge's plate.

"Marjory Valentine's coming," said Mrs. Dennison. "You like her, don't you, Madge?"

"She's a girl," said Madge scornfully; and Harry, with a laugh, stroked her hair again.

"You're a little flirt," said he.

"But why can't Tom?" persisted Madge, as she attacked the banana. It was Mrs. Cormack's gift, but —*non olet.*

For a moment nobody answered. Then Harry Dennison said—not in the least as though he believed it, or expected anybody else to believe it—

"Tom's got to stay and work."

"Have all the gentlemen we know got to stay and work?"

Harry nodded assent.

Mrs. Cormack was leaning forward. A moment later she sank back, hiding a smile behind her napkin; for Madge observed, in a tone of utter contentment,

"Oh, then, Mr Ruston won't come;" and she wagged her head reassuringly at the open-mouthed little ones. They were satisfied, and fell again to eating.

After a few moments, Mrs. Dennison, who had made no comment on her daughter's inference, swept the flock off to bed, praying Berthe to excuse her temporary absence. It was her habit to go upstairs with them when possible, and Harry would see that coffee came.

"Poor Madge!" said Harry, when the door was shut, "what'll she say when Ruston turns up?"

"Then he does go?"

"I think so. We'd asked him to stay with us, and though he can't do that now, he and young Walter Valentine talk of running over for a few days. I hope they will."

Mrs. Cormack, playing with her teaspoon, glanced at her host out of the corner of her eye.

"He can go all the better, as I shall be here," continued Harry. "I can look after Omofaga."

Mrs. Cormack rapped the teaspoon sharply on her cup. The man was such a fool. Harry, dimly recognising her irritation, looked up inquiringly; but she hesitated before she spoke. Would it spoil sport or make sport if she stirred a suspicion in him? A thought threw its weight in the balance. Maggie Dennison's friendship had been a trifle condescending, and the grateful friend pictured her under the indignity of enforced explanations, of protests, even of orders to alter her conduct. But how would Harry take a hint? There were men silly enough to resent such hints. Caution was the word.

"Well, I almost wish he wasn't going," she said at last. "For Maggie's sake, I mean. She wants a complete rest."

"Oh, but she likes him. He amuses her. Why, she's tremendously interested in Omofaga, Mrs. Cormack."

"Ah, but he excites her too. We poor women have nerves, Mr. Dennison. It would be much better for her to hear nothing of Omofaga for a few weeks."

"Has she been talking to you much about it?" asked Harry, beginning to feel anxious at his guest's immensely solemn tone.

Indeed, little Mrs. Cormack spoke for the nonce quite like a family physician.

"Oh, yes, about it and him," she replied. "She's never off the subject. Mr. Loring was half right."

"Tom's objections were based on quite other grounds."

9

"Oh, were they really? I thought—well, anyhow, Mr. Ruston being there will do her no good. She'll like it immensely, of course."

Harry Dennison rubbed his hand over his chin.

"I see what you mean," he said. "Yes, she'd have been better away from everything. But I can't object to Ruston going. I asked him myself."

"Yes, when you were going."

"That makes no difference."

Mrs. Cormack said nothing. She tapped her spoon against the cup once more.

"Why, we should have talked all the more about it if I'd been there."

His companion was still silent, her eyes turned down towards the table. Harry looked at her with perplexity, and when he next spoke, there was a curious appealing note in his voice.

"Surely it doesn't make any difference?" he asked. "What difference can it make?"

No answer came. Mrs. Cormack laid down the spoon and sat back in her chair.

"You mean there'll be no one to make a change for her—to distract her thoughts?"

Mrs. Cormack flung her hands out with an air of impatience.

"Oh, I meant nothing," said she petulantly.

The clock seemed to tick very loud in the silence that followed her words.

"I wish I could go," said Harry at last, in a low tone.

"Oh, I wish you could, Mr. Dennison;" and as she spoke she raised her eyes, and, for the first time, looked full in his face.

Harry rose from his chair; at the same moment his wife re-entered the room. He started a little at the sight of her.

She held a letter in her hand.

"Mr. Ruston will be at Dieppe on the 15th with Walter Valentine," she said, referring to it. "Give me some coffee, Harry."

He poured it out and gave it to her, saying,

"A letter from Ruston? Let's see what he says."

"Oh, there's nothing else," she answered, laying it beside her.

Mrs. Cormack sat looking on.

"May I see?" asked Harry Dennison.

"If you like," she answered, a little surprised; and, turning to Mrs. Cormack, she added, "Mr. Ruston's a man of few words on paper."

"Ah, he makes every word mean something, I expect," returned that lady, who was quite capable of the same achievement herself, and exhibited it in this very speech.

"What does he mean by the postscript?—'Have you found another kingdom yet?'" asked Harry, with a puzzled frown.

" It's a joke, dear."

" But what does it mean ? "

" Oh, my dear Harry, I can't explain jokes."

Harry laid the note down again.

" It's a joke between ourselves," Mrs. Dennison went on. " I oughtn't to have shown you the letter. Come, Berthe, we'll go upstairs."

And Mrs. Cormack had no alternative but to obey.

Left alone, Harry Dennison drew his chair up to the hearthrug. There was no fire, but he acted as though there were, leaning forward with his elbows on his knees, and gazing into the grate. He felt hurt and disconsolate. His old grievance—that people left him out—was strong upon him. He had delighted in the Omofaga scheme, because he had been in the inside ring there—because he was of importance to it— because it showed him to his wife as a mover in great affairs. And now—somehow—he seemed to be being pushed outside there too. What was this joke between themselves? At Dieppe they would have all that out; he would not be in the way there. Then he did not understand what Berthe Cormack would be at. She had looked at him so curiously. He did not know what to make of it, and he wished that Tom Loring were on the other side of the fireplace. Then he could ask him all about it. Tom! Why, Tom had looked at him almost in the same way as Berthe Cormack had—just when he was wringing his hand in farewell. No, it was not the same way—and yet in part the same. Tom's look had pity in it, and no derision. Mrs. Cormack's derision was but touched with pity. Yet both seemed to ask, "Don't you see?" See what? Why had Tom gone away? He could rely on Tom. See what? There was nothing to see.

He sat longer than he meant. It was past ten when he went upstairs. Mrs. Cormack had gone, and his wife was in an armchair by the open window. He came in softly and surprised her with her head thrown back on the cushions and a smile on her lips. And the letter was in her hands. Hearing his step when he was close by her, she sat up, letting the note fall to the ground.

"What a time you've been! Berthe's gone. Were you asleep?"

"No. I was thinking; Maggie, I wish I could come to Dieppe with you."

"Ah, I wish you could," said she graciously. "But you're left in charge of Omofaga."

She spoke as though in that charge lay consolation more than enough.

"I believe you care—I mean you think more about Omofaga than about——"

"Anything in the world?" she asked, in playful mockery.

"Than about me," he went on stubbornly.

"Than about your coming to Dieppe, you mean?"

"I mean, than about me," he repeated.

She looked at him wonderingly.

"My dear man," said she, taking his hand, "what's the matter?"

"You do wish I could come?"

"Must I say?" smiled Mrs. Dennison. "For shame, Harry! You might be on your honey-moon."

He moved away, and flung himself into a chair.

"I don't think it's fair of Ruston," he broke out, "to run away and leave it all to me."

"Why, you told him you could do it perfectly! I heard you say so."

"How could I say anything else, when—when——"

"And originally you were both to be away! After all, you're not stopping because of Omofaga, but because Sir George has got the gout."

Harry Dennison, convicted of folly, had no answer, though he was hurt that he should be convicted out of his wife's mouth. He shuffled his feet about and began to whistle dolefully.

Mrs. Dennison looked at him with smothered impatience. Their little boy behaved like that when he was in a naughty mood—when he wanted the moon, or something of that kind, and thought mother and nurse cruel because it didn't come. Mrs. Dennison

forgot that mother and nurse were fate to her little
boy, or she might have sympathised with his naughty
moods a little better.

She rose now and walked slowly over to her husband. She had a hand on his chair, and was about to
speak, when he stopped his whistling and jerked out
abruptly,

"What did he mean about the kingdom?"

Mrs. Dennison's hand slid away and fell by her
side. Harry caught her look of cold anger. He
leapt to his feet.

"Maggie, I'm a fool," he cried. "I don't know
what's wrong with me. Sit down here."

He made her sit, and half-crouched, half-knelt beside her.

"Maggie," he went on, "are you angry? Damn
the joke! I don't want to know. Are you sorry
I'm not coming?"

"What a baby you are, Harry! Oh, yes, awfully
sorry."

He knew so well what he wanted to say: he
wanted to tell her that she was everything to him,
that to be out of her heart was death: that to feel
her slipping away was a torture: he wanted to woo
and win her over again—win her more truly than he
had even in those triumphant days when she gave
herself to him. He wanted to show her that he understood her—that he was not a fool—that he was

man enough for her! Yes, that she need not turn to Ruston or anybody else. Oh, yes, he could understand her, really he could.

Not a word of it would come. He dared not begin: he feared that he would look—that she would find him—more silly still, if he began to say that sort of thing. She was smiling satirically now—indulgently but satirically, and the emphasis of her purposely childish "awfully" betrayed her estimation of his question. She did not understand the mood. She was accustomed to his admiration — worship would hardly be too strong a word. But the implied demand for a response to it seemed strange to her. Her air bore in upon him the utter difference between his thoughts of her and the way she thought about him. Always dimly felt, it had never pressed on him like this before.

" Really, I'm very sorry, dear," she said, just a little more seriously. " But it's only a fortnight. We're not separating for ever," and her smile broke out again.

With a queer feeling of hopelessness, he rose to his feet. No, he couldn't make her feel it. He had suffered in the same way over his speeches; he couldn't make people feel them either. She didn't understand. It was no use. He began to whistle again, staring out of the open window.

" I shall go to bed, Harry. I'm tired. I've been

seeing that the maid's packed what I wanted, and it's harder work than packing oneself."

" Give me a kiss, Meg," he said, turning round.

She did not do that, but she accepted his kiss, and he, turning away abruptly, shaped his lips to resume his tune. But now the tune wouldn't come. His wife left him alone. The tune came when she was there. Now it wouldn't. Ah, but the words would. He muttered them inaudibly to himself as he stood looking out of the window. They sounded as though they must touch any woman's heart. With an oath he threw himself on to the sofa, trying now to banish the haunting words—the words that would not come at his call, and came, in belated uselessness, to mock him now. He lay still; and they ran through his head. At last they ceased; but, before he could thank God for that, a strange sense of desolation came over him. He looked round the empty, silent room, that seemed larger now than in its busy daylight hours. The house was all still; there might have been one lying dead in it. It might have been the house of a man who had lost his wife.

CHAPTER XI.

AGAINST HIS COMING.

"THE great Napoleon once observed——"

"Don't quote from 'Anecdotes, New and Old,'" interrupted Adela unkindly.

"That when his death was announced," pursued Lord Semingham, who thought it good for Adela to take no notice of such interruptions, "everybody would say *Ouf*. I say '*Ouf*' now," and he stretched his arms luxuriously to their full length. "There's room here," he added, explaining the gesture.

"Well, who's dead?" asked Adela, choosing to be exasperatingly literal.

"Nobody's dead; but a lot of people—and things—are a long way off."

"That's not so satisfactorily final," said Adela.

"No, but it serves for the time. Did you see me on my bicycle this morning?"

"What, going round here?" and Adela waved her hand circularly, as though embracing the broad path that runs round the grass by the sea at Dieppe.

“ Yes—just behind a charming *Parisienne* in a pair of—behind a charming *Parisienne* in an appropriate costume.”

“ Bessie must get one,” said Adela.

“ Good heavens! ”

“ I mean a bicycle.”

“ Oh, certainly, if she likes; but she’d as soon mount Salisbury Spire.”

“ How did you learn ? ”

“ I really beg your pardon,” said Semingham, “ but the fact is—Ruston taught me.”

“ Let’s change the subject,” said Adela, smiling.

“ A charming child, this Marjory Valentine,” observed Semingham. “ She’s too good for young Evan. I’m very glad she wouldn’t have him.”

“ I’m not.”

“ You’re always sorry other girls don’t marry. Heaven knows why.”

“ Well, I’m sorry she didn’t take Evan.”

“ Why ? ”

“ I can’t tell you.”

“ Not—not the forbidden topic ? ”

“ I half believe so.”

“ But she’s here with Maggie Dennison.”

“ Well, everybody doesn’t chatter as you do,” said Adela incisively.

“ I don’t believe it. She—— Hallo ! here she is ! ”

Marjory Valentine came along, bending her slim figure a little, the better to resist a fresh breeze that blew her skirts out behind her, and threatened to carry off her broad-brimmed hat. She had been bathing; the water was warm, and her cheeks glowed with a fine colour. As she came up, both Adela and Lord Semingham put on their eyeglasses.

"An uncommon pretty girl," observed the latter.

"Isn't it glorious?" cried Marjory, yet several yards away. "Walter will enjoy the bathing tremendously."

"When's he coming?"

"Saturday," answered Marjory. "Where is Lady Semingham?"

"Dressing," said Semingham solemnly. "Costume number one, off at 11.30. Costume number two, on at 12. Costume number two, off at 3.30. Costume——"

"After all, she's your wife," said Adela, in tones of grave reproach.

"But for that, I shouldn't have a word to say against it. Women are very queer reasoners."

Marjory sat down next to Adela.

"Women do waste a lot of time on dress, don't they?" she asked, in a meditative tone; "and a lot of thought, too!"

"Hallo!" exclaimed Lord Semingham.

"I mean, thought they might give to really important things. You can't imagine George Eliot——"

"What about Queen Elizabeth?" interrupted Semingham.

"She was a horrible woman," said Adela.

"Phryne attached no importance to it," added Semingham.

"Oh, I forgot! Tell me about her," cried Marjory.

"A strong-minded woman, Miss Marjory."

"He's talking nonsense, Marjory."

"I supplied a historical instance in Miss Valentine's favour."

"I shall look her up," said Marjory, at which Lord Semingham smiled in quiet amusement. He was a man who saw his joke a long way off, and could wait patiently for it.

"Yes, do," he said, lighting a cigarette.

Adela had grown grave, and was watching the girl's face. It was a pretty face, and not a silly one; and Marjory's blue eyes gazed out to sea, as though she were looking at something a great way off. Adela, with a frown of impatience, turned to her other neighbour. She would not be troubled with aspirations there. In fact, she was still annoyed with her young friend on Evan Haselden's account. But it was no use turning to Lord Semingham. His eyes were more than half-closed, and he was beating time gently to the Casino band, audible in the distance. Adela sighed. At last Marjory broke the silence.

"When Mr. Ruston comes," she began, "I shall ask him whether——"

The sentence was not finished.

"When who comes?" cried Adela; and Semingham opened his eyes and stilled his foot-pats.

"Mr. Ruston."

"Is he coming after all? I thought, now that Dennison——"

"Oh, yes—he's coming with Walter. Didn't you know?"

"Is he coming to-day?"

"I suppose so. Aren't you glad?"

"Of course," from Adela, and "Oh, uncommonly," from Lord Semingham, seemed at first sight answers satisfactory enough; but Marjory's inquiring gaze rested on their faces.

"Come for a stroll," said Adela abruptly, and passing her arm through Marjory's, she made her rise. Semingham, having gasped out his conventional reply, sat like a man of stone, but Adela, for all that it was needless, whispered imperatively, "Stay where you are."

"Well, Marjory," she went on, as they began to walk, "I don't know that I am glad after all."

"I believe you don't like him."

"I believe I don't," said Adela slowly. It was a point she had not yet quite decided.

"I didn't use to."

“ But you do now ? ”

“ Yes.”

Adela hated the pregnant brevity of this affirmative.

“ Mamma doesn’t,” laughed Marjory. “ She’s so angry with him carrying off Walter. As if it wasn’t a grand thing for Walter ! So she’s quite turned round about him.”

“ He’s not staying in— with you, I suppose ? ”

“ Oh, no. Though I don’t see why he shouldn’t. Conventions are so stupid, aren’t they ? Mrs. Dennison’s there,” and Marjory looked up with an appeal to calm reason as personified in Adela.

At another time, nineteen’s view of twenty-nine— Marjory’s conception of Maggie Dennison as a sufficing chaperon—would have amused Adela. But she was past amusement. Her patience snapped, as it were, in two. She turned almost fiercely on her companion, forgetting all prudence in her irritation.

“ For heaven’s sake, child, what do you mean ? Do you think he’s coming to see you ? ”

Marjory drew her arm out from Adela’s, and retreated a step from her.

“ Adela ! I never thought——” She did not end, conscious, perhaps, that her flushed face gave her words the lie. Adela swept on.

“ You ! He’s not coming to see you. I don’t believe he's coming to see anyone—no, not even Maggie —I mean no one, at all."

The girl's look marked the fatal slip.

"Oh!" she gasped, just audibly.

"I don't believe he cares *that* for any of us—for anyone alive. Marjory, I didn't mean what I said about Maggie, I didn't indeed. Don't look like that. Oh, what a stupid girl you are!" and she ended with a half-hysterical laugh.

For some moments they stood facing one another, saying nothing. The meaning of Adela's words was sinking into Marjory's mind.

"Let's walk on. People will wonder," said she at last; and she enlaced Adela's arm again. After another long pause, during which her face expressed the turmoil of her thoughts, she whispered,

"Adela, is that why Mr. Loring went away?"

"I don't know why he went away."

"You think me a child, so you say you don't mean it now. You do mean it, you know. You wouldn't say a thing like that for nothing. Tell me what you do mean, Adela." It was almost an order. Adela suddenly realised that she had struck down to a force and a character. "Tell me exactly what you mean," insisted Marjory; "you ought to tell me, Adela."

Adela found herself obeying.

"I don't know about him; but I'm afraid of her,"

she stammered, as if confessing a shameful deed of
her own. A moment later she broke into entreaty.
"Go away, dear. Don't get mixed up in it. Don't
have anything to do with him."

"Do you go away when your friends are in trouble
or in danger?"

Adela felt suddenly small—then wise—then small
because her wisdom was of a small kind. Yet she
gave it utterance.

"But, Marjory, think of—think of yourself. If
you——"

"I know what you're going to say. If I care for
him? I don't. I hardly know him. But, if I did, I
might—I might be of some use. And are you going
to leave her all alone? I thought you were her
friend. Are you just going to look on? Though you
think—what you think!"

Adela caught hold of the girl's hands. There was
a choking in her throat, and she could say nothing.

"But if he sees?" she murmured, when she found
speech.

"He won't see. There's nothing to see. I shan't
show it. Adela, I shall stay. Why do you think
what—what you think?"

People might wonder, if they would—perhaps they
did—when Adela drew Marjory towards her, and
kissed her lips.

"I couldn't, my dear," she said, "but, if you can,
10

for heaven's sake do. I may be wrong, but—I'm uneasy."

Marjory's lips quivered, but she held her head proudly up; then she sobbed a short quick-stifled sob, and then smiled.

" I daresay it's not a bit true," she said.

Adela pressed her hand again, saying,

" I'm an emotional old creature."

" Why did Mr. Loring go away? " demanded Marjory.

" I don't know. He thought it——"

" Best ? Well, he was wrong."

Adela could not hear Tom attacked.

" Maggie turned him out," she said—which account of the matter was, perhaps, just a little one-sided, though containing a part of the truth. Marjory meditated on it for a moment, Adela still covertly looking at her. The discovery was very strange. Half-an-hour ago she had smiled because the girl hinted a longing after something beyond frocks, and had laughed at her simple acceptance of Semingham's joke. Now she found herself turning to her, looking to her for help in the trouble that had puzzled her. In her admiration of the girl's courage, she forgot to wonder at her intuition, her grasp of evil possibilities, the knowledge of Maggie Dennison that her resolve implied. Adela watched her, as, their farewell said, she walked, first quickly, then very slowly, towards the villa which Mrs. Dennison had hired, on the cliff-side, near the old Castle. Then, with a last sigh, she put up her parasol and sauntered back to the Hôtel de Rome. Costume number two would be on by now, and Bessie Semingham ready for luncheon.

Marjory, finally sunk into the slow gait that means either idleness or deep thought, made her way up to the villa. With every step she drew nearer, the burden she had taken up seemed heavier. It was not sorrow for the dawning dream that the storm-cloud had eclipsed that she really thought of. But the task loomed large in its true difficulty, as her first enthusiasm spent itself. If Adela were right, what could she do? If Adela were wrong, what unpardonable offence she might give. Ah, was Adela right? Strange and new as the idea was, there was an unquestioning conviction in her manner that Marjory could hardly resist. Save under the stress of a conviction, speech on such a matter would have been an impossible crime. And Marjory remembered, with a sinking heart, Maggie Dennison's smile of happy triumph when she read out the lines in which Ruston told of his coming. Yes, it was, or it might be, true. But where lay her power to help?

Coming round the elbow of the rising path, she caught sight of Maggie Dennison sitting in the garden. Mrs. Dennison wore white; her pale, clear-cut profile was towards Marjory; she rested her chin on her hand, and her elbow on her knee, and she was looking on the ground. Softly Marjory drew near. An unopened letter from Harry lay on a little table; the children had begun their mid-day meal in the room, whose open window was but a few feet behind; Mrs. Dennison's thoughts were far away. Marjory stopped short. A stronger buffet of fear, a more overwhelming sense of helplessness, smote her. She understood better why Adela had been driven to do nothing—to look on. She smiled for an instant; the idea put itself so whimsically; but she thought that, had Mrs. Dennison been walking over a precipice, it would need all one's courage to interfere with her. She would think it such an impertinence. And Ruston? Marjory saw, all in a minute, his cheerful scorn, his unshaken determination, his rapid dismissal of one more obstacle. She drew in her breath in a long inspiration, and Mrs. Dennison raised her eyes and smiled.

"I believe I felt you there," she said, smiling. "At least, I began to think of you."

Marjory sat near her hostess.

"Did you meet anyone?" asked Mrs. Dennison.

"Adela Ferrars and Lord Semingham."

"Well, had they anything to say?"

"No—I don't think so," she answered slowly.

"What should they have to say in this place? The children have begun. Aren't you hungry?"

“ Not very.”

“ Well, I am,” and Mrs. Dennison arose. “ I forgot it, but I am.”

“ They didn’t know Mr. Ruston was coming.”

“ Didn’t they?” smiled Mrs. Dennison. “ And has Adela forgiven you? Oh, you know, the poor boy is a friend of hers, as he is of mine.”

“ We didn’t talk about it.”

“ And you don’t want to? Very well, we won’t. See, here’s a long letter—it’s very heavy, at least—from Harry. I must read it afterwards.”

“ Perhaps it’s to say he can come sooner.”

“ I expect not,” said Mrs. Dennison, and she opened the letter. “ No; a fortnight hence at the soonest,” she announced, after reading a few lines.

Marjory was both looking and listening closely, but she detected neither disappointment nor relief.

“ He’s seen Tom Loring! Oh, and Tom sends me his best remembrances. Poor Tom! Marjory, does Adela talk about Mr. Loring?”

“ She mentioned him once.”

“ She thinks it was all my fault,” laughed Mrs. Dennison. “ A woman always thinks it’s a woman’s fault; at least, that’s our natural tendency, though we’re being taught to overcome it. Marjory, you look dull! It will be livelier for you when your brother and Mr. Ruston come.”

The hardest thing about great resolves and lofty

moods is their intermixture with everyday life. The intervals, the "waits," the mass of irrelevant trivialities that life inartistically mingles with its drama, flinging down pell-mell a heap of great and small— these cool courage and make discernment distrust itself. Mrs. Dennison seemed so quiet, so placid, so completely the affectionate but not anxious wife, the kind hostess, and even the human gossip, that Marjory wanted to rub her eyes, wondering if all her heroics were nonsense—a girl's romance gone wrong. There was nothing to be done but eat and drink, and talk and lounge in the sun—there was no hint of a drama, no call for a rescue, no place for a sacrifice. And Marjory had been all aglow to begin. Her face grew dull and her eyelids half-dropped as she leant her head on the back of her chair.

"*Déjeuner!*" cried Mrs. Dennison merrily. "And this afternoon we're all going to gamble at *petits chevaux*, and if we win we're going to buy more Omofagas. There's a picture of a speculator's family!"

"Mr. Dennison's not a speculator, is he?"

"Oh, it depends on what you mean. Anyhow, I am;" and Mrs. Dennison, waving her letter in the air and singing softly, almost danced in her merry walk to the house. Then, crying her last words, "Be quick!" from the door, she disappeared.

A moment later she was laughing and chattering to her children. Marjory heard her burlesque complaints over the utter disappearance of an omelette she had set her heart upon.

That afternoon they all played at *petits chevaux*, and the only one to win was Madge. But Madge utterly refused to invest her gains in Omofagas. She assigned no reasons, stating that her mother did not like her to declare the feeling which influenced her, and Mrs. Dennison laughed again. But Adela Ferrars would not look towards Marjory, but kept her eyes on an old gentleman who had been playing also, and playing with good fortune. He had looked round curiously when, in the course of the chaff, they had mentioned Omofaga, and Adela detected in him the wish to look again. She wondered who he was, scrutinising his faded blue eyes and the wrinkles of weariness on his brow. Willie Ruston could have told her. It was Baron von Geltschmidt of Frankfort.

CHAPTER XII.

IT CAN WAIT.

In all things evil and good, to the world, and—a thing quite rare—to himself, Willie Ruston was an unaffected man. Success, the evidence of power and the earnest of more power, gave him his greatest pleasure, and he received it with his greatest and most open satisfaction. It did not surprise him, but it elated him, and his habit was to conceal neither the presence of elation nor the absence of surprise. That irony in the old sense, which means the well-bred though hardly sincere depreciation of a man's own qualities and achievements, was not his. When he had done anything, he liked to dine with his friends and talk it over. He had been sharing the Carlins' unfashionable six o'clock meal at Hampstead this evening, and had taken the train to Baker Street, and was now sauntering home with a cigar. He had talked the whole thing over with them. Carlin had said that no one could have managed the affair so well as he had, and Mrs. Carlin had not once referred to that lost *tabula in naufragio*, the coal business. Yes, his attack on London had been a success. He had known nothing of London, save that its denizens were human beings, and that knowledge, whether in business or society, had been enough. His great scheme was floated; a few months more would see him in Omofaga; there was money to last for a long time to come; and he had been cordially received and even made a lion of in the drawing-rooms. They would look for his name in the papers ("and find it, by Jove," he interpolated). Men in high places would think of him when there was a job to be "put through;" and women, famous in regions inaccessible to the vulgar, would recollect their talks with Mr. Ruston. Decidedly they were human beings, and therefore, raw as he was (he just knew that he had come to them a little raw), he had succeeded.

Yet they were, some of them, strange folk. There were complications in them which he found it necessary to reconnoitre. They said a great many things which they did not think, and, *en revanche*, would often only hint what they did. And—— But here he yawned, and, finding his cigar out, relit it. He was not in the mood for analysing his acquaintance. He let his fancy play more lightly. It was evening, and work was done. He liked London evenings. He had liked bandying repartees with Adela Ferrars (though she had been too much for him if she could have kept her temper) ; he liked talking to Marjory Valentine and seeing her occupied with his ideas. Most of all, he liked trying to catch Maggie Dennison's thought as it flashed out for a moment, and fled to shelter again. He had laughed again and again over the talk that Tom Loring had interrupted—and not less because of the interruption. There was little malice in him, and he bore no grudge against Tom. Even his anger at the Omofaga articles had been chiefly for public purposes and public consumption. It was always somebody's " game " to spoil his game, and one must not quarrel with men for playing their own hands. Tom amused him, and had amused him, especially by his behaviour over that talk. No doubt the position had looked a strange one. Tom had been so shocked. Poor Tom, it must be very serious to be so easily shocked. Mr. Ruston was not easily shocked.

Unaffected, free from self-consciousness, undividedly bent on his schemes, unheeding of everything but their accomplishment, he had spent little time in considering the considerable stir which he had, in fact, created in the circle of his more intimate associates. They had proved pliable and pleasant, and these were the qualities he liked in his neighbours. They said agreeable things to him, and they did what he wanted. He had stayed not (save once, and half in jest, with Maggie Dennison) to inquire why, and

the quasi-real, quasi-burlesque apprehension of him—
burlesqued perhaps lest it should seem too real—
which had grown up among such close observers as
Adela Ferrars and Semingham, would have struck
him as absurd, the outcome of that idle business of
brain which weaves webs of fine fancies round the
obvious, and loses the power of action in the fascina-
tion of self-created puzzles. The *nuances* of a woman's attraction towards a man, whether it be admiration, or interest, or pass beyond—whether it be liking
and just not love—or interest running into love—or
love masquerading as interest, or what-not, Willie
Ruston recked little of. He was a man, and a young
man. He liked women and clever women—yes, and
handsome women. But to spend your time thinking
of or about women, or, worse still, of or about what
women thought of you, seemed poor economy of precious days—amusing to do, maybe, in spare hours,
inevitable now and again—but to be driven or laughed
away when there was work to be done.

Such was the colour of his floating thoughts, and
the loose-hung meditation brought him to his own
dwelling, in a great building which overlooked Hyde
Park. He lived high up in a small, irregular, many-
cornered room, sparely-furnished, dull and pictureless.
The only thing hanging on the walls was a large scale
map of Omofaga and the neighbouring territories; in
lieu of nicnacks there stood on the mantlepiece lumps

of ore, specimens from the mines of Omofaga (would not these convince the most obstinate unbeliever?), and half-smothered by ill-dusted papers, a small photograph of Ruston and a potent Omofagan chief seated on the ground with a large piece of paper before them —a treaty no doubt. A well-worn sofa, second-hand and soft, and a deep arm-chair redeemed the place from utter comfortlessness, but it was plain that beauty in his daily surroundings was not essential to Willie Ruston. He did not notice furniture.

He walked in briskly, but stopped short with his hand still on the knob of the door. Harry Dennison lay on the sofa, with his arm flung across his face. He sprang up on Ruston's entrance.

"Hullo! Been here long? I've been dining with Carlin," said Ruston, and, going to a cupboard, he brought out whisky and soda water.

Harry Dennison began to explain his presence. In the first place he had nothing to do; in the second he wanted someone to talk to; in the third—at last he blurted it out—the first, second, third and only reason for his presence.

"I don't believe I can manage alone in town," he said.

"Not manage? There's nothing to do. And Carlin's here."

"You see I've got other work besides Omofaga," pleaded Harry.

"Oh, I know Dennisons have lots of irons in the fire. But Omofaga won't trouble you. I've told Carlin to wire me if any news comes, and I can be back in a few hours."

Harry had come to suggest that the expedition to Dieppe should be abandoned for a week or two. He got no chance and sat silent.

"It's all done," continued Ruston. "The stores are all on their way. Jackson is waiting for them on the coast. Why, the train will start inland in a couple of months from now. They'll go very slow. though. I shall catch them up all right."

Harry brightened a little.

"Belford said it was uncertain when you would start," he said.

"It may be uncertain to Belford, it's not to me," observed Mr. Ruston, lighting his pipe.

The speech sounded unkind; but Mr. Belford's mind dwelt in uncertainty contentedly.

"Then you think of——?"

"My dear Dennison, I don't 'think' at all. To-day's the 12th of August. Happen what may, I sail on the 10th of November. Nothing will keep me after that—nothing."

"Belford started for the Engadine to-day."

"Well, he won't worry you then. Let it alone, my dear fellow. It's all right."

Clearly Mr. Ruston meant to go to Dieppe. That

was now to Harry Dennison bad news; but he meant to go to Omofaga also, and to go soon; that was good. Harry, however, had still something that he wished to convey—a bit of diplomacy to carry out.

"I hope you'll find Maggie better," he began. "She was rather knocked up when she went."

"A few days will have put her all right," responded Ruston cheerfully.

He was never ill and treated fatigue with a cheery incredulousness. But, at least, he spoke with an utter absence of undue anxiety on the score of another man's wife.

Harry Dennison, primed by Mrs. Cormack's suggestions, went on,

"I wish you'd talk to her as little as you can about Omofaga. She's very interested in it, you know, and —and very excitable—and all that. We want her mind to get a complete rest."

"Hum. I expect, then, I mustn't talk to her at all."

The manifest impossibility of making such a request did not prevent Harry yearning after it.

"I don't ask that," he said, smiling weakly.

"It won't hurt her," said Willie Ruston. "And she likes it."

She liked it beyond question.

"It tires her," Harry persisted. "It—it gets on her nerves. It absorbs her too much."

His face was turned up to Ruston. As he spoke the last words, Ruston directed his eyes, suddenly and rapidly, upon him. Harry could not escape the encounter of eyes; hastily he averted his head, and his face flushed. Ruston continued to look at him, a slight smile on his lips.

"Absorbs her?" he repeated slowly, fingering his beard.

"Well, you know what I mean."

Another long stare showed Ruston's meditative preoccupation. Harry sat uncomfortable under it, wishing he had not let fall the word.

"Well, I'll be careful," said Ruston at last. "Anything else?"

Harry rose. Ruston carried an atmosphere of business about with him, and the visit seemed naturally to end with the business of it. Taking his hat, Harry moved towards the door. Then, pausing, he smiled in an embarrassed way, and remarked,

"You can talk to Marjory Valentine, you know."

"So I can. She's a nice girl."

Harry twirled his hat in his fingers. His brain had conceived more diplomacy.

"It'll be a fine chance for you to win her heart," he suggested with a tentative laugh.

"I might do worse," said Willie Ruston.

"You might—much worse," said Harry eagerly.

"Aren't you rather giving away your friend young Haselden?"

"Who told you, Ruston?"

"Lady Val. Who told you?"

"Semingham."

"Ah! Well, what would Haselden say to your idea?"

"Well, she won't have him—he's got no chance anyhow."

"All right. I'll think about it. Good-night."

He watched his guest depart, but did not accompany him on his way, and, left alone, sat down in the deep arm-chair. His smile was still on his lips. Poor Harry Dennison was a transparent schemer—one of those whose clumsy efforts to avert what they fear effects naught save to suggest the doing of it. Yet Willie Ruston's smile had more pity than scorn in it. True, it had more of amusement than of either. He could have taken a slate and written down all Harry's thoughts during the interview. But whence had come the change? Why had Dennison himself bidden him to Dieppe, to come now, a fortnight later, and beg him not to go? Why did he now desire his wife to hear no more of Omofaga, whose chief delight in it had been that it caught her fancy and imparted to him some of the interest she found in it? Ruston saw in the transformation the working of another mind.

"Somebody's been putting it into his head," he muttered, still half-amused, but now half-angry also.

And, with his usual rapidity of judgment, he darted unhesitatingly to a conclusion. He identified the hand in the business; he recognised whose more subtle thoughts Harry Dennison had stumbled over and mauled in his painful devices. But to none is it given to be infallible, and want of doubt does not always mean absence of error. Forgetting this commonplace truth, Willie Ruston slapped his thigh, leapt up from his chair and, standing on the rug, exclaimed,

"Loring—by Jove!"

It was clear to him. Loring was his enemy; he had displaced Loring. Loring hated him and Omofaga. Loring had stirred a husband's jealousy to further his own grudge. The same temper of mind that made his anger fade away when he had arrived at this certainty, prevented any surprise at the discovery. It was natural in man to seek revenge, to use the nearest weapon, to counter stroke with stroke, not to throw away any advantages for the sake of foibles of generosity. So, then, it was Loring who bade him not go to Dieppe, who prayed him to not to "absorb" Mrs. Dennison in Omofaga, who was ready, notwithstanding his hatred and distrust, to see him the lover of Marjory Valentine sooner than the too engrossing friend of Mrs. Dennison! What a fool they must

11

think him!—and, with this reflection, he put the whole matter out of his head. It could wait till he was at Dieppe, and, taking hold of the great map by the roller at the bottom, he drew it to him. Then he reached and lifted the lamp from the table, and set it high on the mantlepiece. Its light shone now on his path, and with his finger he traced the red line that ran, curving and winding, inwards from the coast, till it touched the blue letters of the "Omofaga" that sprawled across the map. The line ended in a cross of red paint. The cross was Fort Imperial—was to be Fort Imperial, at least; but Willie Ruston's mind overleapt all difference of tenses. He stood and looked, pulling hard and fast at his pipe. He was there—there in Fort Imperial already—far away from London and London folk—from weak husbands and their causes of anxiety—from the pleasing recreations of fascinating society, from the covert attacks of men whose noses he had put out of joint. He forgot them all; their feelings became naught to him. What mattered their graces, their assaults, their weal or woe? He was in Omofaga, carving out of its rock a stable seat, carving on the rock face, above the seat, a name that should live.

At last he turned away, flinging his empty pipe on the table and dropping the map from his hand.

"I shall go to bed," he said. "Three months more of it!"

And to bed he went, never having thought once during the whole evening of a French lady, who liked to get amusement out of her neighbours, and had stayed in town on purpose to have some more talks with Harry Dennison. Had Willie Ruston not been quite so sure that he read Tom Loring's character aright, he might have spared a thought for Mrs. Cormack.

CHAPTER XIII.

A SPASM OF PENITENCE.

Tom Loring had arranged to spend the whole of
the autumn in London. His Omofaga articles had
gained such favourable notice that his editor had
engaged him to contribute a series dealing with
African questions and African companies (and the
latter are in the habit of producing the former), while
he was occupied, on his own account, at the British
Museum, in making way with a treatise of a politico-
philosophical description, which had been in his head
for several years. He hailed with pleasure the
prospect of getting on with it; the leisure afforded
him by his departure from the Dennisons was, in its
way, a consolation for the wrench involved in the
parting. Could he have felt more at ease about the
course of events in his absence, he would have endured
his sojourn in town with equanimity.

Of course, the place was fast becoming a desert,
but, at this moment, chance, which always objects to
our taking things for granted, brought a carriage

exactly opposite the bench on which Tom was seated, and he heard his name called in a high-pitched voice that he recognised. Looking up, he saw Mrs. Cormack leaning over the side of her victoria, smiling effusively and beckoning to him. That everyone should go save Mrs. Cormack seemed to Tom the irony of circumstance. With a mutter to himself, he rose and walked up to the carriage. He then perceived, to his surprise, that it contained, hidden behind Mrs. Cormack's sleeves—sleeves were large that year—another inmate. It was Evan Haselden, and he greeted Tom with an off-hand nod.

"The good God," cried Mrs. Cormack, "evidently kept me here to console young men! Are you left desolate like Mr. Haselden here?"

"Well, it's not very lively," responded Tom, as amiably as he could.

"No, it isn't," she agreed, with the slightest, quickest glance at Evan, who was staring moodily at the tops of the trees.

Tom laughed. The woman amused him in spite of himself. And her failures to extract entertainment from poor heart-broken Evan struck him as humorous.

"But I'm at work," he went on, "so I don't mind."

"Ah! Are you still crushing——?"

"No," interrupted Tom quickly. "That's done."

"I should not have guessed it," said Mrs. Cormack, opening her eyes.

"I mean, I've finished the articles on that point."

"That is rather a different thing," laughed she.

"I'm afraid so," said Tom.

"I wish to heaven it wasn't!" ejaculated Evan suddenly, without shifting his gaze from the tree-tops.

"Oh, he is very very bad," whispered Mrs. Cormack. "Poor young man! Are you bad too?"

"Eh?"

"Oh, but I know."

"Oh, no, you don't," said Tom.

Suddenly Evan rose, opened the carriage door, got out, shut it, and lifted his hat.

"Good-bye," said Mrs. Cormack, smiling merrily.

"Good-bye. Thanks," said Evan, with unchanged melancholy, and, with another nod to Tom, he walked round to the path and strode quickly away.

"How absurd!" said she.

"Not at all. I like to see him honest about it. He's hard hit—and he's not ashamed of it."

"Oh, well," said Mrs. Cormack, shrugging the subject away in weariness of it. "And how do you stand banishment? Will you get in?"

"Yes, if you won't assume——"

"Too great familiarity, Mr. Loring?"

"Oh, I was only going to say—with my affairs.

With me—I should be charmed," and Tom settled himself in the victoria.

He had, now he came to think of it, been really very much bored; and the little woman was quite a resource.

She rewarded his ironical gallantry with a look that told him she took it for what it was worth, but liked it all the same; and, after a pause, asked,

" And you see Mr. Dennison often ?"

" Very seldom, on the contrary. I don't know what he does with himself."

" The poor man! He walks up and down. I hear him walking up and down."

" What does he do that for ?"

" Ah! what? Well, he cannot be happy, can he ?"

" Can't he ?" said Tom, determined to understand nothing.

" You are very discreet," she said, with a malicious smile.

" I'm obliged to be. Somebody must be."

" Mr. Loring," she said abruptly, " you don't like me, neither you nor Miss Ferrars."

" I never answer for others. For myself——"

" Oh, I know. What does it matter? Well, anyhow, I'm sorry for that poor man."

" Your sympathy is very ready, Mrs. Cormack."

" You mean it is too soon—premature ?"

"I mean it's altogether unnecessary, to my humble thinking."

"But I'm not a fool," she protested.

Tom could not help laughing. The laugh, however, rather spoilt his argument.

"Have it your own way," he conceded, conscious of his error, and trying to cover it by a burlesque surrender. "He's miserable."

"Well, he is."

There was a placid certainty about her that disturbed Tom's attitude of incredulity.

"Why is he?" he asked curiously.

"I have talked to him. I know," she answered, with a nod full of meaning.

"Oh, have you?"

"Yes, and he—well, do you want to hear, or will you be angry and despise me as you used?"

"I want to hear."

"What did I use to say? That the man would come? Well, he has come. *Voilà tout!*"

"Oh, so you say. But Harry doesn't think such— I beg pardon, I was about to say, nonsense."

"Yes, he does. At least, he is afraid of it."

"How do you know?"

"I tell you, we have talked. And I saw. He almost cried that he couldn't go to Dieppe, and that somebody else——"

Tom suddenly turned upon her.

“ Who began the talk ? ” he demanded.

“ What do you say ? ”

“ Who began ? ”

“ Oh, what nonsense! Who does begin to talk ?
How do I know? It came, Mr. Loring.”

Tom said nothing.

“ You look as if you didn’t believe me,” she remarked, pouting.

“ I don’t. He’s the most unsuspicious fellow
alive.”

“ Well, if you like, I began. I’m not ashamed.
But I said very little. When he asked me if I thought
it good that she and—the other—should be together
out there and he here—well, was I to say yes ? ”

“ I think,” observed Tom, in quiet and deliberate
tones, “ that it’s a great pity that some women can’t
be gagged.”

“ They can, but only with kisses,” said Mrs. Cormack, not at all offended. “ Oh, don’t be frightened.
I do not wish to be gagged at all. If I did—there is
more than one man in the world.”

Tom despised and half-hated her; but he liked
her good-nature, and, in his heart, admired her for not
flinching. Her shamelessness was crossed with courage.

“ So you’ve made him miserable ? ”

“ Well, I might say, I, a wicked Frenchwoman,
that it is better to be deceived than to be wretched.

But you, an Englishman——! Oh, never, Mr. Loring!"

Tom sat silent a little while.

"I don't know what to do," he said, half in reverie.

"Who thought you would?" asked Mrs. Cormack, unkindly.

"I believe it's all a mare's nest."

"That means a mistake, a delusion?"

"It does."

"Then I don't think you do believe it. And, if you do, you are wrong. It is not all a—a mare's nest."

She pronounced the word with unfamiliar delicateness.

Tom knew that he did not believe that it was all a mare's nest. He would have given everything in the world—save one thing—and that, he thought, he had not got—to believe it.

"Then, if you believed it, why didn't you do something?" he asked rather fiercely.

"What have you all done? I, at least, warned him. Yes, since you insist, I hinted it. But you— you ran away; and your Adela Ferrars, she looks prim and pained, oh! and shocked, and doesn't come so much."

It was a queer source to learn lessons from, and Tom was no less surprised than Adela had been a day or two before at Dieppe.

“What should you do?” he asked, in new-born humility.

“I? Nothing. What is it to me?”

“What should you do, if you were me?”

“Make love to her myself,” smiled Mrs. Cormack. She was having her revenge on Tom for many a scornful speech.

“If you’d held your tongue, it would all have blown over!” he exclaimed in exasperation.

“It will blow over still; but it will blow first,” she said. “If that contents you, hold your tongue.”

Then she turned to Tom, and laid a small forefinger on his arm.

“Mark this,” said she, “he does not care for her. He cares for himself; she is—what would you say? an incident—an accident—I do not know how to say it—to him.”

“Well, if you’re right there——” began Tom in some relief.

“If I’m right there, it will make no difference—at first. But, as you say, it will blow over—and sooner.”

Tom looked at her, and thought, and looked again.

“By Jove, you’re not a fool, Mrs. Cormack,” said he, almost under his breath.

Then he added, louder,

“It’s the wisdom of the devil.”

"Oh, you surpass yourself," she smiled. "Your compliments are magnificent."

"You must have learnt it from him."

"Oh, no. From my husband," said Mrs. Cormack.

The carriage, which during their talk had moved slowly round the circle, stopped again.

Mrs. Cormack turned to Tom. He was already looking at her.

"I don't understand you," said he.

"No? Well, you'll hardly believe it, but that does not surprise me."

"I'm not sure you don't mean well, if you weren't ashamed to confess it," said Tom.

For the first time since he had known her, she blushed and looked embarrassed. Then she began, in a quick tone,

"Well, I talked. I wanted to see how he took it; and it amused me. And—well, our dear Maggie—she is so very magnificent at times. She looks down so calmly—oh! from such a height—on one. She had told me that day—well, never mind that; it was true, I daresay. I don't love truth. I don't see what right people have to say things to me, just because one may know they are true."

"So you made a little mischief?"

"Well, I hear that poor man walking up and down. I want to comfort him. I asked him to come

in, and he refused. Then I offered to go in—he was
very frightened. Oh, *mon Dieu!*" and she laughed
almost hysterically.

This very indirect confession proved in the end to
be all that Mrs. Cormack's penitence could drive her
to, and Tom left her, feeling a little softened towards
her, but hardly better equipped for action. What,
indeed, could be done? Tom's sense of futility expressed itself in a long letter to Adela Ferrars. As
he had no suggestions for present action, he took
refuge in future promises.

"It will be very awkward for me to come, but if,
as time goes on, you think I should be any good, I
will come."

And Adela, when she read it, was tempted to send
for him on the spot; he would have been of no use,
but he would have comforted her. But then his presence would unquestionably exasperate Maggie Dennison. Adela decided to wait.

Now, by the time Tom Loring's letter reached
Dieppe, young Sir Walter and Willie Ruston were on
the boat, and they arrived hard on its heels. They
took up their abode at a hotel a few doors from where
the Seminghams were staying, and Walter at once
went round to pay his respects.

Ruston stayed in to write letters. So he said; but
when he was alone he stood smoking at the window
and looking at the people down below. Presently, to

his surprise, he saw the same old gentleman whom Adela had noticed in the Casino.

"The Baron, by Jove!" he exclaimed. "Now, what brings him here?"

The Baron was sauntering slowly by, wrapped in a cloak, and leaning heavily on a malacca cane. In a moment Willie Ruston was down the stairs and after him.

Hearing his name cried, the Baron stopped and turned round.

"What chance brings you here?" asked Willie, holding out his hand.

"Oh, hardly chance," said the Baron. "I always go to some seaside place, and I thought I might meet friends here," and he smiled significantly.

"Yes," said Ruston, after a pause; "I believe I did mention it in Threadneedle Street. I went in there the other day."

By the general term Threadneedle Street he meant to indicate the offices of the Baron's London correspondents, which were situate there.

"They keep you informed, it seems?"

"I live by being kept informed," said the Baron.

Ruston was walking by him, accommodating his pace to the old man's feeble walk.

"You mean you came to see me?" he asked.

"Well, if you'll forgive the liberty—in part."

"And why did you want me?"

"Oh, I've not lost all interest in Omofaga."

"No, you haven't," said Ruston. "On the contrary, you've been increasing your interest."

The Baron stopped and looked at him.

"Oh, you know that?"

"Certainly."

The Baron laughed.

"Then you can tell me whether I shall lose my money," he said.

"Do you ever lose your money, Baron?"

"But am I to hear about Omofaga?" asked the Baron, countering question by question.

"As much as you like," answered Ruston, with the indifference of perfect candour.

"Ah, by the way, I have heard about it already. Who are the ladies here who talk about it?"

Willie Ruston gave a careful catalogue of all the persons in Dieppe who were interested in the Omofaga Company. The Baron identified the Seminghams and Adela. Then he observed,

"And the other lady is Mrs. Dennison, is she?"

"She is. I'm going to her house to-morrow. Shall I take you?"

"I should be charmed."

"Very well. To-morrow afternoon."

"And you'll dine with me to-night?"

Ruston was about to refuse; but the Baron added, half seriously,

"I've come a long way to see you."

"All right, I'll come," he said. Then he paused a moment, and looked at the Baron curiously. "And perhaps you'll tell me then," he added.

"Why I've come?"

"Yes; and why you've been buying. You were bought out. What do you want to come in again for?"

"I'll tell you all that now," said the Baron. "I've come because I thought I should like to see some more of you; and I've been buying because I fancy you'll make a success of it."

Willie Ruston pulled his beard thoughtfully.

"Don't you believe me?" asked the Baron.

"Let's wait a bit," suggested Ruston. Then, with a sudden twinkle of his eye, his holiday mood seemed to come back again. Seizing the Baron's arm, he pressed it, and said with a laugh, "I say, Baron, if you want to get control over Omofaga——"

"But, my dear friend——" protested the Baron.

"If you do—I only say 'if'—I'm not the only man you've got to fight. Well, yes, I am the only man."

"My dear young friend, I don't understand you," pleaded the Baron.

"We'll go and see Mrs. Dennison to-morrow," said Willie Ruston.

CHAPTER XIV.

THE THING OR THE MAN.

"Well?"

It was the morning of the next day, Mrs. Dennison sat in her place in the little garden on the cliff, and Willie Ruston stood just at the turn of the mounting path, where Marjory had paused to look at her friend.

"Well, here I am," said he.

She did not move, but held out her hand. He advanced and took it.

"I met your children down below," he went on, "but they would hardly speak to me. Why don't they like me?"

"Never mind the children."

"But I do mind. Most children like me."

"How is everything?"

"In London? Oh, first-rate. I saw your husband the——"

"I mean, how is Omofaga?"

"Capital; and here?"

12   (173)

"It has been atrociously dull. What could you expect?"

"Well, I didn't expect that, or I shouldn't have come."

"Are the stores started?"

"I thought it was holiday time? Well, yes, they are."

She had been looking at him ever since he came, and at last he noticed it.

"Do I look well?" he asked in joke.

"You know, it's rather a pleasure to look at you," she replied. "I've been feeling so shut in," and she pushed her hair back from her forehead, and glanced at him with a bright smile. "And it's really going well?"

"So well," he nodded, "that everything's quiet, and the preparations well ahead. In three months" (and his enthusiasm began to get hold of him) "I shall be off; in two more I hope to be actually there, and then—why, forward!"

She had listened at first with sparkling eyes; as he finished, her lips drooped, and she leant back in her chair. There was a moment's silence; then she said in a low voice,

"Three months!"

"It oughtn't to take more than two, if Jackson has arranged things properly for me."

Evidently he was thinking of his march up country; but it was the first three months that were in her mind. She had longed to see the thing really started, hastened by all her efforts the hour that was to set him at work, and dreamt of the day when he should set foot in Omofaga. Now all this seemed assured, imminent, almost present; yet there was no exultation in her tone.

"I meant, before you started," she said slowly.

He looked up in surprise.

"I can't manage sooner," he said, defending himself. "You know I don't waste time."

He was still off the scent; and even she herself was only now, for the first time and as yet dimly, realising her own mind.

"I have to do everything myself," he said. "Dear old Carlin can't walk a step alone, and the Board"— he paused, remembering that Harry Dennison was on the Board—"well, I find it hard to make them move as quick as I want. I had to fix a date, and I fixed the earliest I could be absolutely sure of."

"Why don't they help you more?" she burst out indignantly.

"Oh, I don't want help."

"Yes, but I helped you!" she exclaimed, leaning forward, full again of animation.

"I can't deny it," he laughed. "You did indeed."

"Yes," she said, and became again silent.

"*Apropos*," said he. "I want to bring someone to see you this afternoon—Baron von Geltschmidt."

"Who?"

"He was the German capitalist, you know."

"What! Why, what's he doing here?"

"He came to see me—so he says. May I bring him?"

"Why, yes. He's a great—a great man, isn't he?"

"Well, he's a great financier."

"And he came to see you?"

"So he says."

"And don't you believe him?"

"I don't know. I want your opinion," answered Ruston, with a smile.

"Are you serious?" she asked quickly. "I mean, do you really want my opinion, or are you being polite?"

"I don't think *you* a fool, you know," said Willie Ruston.

She flashed a glance of understanding, mingled with reproach, at him, and, leaning forward again, said,

"Has he come about Omofaga?"

"That you might tell me too—or will you want all Omofaga if you do so much?"

For a moment she smiled in recollection. Then her face grew sad.

"Much of Omofaga I shall have!" she said.

"Oh, I'll write," he promised carelessly.

"Write!" she repeated in low, scornful tones. "Would you like to be written to about it? It'll happen to you, and I'm to be written to!"

"Well, then, I won't write."

"Yes, do write."

Willie Ruston smiled tolerantly, but his smile was suddenly cut short, for Mrs. Dennison, not looking at him but out to sea, asked herself in a whisper, which was plainly not meant for him though he heard it,

"How shall I bear it?"

He had been tilting his chair back; he brought the front legs suddenly on to the ground again and asked,

"Bear what?"

She started to find he had heard, but attempted no evasion.

"When you've gone," she answered in simple directness.

He looked at her with raised eyebrows. There was no embarrassment in her face, and no tremble in her voice; and no passion could he detect in either.

"How flat it will all be," she added in a tone of utter weariness.

He was half-pleased, half-piqued at the way she seemed to look at him. It not only failed to satisfy him, but stirred a new dissatisfaction. It hinted much, but only, it seemed to him, to negative it. It left Omofaga still all in all, and him of interest only because he would talk of and work for Omofaga, and keep the Omofaga atmosphere about her. Now this was wrong, for Omofaga existed for him, not he for Omofaga; that was the faith of true disciples.

"You don't care about me," he said. "It's all the Company — and only the Company because it gives you something to do. Well, the Company'll go on (I hope), and you'll hear about our doings."

She turned to him with a puzzled look.

"I don't know what it is," she said with a shake of her head. Then, with a sudden air of understanding, as though she had caught the meaning that before eluded her, she cried, "I'm just like you, I believe. If I went to Omofaga, and you had to stay——"

"Oh, it would be the deuce!" he laughed.

"Yes, yes. Well, it is—the deuce," she answered, laughing in return. But in a moment she was grave again.

Her attraction for him—the old special attraction of the unknown and unconquered —- came strongly upon him, and mingled more now with pleasure in her. Her silence let him think; and he began to think how wasted she was on Harry Dennison. Another thought followed, and to that he gave utterance.

"But you've lots of things you could do at home; you could have plenty to work at, and plenty of—of influence, and so on."

"Yes, but—oh, it would come to Mr. Belford! Who wants to influence Mr. Belford? Besides, I've grown to love it now, haven't you?"

"Omofaga?"

"Yes! It's so far off—and most people don't believe in it."

"No, confound them! I wish they did!"

"Do you? I'm not sure I do."

She was so absorbed that she had not heard an approaching step, and was surprised to see Ruston jump up while her last sentence was but half said.

"My dear Miss Valentine," he cried, his face lighting up with a smile of pleasure, "how pleasant to meet you again!"

There was no mistaking the sincerity of his greeting. Marjory blushed as she gave him her hand, and he fixed his eyes on her in undisguised approval.

"You're looking splendid," he said. "Is it the air or the bathing or what?"

Perhaps it was both in part, but, more than either, it was a change that worked outwards from within, and was giving to her face the expression without which mere beauty of form or colour is poor in allurement. The last traces of what Lord Semingham meant by "insipidity" had been chased away. Ruston felt the change though he could not track it.

Marjory, a bad dissembler, greeted him nervously, almost coldly; she was afraid to let her gaze rest on

him or on Mrs. Dennison for long, lest it should hint
her secret. Her manner betrayed such uneasiness
that Ruston noticed it. Mrs. Dennison did not, for
something in Ruston's face had caught her attention.
She had seen many expressions in his eyes as he
looked at her—of sympathy, amusement, pleasure,
even (what had pleased her most) puzzle, but never
what she saw now. The look now was a man's homage to beauty—it differs from every other—a lover
hardly seems to have it unless his love be beautiful—
and she had never yet seen it when he looked at her.
She turned away towards the sea, grasping the arm of
her chair with a sudden grip that streaked her fingers
red and white. Marjory also saw, and a wild hope
leapt up in her that her task needed not the doing.
But a moment later Ruston was back in Omofaga—
young Sir Walter being his bridge for yet another
transit.

"How's Mr. Dennison?" asked Marjory, when he
gave her an opportunity.

"Oh, he's all right. You'd have heard, I suppose,
if he hadn't been?"

It was true. Marjory recognised the inappropri-
ateness of her question, but Mrs. Dennison came to
the rescue.

"Marjory wants a personal impression," she said.
"You know she and my husband are great allies!"

"Well," laughed Ruston, "he was a little cross

with me because I would come to Dieppe. I should have felt the same in his place; but he's well enough, I think."

"I was going down to find Lady Semingham," said Marjory. "Are you coming down this morning, Maggie?"

"Maggie" was something new—adopted at Mrs. Dennison's request.

"I think not, dear."

"I am," said Ruston, taking up his walking stick. "I shall be up with the Baron this afternoon, Mrs. Dennison. Come along, Miss Valentine. We've been having no end of palaver about Omofaga," and as they disappeared down the cliff Mrs. Dennison heard his voice talking eagerly to Marjory.

She felt her heart beating quickly. She had to conquer a strange impulse to rise and hurry after them. She knew that she must be jealous—jealous, she said to herself, trying to laugh, that he should talk about Omofaga to other people. Nonsense! Why, he was always talking of it! There was a stronger feeling in her, less vague, of fuller force. It had come on her when he spoke of his going to Africa, but then it was hard to understand, for with all her heart she thought she was still bent on his going. It spoke more clearly now, stirred by the threat of opposition. At first it had been the thing—the scheme—the idea —that had caught her; she had taken the man for the thing's sake, because to do such a thing proved him a man after her pattern. But now, as she sat in the little garden, she dimly traced her change—she loved the scheme because it was his. She did not shrink from testing it. "Yes," she murmured, "if he gave it up now, I should go on with him to something else." Then came another step—why should he not give it up? Why should he go into banishment—he who might go near to rule England? Why should he empty her life by going? But if he went—and she could not persuade herself that she had power to stop his going—he must go from her side, it must be she who gave him the stirrup-cup, she towards whom he would look across the sea, she for whom he would store up his brief, grim tales of victory, in whose eyes he would see the reflection of his triumphs. Could she fill such a place in his life? She knew that she did not yet, but she believed in herself. "I feel large enough," she said with a smile.

Yet there was something that she had not yet touched in him—the thing which had put that look in his eyes, a thing that for the moment at least Marjory Valentine had touched. Why had she not? She answered, with a strong clinging to self-approbation, that it was because she would not. She told herself that she had asked nothing from her intercourse with him save the play of mind on mind—it was her mind and nothing else that her own home failed to satisfy.

She recalled the scornful disgust with which she had listened to Semingham when he hinted to her that there was only one way to rule a man. It seemed less disgusting to her now than when he spoke. For, in the light of that look in his eyes, there stood revealed a new possibility—always obvious, never hitherto thought of—that another would take and wield the lower mighty power that she had disdained to grasp, and by the might of the lower wrest from her the higher. Was not the lower solidly based in nature, the higher a fanciful structure resting in no sound foundation? The moment this spectre took form before her—the moment she grasped that the question might lie between her and another—that it might be not what she would take but what she could keep—her heart cried out, to ears that shrank from the tumultuous reckless cry, that less than all was nothing, that, if need be, all must be paid for all. And, swift on the horror of her discovery, came the inevitable joy in it—joy that will be silenced by no reproofs, not altogether abashed by any shame, that no pangs can rob utterly of its existence—a thing to smother, to hide, to rejoice in.

Yet she would not face unflinchingly what her changing mind must mean. She tried to put it aside —to think of something, ah! of anything else, of anything that would give her foothold.

"I love my husband," she found herself saying. "I love poor old Harry and the children." She repeated it again and again, praying the shibboleth to show its saving virtue. It was part of her creed, part of her life, to be a good wife and mother—part of her traditions that women who were not that were nothing at all, and that there was nothing a woman might take in exchange for this one splendid, all-comprehending virtue. To that she must stand—it was strange to be driven to argue with herself on such a point. She mused restlessly as she sat; she listened eagerly for her children's footsteps mounting the hill; she prayed an interruption to rescue her from her thoughts. Just now she would think no more about it; it was thinking about it that did all the harm. Yet while she was alone she could not choose but surrender to the thought of it—to the thought of what a price she must pay for her traditions and her creed. The payment, she cried, would leave life an empty thing. Yet it must be paid—if it must. Was it now come to that? Was this the parting of the roads?

"I must, yet I cannot! I must not, yet I must." It was the old clash of powers, the old conflict of commands, the old ruthless will of nature that makes right too hard and yet fastens anguish upon sin—that makes us yearn for and hate the higher while we love and loathe the lower.

CHAPTER XV.

THE WORK OF A WEEK.

MUCH went to spoil the stay at Dieppe, but the only overt trouble was the feeble health of the Baron von Geltschmidt. The old man had rapidly made his way into the liking of his new acquaintances. Semingham found his dry, worldly-wise, perhaps world-weary, humour an admirable sauce to conversation; Adela Ferrars detected kindness in him; his gallant deference pleased Lady Semingham. They were all grieved when the cold winds laid hold of him, forced him to keep house often, and drove him to furs and a bath-chair, even when the sun shone most brightly. Although they liked him, they implored him to fly south. He would not move, finding pleasure in them, and held fast by an ever-increasing uneasy interest in Willie Ruston. Adela quarrelled with him heartily and energetically on this score. To risk health because anyone was interesting was absurd; to risk it on Ruston's account most preposterous. "I'd be ill to get away from him," she declared. The Baron was obstinate, fatalistic as to his health, infatuated in his folly; stay he would, while Ruston stayed. Yet what Ruston did, pleased him not; for the better part of the man—what led him to respond to kindness or affection, and abate something of his hardness where he met no resistance—seemed to be conspiring with his old domineering mood to lead him beyond all power of warning or recall.

A week had passed since Ruston paid his first visit to Mrs. Dennison in the cottage on the cliff. It was a bright morning. The Baron was feeling stronger; he had left his chair and walked with Adela to a seat. There they sat side by side, in the occasional talk and easy silences of established friendship. The Baron smoked his cigar; Adela looked idly at the sea; but suddenly the Baron began to speak.

"I had a talk with our friend, Lord Semingham, this morning," said he.

"About anything in particular?"

"I meant it to be, but he doesn't like talk that leads anywhere in particular."

"No, he doesn't," said Adela, with a slight smile.

The Baron sat silent for a moment, then he said,

"May I talk to you, Miss Ferrars?" and he looked at her inquiringly.

"Why, of course," she answered. "Is it about yourself, Baron? You're not worse, are you?"

He took no notice of her question, but pointed towards the cliff.

" What is happening up there? " he asked.

Adela started. She had not realised that he meant to talk on that subject.

He detected her shrinking and hastened to defend himself.

" Or are we to say nothing? " he asked. " Nothing? When we all see! Don't you see? Doesn't Miss Valentine see? Is she so sad for nothing? Oh, don't shake your head. And the other—this Mrs. Dennison? Am I to go on? "

" No," said Adela sharply; and added, a moment later, " I know."

" And what does he mean? "

" He? " cried Adela. " Oh, he's not human."

" Nay, but he's terribly human," said the old Baron.

Adela looked round at him, but then turned away.

" I know what I would say, but I may not say it," pursued the Baron. " To you I may not say it. I know him. He will take, if he is offered."

His voice sank to a whisper.

" Then God help her," murmured Adela under her breath, while her cheeks flamed red.

" Yes, he will take, and he will go. Ah, he is a man to follow and to believe in—to trust your money, your fortune, your plans, even your secrets to; but——"

He paused, flinging away his extinct cigar.

" Well?" asked Adela in a low tone, eager in spite of her hatred of the topic.

" Never your love," said he; and added, "yet I believe I, who am old enough to know better, and too old to learn better, have almost given him mine. Well, I am not a woman."

" He can't hurt you," said Adela.

" Yes, he can," said the Baron with a dreary smile. Adela was not thinking of her companion.

" Why do you talk of it?" she asked impatiently.

" I know I was wrong."

" No, no. I mean, why do you talk of it now?"

" Because," said the Baron, "he will not. Have you seen no change in him this week? A week ago, he laughed when I talked to him. He did not mind me speaking—it was still a trifle—nonsense—a week ago; if you like, an amusement, a pastime!"

" Well, and now?"

" Now he tells me to hold my tongue. And yet I am glad for one thing. That girl will not have him for a husband."

" Glad! Why, Baron, don't you see——"

" Yes, I see. Still I am glad."

" I can't go on talking about it; but is there no hope?"

"Where is it? For the time—mind you for the time—he is under that other woman's power."

"She's under his, you mean."

"I mean both. She was a friend of yours. Yes. She is not altogether a bad woman; but she has had a bad fortune. Ah, there she is, and he with her."

As he spoke, Mrs. Dennison and Ruston came by. Mrs. Dennison flung them a glance of recognition; it was hardly more, and even for so much she seemed to grudge the interruption. Ruston's greeting was more ceremonious; he smiled, but his brows contracted a little, and he said to his companion,

"Miss Ferrars isn't pleased with me."

"That hurts?" she asked lightly.

"No," he answered, after a short pause, "I don't know that it does."

But the frown dwelt a little longer on his face.

"Sit down here," she said, and they sat down in full view of Adela and the Baron, about twenty yards off.

"She's mad," murmured Adela, and the Baron muttered assent.

It was the time of the morning when everybody was out. Presently Lord and Lady Semingham strolled by—Lady Semingham did not see Maggie Dennison, her husband did, and Adela caught the look in his eye. Then down from the hill and on to the grass came Marjory Valentine. She saw both

13

couples, and, for a perceptible moment, stood wavering between them. She looked pale and weary. Mrs.
Dennison indicated her with the slightest gesture.

"You were asking for her. There she is," she
said to Willie Ruston.

"Well, I think I'll go and ask her."

"What?"

"To come for a walk."

"Now?"

"Why not?" he asked with a surprised smile.

As he spoke, Marjory's hesitation ended; she joined
Adela and the Baron.

"How rude you are!" exclaimed Mrs. Dennison
angrily, "you asked me to come out with you."

"So I did. By Jove, so I did! But you don't
walk, do you? And I feel rather like a walk now."

"Oh, if you prefer her society——"

"Her prattle," he said, smiling, "amuses me.
You and I always discuss high matters, you see."

"She doesn't prattle, and you know it."

He looked at her for a moment. He had gone so
far as to rise, but he resumed his seat.

"What's the matter?" he asked tolerantly.

Maggie Dennison's lip quivered. The week that
had passed had been a stormy one to her. There had
been a breaking-down of barriers—barriers of honour,
conscience, and pride. All she could do to gain or
keep her mastery she had done. She had all but

thrown herself at his feet. She hated to think of the things she had said or half-said; and she had seen Marjory's eyes look wondering horror and pitying contempt at her. Of her husband she would not think. And she had won in return—she knew not what. It hung still in the balance. Sometimes he would seem engrossed in her; but again he would turn to Marjory or another with a kind of relief, as though she wearied him. And of her struggles, of the great humiliations she suffered, of all she sacrificed to him, he seemed unconscious. Yet, cost what it might, she could not let him go now. The screen of Omofaga was dropped; she knew that it was the man whose life she was resolute to fill; whether she called it love for him or what else mattered little; it seemed rather a mere condition of existence, necessary yet not sweet, even revolting; but its alternative was death.

She had closed her eyes for a moment under the stress of her pain. When she opened them, he was looking at her. And the look she knew was at last in his eyes. She put up her hand to ward it off; it woke her horror, but it woke her delight also. She could not choose whether to banish it, or to live in it all her life. She tried to speak, but her utterance was choked.

" Why, I believe you're—jealous," said Willie Ruston. " But then they always say I'm a conceited chap."

He spoke with a laugh, but he looked at her intently. The little scene was the climax of a week's gradual betrayal. Often in all the hours they had spent together, in all the engrossing talks they had had, something of the kind had appeared and disappeared; he had wondered at her changefulness, her moods of expansion and of coldness—a rapturous greeting of him to be followed by a cold dismissal—an eager sympathy alternating with wilful indifference. She had, too, fits of prudence, when she would not go with him—and then spasms of recklessness when her manner seemed to defy all restraint and mock at the disapproval of her friends. On these puzzles—to him, preoccupied as he was and little versed in such matters, they had seemed such—the present moment shed its light. He recalled, with understanding, things that had passed meaninglessly before his eyes, that he seemed to have forgotten altogether; the ambiguous things became plain; what had been, though plain, yet strange, fell into its ordered place and became natural. The new relation between them proclaimed itself the interpretation and the work of the bygone week.

Her glove lay in her lap, and he touched it lightly; the gesture speaking of their sudden new familiarity.

Her reproach was no less eloquent; she rebuked not the thing, but the rashness of it.

"Don't do that. They're looking," she found voice to whisper.

He withdrew his hand, and, taking off his hat, pushed the hair back from his forehead. Presently he looked at her with an almost comical air of perplexity; she was conscious of the glance, but she would not meet it. He pursed his lips to whistle.

"Don't," she whispered sharply. "Don't whistle." A whistle brought her husband to her mind.

The checked whistle rudely reflected his mingled feelings. He wished that he had been more on his guard—against her and against himself. There had been enough to put him on his guard; if he had been put on his guard, this thing need not have happened. He called the thing in his thoughts "inconvenient." He was marvellously awake to the inconvenience of it; it was that which came uppermost in his mind as he sat by Maggie Dennison. Yet, in spite of a phrase that sounded so cold and brutal, his reflections paid her no little compliment; for he called the revelation inconvenient all the more, and most of all, because he found it of immense interest, because it satisfied suddenly and to the full a sense of interest and expectation that had been upon him, because it seemed to make an immense change in his mind and to alter the conditions of his life. Had it not done all this, its inconvenience would have been much less—to him and save in so far as he grieved for her—nay, it would have been, in reality, nothing. It was inconvenient because it twisted his purposes, set him at jar with himself, and cut across the orderly lines he had laid down—and because, though it did all this, he was not grieved nor angry at it.

He rose to his feet. Mrs. Dennison looked up quickly.

"I shall go for my walk now," he said, and he added in answer to her silent question, "Oh, yes, alone. I've got a thing or two I want to think about."

Her eyes dropped as he spoke. He had smiled, and she, in spite of herself, had smiled in answer; but she could not look at him while she smiled. He stood there for an instant, smiling still; then he grew grave, and turned to walk away. Her sigh witnessed the relaxation of the strain. But, after one step, he faced her again, and said, as though the idea had just struck him,

"I say, when does Dennison come?"

"In a week," she answered.

For just a moment again, he stood still, thoughtfully looking at her. Then he lifted his hat, wheeled round, and walked briskly off towards the jetty at the far end of the expanse of grass. Adela Ferrars, twenty yards off, marked his going with a sigh of relief.

Mrs. Dennison sat where she was a little while longer. Her agitation was quickly passing, and there followed on it a feeling of calm. She seemed to have resigned charge of herself, to have given her conduct into another's keeping. She did not know what he would do; he had uttered no word of pleasure or pain, praise or blame; and that question at the last— about her husband—was ambiguous. Did he ask it, fearing Harry's arrival, or did he think the arrival of her husband would end an awkward 'position and set him free? Really, she did not know. She had done what she could—and what she could not help. He must do what he liked—only, knowing him, she did not think that she had set an end to their acquaintance. And that for the moment was enough.

"A woman, Bessie," she heard a voice behind her saying, "may be anything from a cosmic force to a clothes-peg."

"I don't know what a cosmic force is," said Lady Semingham.

"A cosmic force? Why——"

"But I don't want to know, Alfred. Why, Maggie, that's a new shade of brown on your shoes. Where do you get them?"

Mrs. Dennison gave her bootmaker's address, and Lady Semingham told her husband to remember it. She never remembered that he always forgot such things.

The arrival of the Seminghams seemed to break the spell which had held Mrs. Dennison apart from the group over against her. Adela strolled across, followed by Marjory, and the Baron on Marjory's arm. The whole party gathered in a cluster; but Marjory hung loosely on the outskirts of the circle, and seemed scarcely to belong to it.

The Baron seated himself in the place Willie Ruston had left empty. The rest stood talking for a minute or two, then Semingham put his hand in his pocket and drew out a folded sheet of tracing-paper.

"We're all Omofagites here, aren't we?" he said; "even you, Baron, now. Here's a plan Carlin has just sent me. It shows our territory."

Everybody crowded round to look as he unfolded it. Mrs. Dennison was first in undisguised eagerness; and Marjory came closer, slipping her arm through Adela Ferrars'.

"What does the blue mean?" asked Adela.

"Native settlements."

"Oh! And all that brown?—it's mostly brown."

"Brown," answered Semingham, with a slight smile, "means unexplored country."

"I should have made it all brown," said Adela, and the Baron gave an appreciative chuckle.

"And what are these little red crosses?" asked Mrs. Dennison, laying the tip of her finger on one.

"Eh? What, those? Oh, let me see. Here, just hold it while I look at Carlin's letter. He explains it all," and Lord Semingham began to fumble in his breast-pocket.

"Dear me," said Bessie Semingham, in a tone of delicate pleasure, "they look like tombstones."

"Hush, hush, my dear lady," cried the old Baron; "what a bad omen!"

"Tombstones," echoed Maggie Dennison thoughtfully. "So they do—just like tombstones."

A pause fell on the group. Adela broke it.

"Well, Director, have you found your directions?" she asked briskly.

"It was a momentary lapse of memory," said Semingham with dignity. "Those—er—little——"

"No, not tombstones," interrupted the Baron earnestly.

"Little—er—signposts are, of course, the forts belonging to the Company. What else should they be?"

"Oh, *forts*," murmured everybody.

"They are," continued Lord Semingham apologetically, "in the nature of a prophecy at present, as I understand."

"A very bad prophecy, according to Bessie," said Mrs. Dennison.

"I hope," said the Baron, shaking his head, "that the official name is more correct than Lady Semingham's."

"So do I," said Marjory; and added, before she could think not to add, and with unlucky haste, "my brother's going out, you know."

Mrs. Dennison looked at her. Then she crossed over to her, saying to Adela,

"You never let me have a word with my own guest, except at breakfast and bedtime. Come and walk up and down with me, Marjory."

Marjory obeyed; the group began to scatter.

"But didn't they look like tombstones, Baron?" said Bessie Semingham again, as she sat down and made room for the old man beside her. When she had an idea she liked it very much. He began to be voluble in his reproof of her gloomy fancies; but she merely laughed in glee at her ingenuity.

Adela, by a gesture, brought Semingham to her side and walked a few paces off with him.

"Will you go with me to the post-office?" she said abruptly.

"By all means," he answered, feeling for his glass.

"Oh, you needn't get your glass to spy at me with."

"Dear, dear, you use one yourself!"

"I'll tell you myself why I'm going. You're going to send a telegram."

"Am I?"

"Yes; to invite someone to stay with you. Lord Semingham, when you find a woman relies on a man —on one man only—in trouble, what do you think?"

She asked the question in a level voice, looking straight before her.

“ That she’s fond of him.”

“ And does he—the man—think the same ? ”

“ Generally. I think most men would. They’re seldom backward to think it, you know.”

“ Then,” she said steadily, “ you must think, and he must think, what you like. I can’t help it. I want you to wire and ask a man to come and stay with you.”

He turned to her in surprise.

“ Tom Loring,” she said, and the moment the name left her lips Semingham hastily turned his glance away.

“ Awkward—with the other fellow here,” he ventured to suggest.

“ Mr. Ruston doesn’t choose your guests.”

“ But Mrs.——”

“ Oh, fancy talking of awkwardness now ! He used to influence her once, you know. Perhaps he might still. Do let us try,” and her voice trembled in earnestness.

“ We’ll try. Will he come ? He’s very angry with her.”

And Adela answered, still looking straight in front of her,

“ I’m going to send him a wire, too.”

“ I’m very glad to hear it,” said Lord Semingham.

CHAPTER XVI.

THE LAST BARRIERS.

Willie Ruston rested his elbows on the jetty-wall and gazed across the harbour entrance. He had come there to think; and deliberate thinking was a rare thing for him to set his head to. His brain dealt generally—even with great matters, as all brains deal with small—in rapid half-unconscious beats; the process coalescing so closely with the decision as to be merged before it could be recognised. But about this matter he meant to think; and the first result of his determination was (as it often is in such a case) that nothing at all relevant would stay by him. There was a man fishing near, and he watched the float; he looked long at the big hotel at Puys, which faced him a mile away, and idly wondered whether it were full; he followed the egress of a fishing boat with strict attention. Then, in impatience, he turned round and sat down on the stone bench and let his eyes see nothing but the flags of the pavement. Even then he hardly thought; but after a time he became vaguely occupied with Maggie Dennison, his mind playing to and fro over her voice, her tricks of manner, her very gait, and at last settling more or less resolutely on the strange revelation of herself which she had gradually made and had consummated that day. It changed his feelings towards her; but it did not change them to contempt. He had his ideas, but he did not make ideal figures out of humanity; and humanity could go very far wrong and sink very deep in its lower possibilities without shocking him. Nor did he understand her, nor realise how great a struggle had brought what he saw to birth. It seemed to him a thing not unnatural, even in her, who was in much unlike most other women. There are dominions that are not to be resisted, and we do not think people weak simply because they are under our own influence. His surprise was reserved for the counter-influence which he felt, and strove not to acknowledge; his contempt for the disturbance into which he himself was thrown. At that he was half-displeased, puzzled, and alarmed; yet that, too, had its delight.

"What rot it is!" he muttered, in the rude dialect of self-communion, which sums up a bewildering conflict in a word of slang.

He was afraid of himself—and his exclamation betrayed the fear. Men of strong will are not all will; the strong will has other strong things to fight, and

the strong head has mighty rebels to hold down.
That he felt; but his fear of himself had its limits.
He was not the man—as he saw very well at this moment, and recognised with an odd mixture of pride
and humiliation—to give up his life to a passion.
Had that been the issue clearly and definitely set before him he would not have sat doubtful on the jetty.
He understood what of nobility lay in such a tempera-
ment, and his humiliation was because it made no
part of him; but the pride overmastered, and at last
he was glad to say to himself that there was no danger
of his losing all for love. Indeed, was he in love? In
love in the grand sense people talked and wrote about
so much? Well, there were other senses, and there
were many degrees. The question he weighed, or
rather the struggle which he was undergoing, was between resisting or yielding before a temptation to take
into his life something which should not absorb it, but
yet in a measure alter it, which allured him all the
more enticingly because, judging as he best could, he
could see no price which must be paid for it—well,
except one. And, as the one came into his mind, it
made him pause, and he mused on it, looking at it in
all lights. Sometimes he put the price as an act of
wrong which would stain him—for, apart from other,
maybe greater, maybe more fanciful obstacles, Harry
Dennison held him for a friend—sometimes as an act
of weakness which would leave him vulnerable. And,

after these attempted reasonings, he would fall again to thinking of Maggie Dennison, her voice, her manner, and the revelation of herself; and in these picturings the reasoning died away.

There are a few deliberate sinners, a few by whom "Evil, be thou my Good" is calmly uttered as a dedication and a sacrament, but most men do not make up their minds to be sinners or determine in cool resolve to do acts of the sort that lurked behind Willie Ruston's picturings. They only fail to make up their minds not to do them. Ruston, in a fury of impatience, swept all his musings from him—it led to nothing. It left him where he was. He was vexing himself needlessly; he told himself that he could not decide what he ought to do. In truth, he did not choose to decide what it was that he chose to do. And with the thoughts that he drove away went the depression they had carried with them. He was confident again in himself, his destiny, his career; and in its fancied greatness, the turmoil he had suffered sank to its small proportions. He returned to his old standpoint, and to the old medley of pride and shame it gave him; he might be of supreme importance to Maggie Dennison, but she was only of some importance to him. He could live without her. But, at present, he regarded her loss as a thing not necessary to undergo.

It was late in the day that he met young Sir Walter, who ran to him, open-mouthed with news. Walter was afraid that the news would be unpalatable, and could not understand such want of tact in Semingham. To ask Tom Loring while Ruston was there argued a bluntness of perception strange to young Sir Walter. But, be the news good or bad, he had only to report; and report it he did straightway to his chief. Willie Ruston smiled, and said that, if Loring did not mind meeting him, he did not mind meeting Loring; indeed, he would welcome the opportunity of proving to that unbeliever that there was water somewhere within a hundred miles of Fort Imperial (which Tom in one of those articles had sturdily denied). Then he flirted away a stone with his stick and asked if anyone had yet told Mrs. Dennison. And, Sir Walter thinking not, he said,

"Oh, well, I'm going there. I'll tell her."

"She'll know why he's coming," said Walter, nodding his head wisely.

"Will she? Do you know?" asked Ruston with a smile—young Sir Walter's wisdom was always sure of that tribute from him.

"If you'd seen Adela Ferrars, you'd know too. She tries to make believe it's nothing, but she's—oh, she's——"

"Well?"

"She's all of a flutter," laughed Walter.

" You've got to the bottom of that," said Ruston in a tone of conviction.

"Still, I think it's inconsiderate of Loring; he must know that Mrs. Dennison will find it rather awkward. But, of course, if a fellow's in love, he won't think of that."

" I suppose not," said Willie Ruston, smiling again at this fine scorn.

Then, with a sudden impulse, struck perhaps with an envy of what he laughed at, he put his arm through his young friend's, and exclaimed, with a friendly confidential pressure of the hand,

" I say, Val, I wish the devil we were in Omofaga, don't you ? "

" Rather ! " came full and rich from his companion's lips.

" With a few thousand miles between us and everything—and everybody ! "

Young Sir Walter's eyes sparkled.

" Off in three months now," he reminded his leader exultingly.

It could not be. The Fates will not help in such a fashion, it is not their business to cut the noose a man ties round his neck—happy is he if they do not draw it tight. With a sigh, Willie Ruston dropped his companion's arm, and left him with no other farewell than a careless nod. Of Tom Loring's coming he thought little. It might be that Sir Walter had

14

seen most of its meaning, and that Semingham was
acting as a benevolent match-maker—a character
strange for him, and amusing to see played—but, no
doubt, there was a little more. Probably Tom had
some idea of turning him from his path, of combating
his influence, of disputing his power. Well, Tom had
tried that once, and had failed; he would fail again.
Maggie Dennison had not hesitated to resent such
interference; she had at once (Ruston expressed it to
himself) put Tom in his right place. Tom would be
no more to her at Dieppe than in London—nay, he
would be less, for any power unbroken friendship and
habit might have had then would be gone by now.
Thus, though he saw the other meaning, he made light
of it, and it was as a bit of gossip concerning Adela
Ferrars, not as tidings which might affect herself, that
he told Mrs. Dennison of Tom's impending arrival.

On her the announcement had a very different
effect. For her the whole significance lay in what
Ruston ignored, and none in what had caught his
fancy. He was amazed to see the rush of colour to
her cheeks.

"Tom Loring coming here!" she cried in something like horror.

Again, and with a laugh, Ruston pointed out the
motive of his coming, as young Sir Walter had interpreted it; but he added, as though in concession, and
with another laugh,

“Perhaps he wants to keep his eye on me, too. He doesn’t trust me further than he can see me, you know.”

Without looking at him or seeming to listen to his words, she asked, in low, indignant tones,

“How dare he come?”

Willie Ruston opened his eyes. He did not understand so much emotion spent on such a trifle. Say it was bad taste in Loring to come, or an impertinence! Well, it was not a tragedy at all events. He was almost angry with her for giving importance to it; and the importance she gave set him wondering. But before he could translate his feeling into words, she turned to him, leaning across the table that stood between them, and clasping her hands.

“I can’t bear to have him here now,” she murmured.

“What harm will he do? You needn’t see anything of him,” rejoined Ruston, more astonished at each new proof of disquietude in her.

But Tom Loring was not to be so lightly dismissed from her mind; and she did not seem to heed when Ruston added, with a laugh,

“You got rid of him once, didn’t you? I should think you could again.”

“Ah, then! That was different.”

He looked at her curiously. She was agitated, but there seemed to be more than agitation. As he read it, it was fear; and discerning it, he spoke in growing surprise and rising irritation.

"You look as if you were afraid of him."

"Afraid of him?" she broke out. "Yes, I am afraid of him."

"Of Loring?" he exclaimed in sheer wonder. "Why, in heaven's name? Loring's not——"

He was going to say "your husband," but stopped himself.

"I can't face him," she whispered. "Oh, you know! Why do you torment me? Or don't you know? Oh, how strange you are!"

And now there was fear in her eyes when she looked at Ruston.

He sat still a moment, and then in slow tones he said,

"I don't see what concern your affairs are of Loring's, or mine either, by God!"

At the last word his voice rose a little, and his lips shut tight as it left them.

"Oh, it's easy for you," she said, half in anger at him, half in scorn of herself. "You don't know what he is—what he was—to me."

"What was Loring to you?" he asked in sharp, imperious tones—tones that made her hurriedly cry,

"No, no; not that, not that. How could you think that of me?"

"What then?" came curt and crisp from him, her reproach falling unheeded.

"Oh, I wish—I wish you could understand just a little! Do you think it's all nothing to me? Do you think I don't mind?"

"I don't know what it is to you," he said doggedly. "I know it's nothing to Loring."

"I don't believe," she went on, "that he's coming because of Adela at all."

And as she spoke, she met his eyes for a moment, and then shrank from them.

"Come, shall we speak plainly?" he asked with evident impatience.

"Ah, you will, I know," she wailed, with a smile and a despairing gesture. She loved and dreaded him for it. "Not too plainly, Willie!"

His mouth relaxed.

"Why do you worry about the fellow?" he asked.

"Well, I'll speak plainly, too," she cried. "He's not a fool; and he's an honest man. That's why I don't want him here;" and enduring only till she had flung out the truth, she buried her face in her hands.

"I've had enough of him," said Willie Ruston, frowning. "He's always got in my way; first about the Company—and now——"

He broke off, pushing his chair back, and rising to his feet. He walked to the window of the little sitting-room where they were; the sun was setting over the sea, and early dusk gathering. It was still, save for the sound of the waves.

"Is there nobody at home?" he asked, with his back towards her.

"No. Marjory and the children have gone down to the *Rome* to have tea with Bessie Semingham."

He waited a moment longer, looking out, then he came back and stood facing her. She was leaning her head on her hand. At last she spoke in a low voice.

"He's Harry's friend," she said, "and he used to be mine; and he trusted me."

Willie Ruston threw his head back with a little sharp jerk.

"Oh, well, I didn't come to talk about Tom Loring," he said. "If you value his opinion so very much, why, you must keep it; that's all," and he moved towards where his hat was lying. "But I'm afraid I can't share my friends with him."

"Oh, I know you won't share anything with anybody," said Maggie Dennison, her voice trembling between a sob and a laugh.

He turned instantly. His face lighted up, and the sun, casting its last rays on her eyes, made them answer with borrowed brilliance.

"I won't share you with Loring, anyhow," he cried, walking close up to her, and resting his hand on the table.

She laid hers gently on it.

"Don't go to Omofaga, Willie," she said.

For a moment he sheerly stared at her; then he burst into a merry unrestrained peal of laughter. Next he lifted her hand and kissed it.

"You are the most wonderful woman in the world," said he, his mouth quivering with amusement.

"Oh!" she exclaimed, throwing her arms wide for a moment.

"Well, what's the matter? What have I done wrong now?"

She rose and walked up and down the room.

"I wish I'd never seen you," she said from the far end of it.

"I wish I'd never seen—Tom Loring."

"Ah, that's the only thing!" she cried. "I may live or I may die, or I may—do anything you like; but I mustn't have another friend! I mustn't give a thought to what anybody else thinks of me!"

"You mustn't balance me against Tom Loring," he answered between his teeth, all signs of his merriment gone now.

For a moment—not long, but seeming very long— there was silence in the room; and, while the brief stillness reigned, she fought a last battle against him, calling loyalty and friendship to her aid, praying their alliance against the overbearing demand he made on her—against his roughness, his blindness to all she suffered for him. But the strife was short. Lifting her hands above her head, and bringing them down through the air as with a blow, she cried,

"My God, I balance nothing against you!"

Her reward—her only reward—seemed on the instant to be hers. Willie Ruston was transformed; his sullenness was gone; his eyes were alight with triumph; the smile she loved was on his lips, and he had forgotten those troubled, useless, mazy musings on the jetty. He took a quick step towards her, holding out both his hands. She clasped them.

"Nothing?" he asked in a low tone. "Nothing, Maggie?"

She bowed her head for answer; it was the attitude of surrender, of helplessness, and of trust, and it appealed to the softer feeling in him which her resistance had smothered. He was strongly moved, and his face was pale as he drew her to him and kissed her lips; but all he said was,

"Then the deuce take Tom Loring!"

It seemed to her enough. The light devil-may-care words surely covered a pledge from him to her— something in return from him to her. At last, surely he was hers, and her wishes his law. It was her moment; she would ask of him now the uttermost wish of her heart—the wish that had displaced all else—

the passionate wish not to lose him—not, as it were,
to be emptied of him.

"And Omofaga?" she whispered.

His eyes looked past her, out into the dim twilight,
into the broad world—the world that she seemed to
ask him to give for her, as she was giving her world
for him. He laughed again, but not as he had laughed
before. There was a note of wonder in his laugh now
—of wonder that the prayer seemed now not so utterly
absurd—that he could imagine himself doing even
that—spoiling his heart of its darling ambition—for
her. Yet, even in that moment of her strongest sway,
as her arms were about him, he was swearing to himself that he would not.

She did not press for an answer. A glance into
his distant eyes gave her one, perhaps, for she sighed
as though in pain. Hearing her, he bent his look
on her again. Though he might deny that last
boon, he had given her much. So she read; and,
drawing herself to her full height, she released one
of her hands from his, and held it out to him. For
a moment he hesitated; then a slow smile breaking
on his face, he bent and kissed it, and she whispered
over his bent head, half in triumph, half in apology
for bidding him bend his head even in love,

"I like pretending to be queen—even with you,
Willie."

Her flattery, so sweet to him, because it was wrung

from her all against her will, and was for him alone of men, thrilled through him and he was drawing her to him again when the merry chatter of a child struck on their ears from the garden.

She shrank back.

"Hark!" she murmured. "They're coming."

"Yes," he said, with a frown. "I shall come to-morrow, Maggie."

"To-morrow? Every day?" said she.

"Well, then, every day. But to-morrow all day."

"Ah, yes, all day to-morrow."

"But I must go now."

"No, no, don't go," she said quickly. "Sit down; see, sit there. Don't look as if you'd thought of going."

He did as she bade him, trying to assume an indifferent air.

She, too, sat down, her eyes fixed on the door. A strange look of pain and shame spread over her face. She must bend to deceive her children, to dread detection, to play little tricks and weave little devices against the eyes of those for whom she had been an earthly providence—the highest, most powerful, and best they knew. Willie Ruston did not follow the thought that stamped its mark on her face then, nor understand why, with a sudden gasp, she dashed her hand across her eyes and turned to him with trembling lips, crying, in low tones,

" Ah, but I have you, Willie ! "

Before he could answer her appeal, the voices were in the passage. Her face grew calm, save for a slight frown on her brow. She shaped her lips into a smile to meet the incomers. She shot a rapid glance of caution and warning at him. The door was flung open, and the three children rushed in, Madge at their head. Madge, seeing Willie Ruston, stopped short, and her laughter died away. She turned and said,

" Marjory, here's Mr. Ruston."

None could mistake her tone for one of welcome.

Marjory Valentine came forward. She looked at neither of them, but sat down near the table.

" Well, Madge," said Mrs. Dennison, " there's good news for you, isn't there ? Your friend's coming."

Madge, finding (as she thought) sympathy, came to her mother's knee.

" Yes, I'm glad," she said. " Are you glad, mother?"

" Oh, I don't mind," answered Mrs. Dennison, kissing her; but she could not help one glance at Willie Ruston. Bitterly she repented it, for she found Marjory Valentine following it with her open sorrowful eyes. She rose abruptly, and Ruston rose also, and with brief good-nights—Madge being kissed only on strong persuasion—took his leave. The children flocked away to take off their hats, and Marjory was left alone with her hostess.

The girl looked pale, weary, and sad. Mrs. Dennison was stirred to an impulse of compassion. Walking up to where she sat, she bent down as though to kiss her. Marjory looked up. There was a question —it seemed to be a question—in her face. Mrs. Dennison flushed red from neck to forehead, and then grew paler than the pallor she had pitied. The girl's unspoken question seemed to echo hauntingly from every corner of the little room, Are your lips—clean?

CHAPTER XVII.

Slow in forming, swift in acting; slow in the making, swift in the working; slow to the summit, swift down the other slope; it is the way of nature, and the way of the human mind. What seemed yesterday unborn and impossible, is to-day incipient and a great way off, to-morrow complete, present, and accomplished. After long labour a thing springs forth full grown; to deny it, or refuse it, or fight against it, seems now as vain as a few hours ago it was to hope for it, or to fear, or to imagine, or conceive it. In like manner, the slow, crawling, upward journey can be followed by every eye; its turns, its twists, its checks, its zigzags may be recorded on a chart. Then is the brief pause—on the summit—and the tottering incline towards the declivity. But how describe what comes after? The dazzling rush that beats the eye, that in its fury of advance, its paroxysm of speed, is void of halts or turns, and, darting from point to point, covers and blurs the landscape till there seems nothing but the moving thing; and that again, while the watcher still tries vainly to catch its whirl, has sprung, and reached, and ceased; and, save that there it was and here it is, he would not know that its fierce stir had been.

Such a race runs passion to its goal, when the reins hang loose. Hours may do what years have not done, and minutes sum more changes than long days could stretch to hold. The world narrows till there would seem to be nothing else existent in it—nothing of all that once held out the promise (sure as it then claimed to be) of escape, of help, or warning. The very promise is forgotten, the craving for its fulfilment dies away. "Let me alone," is the only cry; and the appeal makes its own answer, the entreaty its own concession.

Some thirty hours had passed since the last recorded scene, and Marjory Valentine was still under Mrs. Dennison's roof. It had been hard to stay, but the girl would not give up her self-imposed hopeless task. Helpless she had proved, and hopeless she had become. The day had passed with hardly a word spoken between her and her hostess. Mrs. Dennison had been out the greater part of the time, and, when out, she had been with Ruston. She had come in to dinner at half-past seven, and at nine had gone to her room, pleading fatigue and a headache. Marjory had sat up a little longer, with an unopened book on her knee. Then she also went to bed, and tried vainly to sleep. She had left her bed now, and, wrapped in a dressing-gown, sat in a low arm-chair near the window. It was a dark and still night; a thick fog hung over the little garden; nothing was to be heard save the gentle roll of a quiet sea, and the occasional blast of a steam whistle. Marjory's watch had stopped, but she guessed it to be somewhere in the small hours of the morning—one o'clock, perhaps, or nearing two. There was an infinite weary time, then, before the sun would shine again, and the oppression of the misty darkness be lifted off. She hated the night—this night—it savoured not of rest to her, but of death; for she was wrought to a nervous strain, and felt her imaginings taking half-bodily shapes about her, so that she was fearful of looking to the right hand or the left. Sleep was impossible; to try to sleep like a surrender to the mysterious enemies round her. Time seemed to stand still; she counted sixty once, to mark a minute's flight, and the counting took an eternity. The house was utterly noiseless, and she shivered at the silence. She would have given half her life, she felt, for a ray of the sun; but half a life stretched between her and the first break of morning. Sitting there, she heaped terrors round her; the superstitions that hide their heads before daytime mockery reared them now in victory and made a prey of her. The struggle she had in her weakness entered on seemed less now with human frailty than against the strong and evil purpose of some devil; in face of which she was naught. How should she be? She had not, she told herself in morbid upbraiding, even a pure motive in the fight; her hatred of the sin had been less keen had she not once desired the love of him that caused it, and when she arrested Maggie Dennison's kiss, she shamed a rival in rebuking an unfaithful wife. Then she cried rebelliously against her anguish. Why had this come on her, darkening bright youth? Why was she compassed about with trouble? And why—why —why did not the morning come?

The mist was thick and grey against the window. A fog-horn roared, and the sea, regardless, repeated its even beat; behind the feeble interruptions there sounded infinite silence. She hid her face in her hands. Then she leapt up and flung the window open wide. The damp fog-folds settled on her face, but she heard the sea more plainly, and there were sounds in the air about her. It was not so terribly quiet. She peered eagerly through the mist, but saw nothing save vague tremulous shapes, vacant of identity. Still the world, the actual, earthly, healthy world, was there—a refuge from imagination.

She stood looking; and, as she looked, one shape seemed to grow into a nearer likeness of something definite. It was motionless; it differed from the rest only in being darker and of rather sharper outline.

It must be a tree, she thought, but remembered no tree there; the garden held only low-growing shrubs. A post? But the gate lay to the right, and this stood on her left hand, hard by the door of the house. What then? The terror came on her again, but she stood and looked, longing to find some explanation for it—some meaning on which her mind could rest, and, reassured, drive away its terrifying fancies. For the shape was large in the mist, and she could not tell what it might mean. Was it human? On her superstitious mood the thought flashed bright with sudden relief, and she cried beseechingly,

"Who is it? Who is there?"

A human voice in answer would have been heaven to her, but no answer came. With a stifled cry, she shut the window down, and stood a moment, listening—eager, yet fearful, to hear. Hark! Yes, there was a sound! What was it? It was a footstep on the gravel—a slow, uncertain, wavering, intermittent step, as though of someone groping with hesitating feet and doubtful resolution through the mist. She must know what it was—who it was—what it meant. She started up again, laying both hands on the window-sash. But then terror conquered curiosity; gasping as if breath failed her and something still pursued, she ran across the room and flung open the door. She must find someone—Maggie or someone.

On the threshold she paused in amazement. The

15

door of Mrs. Dennison's room was open, and Maggie stood in the doorway, holding a candle, behind which her face gleamed pale and her eyes shone. She was muffled in a long white wrapper, and her dark hair fell over her shoulders. The candle shook in her hand, but, on sight of Marjory, her lips smiled beneath her deep shining eyes. Marjory ran to her crying,

"Is it you, Maggie?"

"Who should it be?" asked Mrs. Dennison, still smiling, so well as her fast-beating breath allowed her. "Why aren't you in bed?"

The girl grasped her hand, and pushed her back into the room.

"Maggie, I—— Hark! there it is again! There's something outside—there, in the garden! If you open the window——"

As she spoke, Mrs. Dennison darted quick on silent naked feet to the window, and stood by it; but she seemed rather to intercept approach to it than to think of opening it. Indeed there was no need. The slow uncertain step sounded again; there were five or six seeming footfalls, and the women stood motionless, listening to them. Then there was stillness outside, matching the hush within; till Maggie Dennison, tearing the wrapper loose from her throat, said in low tones,

"I hear nothing outside;" and she put the candle on the table by her. "You can see nothing for the fog," she added as she gazed through the glass. Her tone was strangely full of relief.

"I opened the window," whispered Marjory, "and I saw—I thought I saw—something. And then I heard —that. You heard it, Maggie?"

The girl was standing in the middle of the room, her eyes fixed on Mrs. Dennison, who leant against the window-sash with a strained, alert, watchful look on her face.

"I heard you open the window and call out something," she said. "That's all I heard."

"But just now—just now as we stood here?"

Mrs. Dennison did not answer for a moment; her ear was almost against the panes, and her face was like a runner's as he waits for the starter's word. There was nothing but the gentle beat of the sea. Mrs. Dennison pushed her hair back over her shoulders and sighed; her tense frame relaxed, and the fixed smile on her lips seemed, in broadening, to lose something of its rigidity.

"No, I didn't, you silly child," she said. "You're full of fancies, Marjory."

The curl of her lip and the shrug of her shoulders won no attention.

"It went across the garden from the door—across towards the gate," said Marjory, "towards the path down. I heard it. It came from near the door. I heard it."

Mrs. Dennison shook her head. The girl sprang forward and again caught her by the arm.

"You heard too?" she cried. "I know you heard!" and a challenge rang in her voice.

"I didn't hear," she repeated impatiently, "but I daresay you did. Perhaps it was a man—a thief, or somebody lost in the fog. Would you like me to wake the footman? I can tell him to take a lantern and look if anyone's in the garden."

Marjory took no notice of the offer.

"But if it was anyone, he'll have gone now," continued Maggie Dennison, "your opening the window will have frightened him. You made such a noise— you woke me up."

"Were you asleep?" came in quick question.

"Yes," answered Mrs. Dennison steadily, "I was asleep. Couldn't you sleep?"

"Sleep? No, I couldn't sleep. I was afraid."

"You're as bad as the children," said Mrs. Dennison, laughing gently. "Come, go back to bed. Shall I come and sit by you till it's light?"

The girl seemed not to hear; she drew nearer, searching Mrs. Dennison's face with suspicious eyes. Maggie could not face her; she dropped her glance to the floor and laughed nervously and fretfully. Suddenly Marjory threw herself on the floor at her friend's feet.

"Maggie, come away from here," she beseeched.

"Do come; do come away directly. Maggie, dear, I love you so, and—and I was unkind last night. Do come, darling! We'll go back together—back home," and she burst into sobbing.

Maggie Dennison stood passive and motionless, her hands by her side. Her lips quivered and she looked down at the girl kneeling at her feet.

"Won't you come?" moaned Marjory. "Oh, Maggie, there's still time!"

Mrs. Dennison knew what she meant. A strange smile came over her face. Yes, there was time; in a sense there was time, for the uncertain footfalls had not reached their goal—arrested by that cry from the window, they had stopped—wavered—retreated—and were gone. Because a girl had not slept, there was time. Yet what difference did it make that there was still time—to-night? Since to-morrow was coming and must come.

"Time!" she echoed in a whisper.

"For God's sake, come, Maggie! Come to-morrow—you and the children. Come back with them to England! Maggie, I can't stay here!"

Mrs. Dennison put out her hands and took Marjory's.

"Get up," she said, almost roughly, and dragged the girl to her feet. "You can go, Marjory; I—I suppose you're not happy here. You can go."

"And you?"

"I shan't go," said Maggie Dennison.

Marjory, standing now, shrank back from her.

"You won't go?" she whispered. "Why, what are you staying for?"

"You forget," said Mrs. Dennison coldly. "I'm waiting for my husband."

"Oh!" moaned Marjory, a world of misery and contempt in her voice.

At the tone Mrs. Dennison's face grew rigid, and, if it could be, paler than before; she had been called "liar" to her face, and truly. It was lost to-night her madness mourned—hoped for to-morrow that held her in her place.

The fog was lifting outside; the darkness grew less dense; a distant, dim, cold light began to reveal the day.

"See, it's morning," said Mrs. Dennison. "You needn't be afraid any longer. Won't you go back to your own room, Marjory?"

Marjory nodded. She wore a helpless bewildered look, and she did not speak. She started to cross the room, when Mrs. Dennison asked her,

"Do you mean to go this morning? I suppose the Seminghams will take you, if you like. We can make some excuse if you like."

Marjory stood still, then she sank on a chair near her, and began to sob quietly. Mrs. Dennison slowly walked to her, and stood by her. Then, gently and timidly, she laid her hand on the girl's head.

"Don't cry," she said. "Why should you cry?"

Marjory clutched her hand, crying,

"Maggie, Maggie, don't, don't!"

Mrs. Dennison's eyes filled with tears. She let her hand lie passive till the girl released it, and, looking up, said,

"I'm not going, Maggie. I shall stay. Don't send me away! Let me stay till Mr. Dennison comes."

"What's the use? You're unhappy here."

"Can't I help you?" asked the girl, so low that it seemed as though she were afraid to hear her own voice.

Mrs. Dennison's self-control suddenly gave way.

"Help!" she cried recklessly. "No, you can't help. Nobody can help. It's too late for anyone to help now."

The girl raised her head with a start.

"Too late! Maggie, you mean——?"

"No, no, no," cried Mrs. Dennison, and then her eager cry died swiftly away.

Why protest in horror? By no grace of hers was it that it was not too late. The girl's eyes were on her, and she stammered,

"I mean nothing—nothing. Yes, you must go. I hate—no, no! Marjory, don't push me away! Let me touch you! There's no reason I shouldn't touch you. I mean, I love you, but—I can't have you here."

"Why not?" came from the girl in slow, strong tones.

A moment later, she sprang to her feet, her eyes full of new horror, as the vague suspicion grew to a strange undoubting certainty.

"Who was it in the garden? Who was out there? Maggie, if I hadn't——?"

She could not end. On the last words her voice sank to a fearful whisper; when she had uttered them —with their unfinished, yet plain and naked, question —she hid her face in her hands, listening for the answer.

A minute—two minutes—passed. There was no sound but Maggie Dennison's quick breathings; once she started forward with her lips parted as if to speak, and a look of defiance on her face; once too, entreaty, hope, tenderness dawned for a moment. In anger or in sorrow, the truth was hard on being uttered; but the impulse failed. She arrested the words on her lips, and with an angry jerk of her head, said petulantly,

"Oh, you're a silly girl, and you make me silly too. There's nothing the matter. I don't know who it was or what it was. Very likely it was nothing. I heard nothing. It was all your imagination." Her voice grew harder, colder, more restrained as she went on. "Don't think about what I've said to-night—and don't chatter about it. You upset me with your fancies. Marjory, it means nothing."

The last words were imperative in their insistence, but all the answer Marjory made was to raise her head and ask,

"Am I to go?" while her eyes added, too plainly for Maggie Dennison not to read them, "You know the meaning of that."

Under the entreaty and the challenge of her eyes, Mrs. Dennison could not give the answer which it was her purpose to give—the answer which would deny the mad hope that still filled her, the hope which still cried that, though to-night was gone, there was to-morrow. It was the answer she must make to all the world—which she must declare and study to confirm in all her acts and bearing. But there—alone with the girl—under the compelling influence of the reluctant confidence—that impossibility of open falsehood—which the time and occasion seemed strangely to build up between them—she could not give it plainly. She dared not bid the girl stay, with that hope at her heart; she dared not cast away the cloak by bidding her go.

"You must do as you like," she said at last. "I can't help you about it."

Marjory caught at the narrow chance the answer left her; with returning tenderness she stretched out her hands towards her friend, saying,

" Maggie, do tell me! I shall believe what you tell me."

Mrs. Dennison drew back from the contact of the outstretched hands. Marjory rose, and for an instant they stood looking at one another. Then Marjory turned, and walked slowly to the door. To her own room she went, to fear and to hope, if hope she could.

Mrs. Dennison was left alone. The night was far gone, the morning coming apace. Her lips moved, as she gazed from the window. Was it in thanksgiving for the escape of the night, or in joy that the morrow was already to-day? She could not tell; yes, she was glad—surely she was glad? Yet, as at last she flung herself upon her bed, she murmured, " He'll come early to-day," and then she sobbed in shame.

CHAPTER XVIII.

ON THE MATTER OF A RAILWAY.

Willie Ruston was half-dressed when the chamber-maid knocked at his door. He opened it and took from her three or four letters. Laying them on the table he finished his dressing—with him a quick process, devoid of the pleasant lounging by which many men cheat its daily tiresomeness. At last, when his coat was on, he walked two or three times up and down the room, frowning, smiling for an instant, frowning long again. Then he jerked his head impatiently as though he had had too much of his thoughts, and, going to the table, looked at the addresses on his letters. With a sudden access of eagerness he seized on one and tore it open. It bore Carlin's handwriting, and he groaned to see that the four sides were close-filled. Old Carlin was terribly verbose and roundabout in his communications, and a bored look settled on Willie Ruston's face as he read a wilderness of small details, skirmishes with unruly clerks, iniquities of office-boys, lamentations on the apathy of the public, and lastly, a conscientious account of the health of the writer's household. With a sigh he turned the second page.

"By the way," wrote Carlin, "I have had a letter from Detchmore. He draws back about the railway, and says the Government won't sanction it."

Willie Ruston raced through the rest, muttering to himself as he read, "Why the deuce didn't he wire? What an old fool it is!" and so forth. Then he flung down the letter, put his hands deep in his pockets and stood motionless for a few moments.

"I must go at once," he said aloud.

He stood thinking, and a rare expression stole over his face. It showed a doubt, a hesitation, a faltering —the work and the mark of the day and the night that were gone. He walked about again; he went to the window and stared out, jangling the money in his pockets. For nearly five minutes that expression was on his face. For nearly five minutes—and it seemed no short time—he was torn by conflicting forces. For nearly five minutes he wavered in his allegiance, and Omofaga had a rival that could dispute its throne. Then his brow cleared and his lips shut tight again. He had made up his mind; great as the thing was that held him where he was, yet he must go, and the thing must wait. Wheeling round, he took up the letter and, passing quickly through the door, went to young Sir Walter's room, with the face of a man who knows grief and vexation but has set wavering behind him.

It was an hour later when Adela Ferrars and the Seminghams sat down to their coffee. A fourth plate was laid at the table, and Adela was in very good spirits. Tom Loring had arrived; they had greeted him, and he was upstairs making himself fit to be seen after a night-voyage; his boat had lain three hours outside the harbour waiting for the fog to lift. "I daresay," said Tom, "you heard our horn bellowing." But he was here at last, and Adela was merrier than she had been in all her stay at Dieppe. Semingham also was happy; it was a great relief to feel that there was someone to whom responsibility properly, or at least more properly, belonged, and an end, therefore, to all unjustifiable attempts to saddle mere onlookers with it. And Lady Semingham perceived that her companions were in more genial mood than lately had been their wont, and expanded in the warmer air. When Tom came down nothing could exceed the *empressement* of his welcome.

The sun had scattered the last remnants of fog, and, on Semingham's proposal, the party passed from the table to a seat in the hotel garden, whence they could look at the sea. Here they became rather more silent; for Adela began to feel that the hour of explanation was approaching, and grew surer and surer that to her would be left the task. She believed that

Tom was tactful enough to spare her most of it, but something she must say—and to say anything was terribly difficult. Lord Semingham was treating the visit as though there were nothing behind; and his wife had no inkling that there was anything behind. The wife's genius for not observing was matched by the husband's wonderful power of ignoring; and if Adela had allowed herself to translate into words the exasperated promptings of her quick temper, she would have declared a desire to box the ears of both of them. It would have been vulgar, but entirely satisfactory.

At last Tom, with carefully-prepared nonchalance, asked,

"Oh, and how is Mrs. Dennison?"

Bessie Semingham assumed the question to herself.

"She's very well, thank you, Mr. Loring. Dieppe has done her a world of good."

Adela pursed her lips together. Semingham, catching her eye, smothered a nascent smile. Tom frowned slightly, and, leaning forward, clasped his hands between his knees. He was guilty of wishing that Bessie Semingham had more pressing avocations that morning.

"You see," she chirruped, "Marjory's with her, and the children dote on Marjory, and she's got Mr. Ruston and Walter to wait on her—you know Maggie always likes somebody in her train. Well, Alfred, why shouldn't I say that? I like to have someone myself."

"I didn't speak," protested Semingham.

"No, but you looked funny. I always say about Maggie, Mr. Loring, that——"

All three were listening in some embarrassment; out of the mouths of babes come sometimes alarming things.

"That without any apparent trouble she can make her clothes look better than anybody I know."

Lord Semingham laughed; even Adela and Tom smiled.

"What a blessed irrelevance you have, my dear," said Semingham, stroking his wife's small hand.

Lady Semingham smiled delightedly and blushed prettily. She enjoyed Alfred's praise. He was so *difficile* as a rule. The exact point of the word "irrelevance" she did not stay to consider; she had evidently said something that pleased him. A moment later she rose with a smile, crying,

"Why, Mr. Ruston, how good of you to come round so early!"

Willie Ruston shook hands with her in hasty politeness. A nod to Semingham, a lift of the hat to Adela, left him face to face with Tom Loring, who got up slowly.

"Ah, Loring, how are you?" said Willie holding

out his hand. "Young Val told me you were to arrive to-day. How did you get across? Uncommon foggy, wasn't it?"

By this time he had taken Tom's hand and shaken it, Tom being purely passive.

"By the way, you're all wrong about the water, you know," he continued, in sudden remembrance. "There's enough water to supply Manchester within ten miles of Fort Imperial. What? Why, man, I'll show you the report when we get back to town; good water, too. I had it analysed, and—well, it's all right; but I haven't time to talk about it now. The fact is, Semingham, I came round to tell you that I'm off."

"Off?" exclaimed Semingham, desperately fumbling for his eyeglass.

Adela clasped her hands, and her eyes sparkled. Tom scrutinised Willie Ruston with attentive eyes.

"Yes; to-day—in an hour; boat goes at 11·30. I've had a letter from old Carlin. Things aren't going well. That ass Detch—— By Jove, though, I forgot you, Loring! I don't want to give you materials for another of those articles."

His rapidity, his bustle, his good humour were all amazing.

Tom glanced in bewilderment at Adela. Adela coloured deeply. She felt that she had no adequate reason to give for having summoned Tom Loring to

Dieppe, unless (she brightened as the thought struck her) Tom had frightened Ruston away.

Willie seized Semingham's arm, and began to walk him (the activity seemed all on Willie's part) quickly up and down the garden. He held Carlin's letter in his hand, and he talked eagerly and fast, beating the letter with his fist now and again. Bessie Semingham sat down with an amiable smile. Adela and Tom were close together. Adela lifted her eyes to Tom's in question.

" What ? " he asked.

" Do you think it's true?" she whispered.

" He's the finest actor alive if it isn't," said Tom, watching the beats of Ruston's fist.

" Then thank heaven ! But I feel so foolish."

" Hush ! here they come," said Tom.

There was no time for more.

" Tom, there's riches in it for you if we told you," laughed Semingham; "but Ruston's going to put it all right."

Tom gave a not very easy laugh.

" Fancy old Carlin not wiring!" exclaimed Willie Ruston.

" Shall I sell?" asked Adela, trying to be frivolous.

" Hold for your life, Miss Ferrars," said Willie; and going up to Bessie Semingham he held out his hand.

16

"What, are you really off? It's too bad of you, Mr. Ruston! Not that I've seen much of you. Maggie has quite monopolised you."

Adela and Tom looked at the ground. Semingham turned his back; his smile would not be smothered.

"Of course you're going to say good-bye to her?" pursued Lady Semingham.

Tom looked up, and Adela followed his example. They were rewarded—if it were a reward—by seeing a slight frown—the first shadow since he had been with them—on Ruston's brow. But he answered briskly, with a glance at his wathe,

"I can't manage it. I should miss the boat. I must write her a line."

"Oh, she'll never forgive you," cried Lady Semingham.

"Oh, yes, she will," he laughed. "It's for Omofaga, you know. Good-bye. Good-bye. I'm awfully sorry to go. Good-bye."

He was gone. It was difficult to realise at first. His presence, the fact of him, had filled so large a space; it had been the feature of the place from the day he had joined them. It had been their interest and their incubus.

For a moment the three stood staring at one another; then Semingham, with a curious laugh, turned on his heel and went into the house. His wife unfolded yesterday's *Morning Post* and began to read.

"Come for a stroll," said Tom Loring to Adela.

She accompanied him in silence, and they walked a hundred yards or more before she spoke.

"What a blessing!" she said then. "I wonder if your coming sent him away?"

"No, it was genuine," declared Tom, with conviction.

"Then I was very wrong, or he's a most extraordinary man. I can't talk to you about it, Mr. Loring, but you told me I might send. And I did think it —desirable—when I wrote. I did, indeed. I hope you're not very much annoyed?"

"Annoyed! No; I was delighted to come. And I am still more delighted that it looks as if I wasn't wanted."

"Oh, you're wanted, anyhow," said Adela.

She was very happy in his coming, and could not help showing it a little. Fortunately, it was tolerably certain (as she felt sometimes, intolerably certain) that Tom Loring would not notice anything. He never seemed to consider it possible that people might be particularly glad to see him.

"And you can stay, can't you?" she added.

"Oh, yes; I can stay a bit. I should like to. What made you send?"

"You know. I can't possibly describe it."

" Did Semingham notice it too ? "

" Yes, he did, Mr. Loring.   I distrust that man—
Mr. Ruston I mean—utterly.   And Maggie——"

" She's wrapped up in him ? "

" Terribly.   I tried to think it was his wretched
Omofaga ; but it's not; it's him."

" Well, he's disposed of."

" Yes, indeed," she sighed, in complacent ignorance.

" I must go and see her, you know," said Tom,
wrinkling his brow.

Adela laughed.

" What'll she say to me ? " asked Tom anxiously.

" Oh, she'll be very pleasant."

" I shan't," said Tom with sudden decision.

Adela looked at him curiously.

" You mean to—to give her ' a bit of your mind ? ' "

" Well, yes," he answered, smiling.   " I think so ;
don't you ? "

" I should like to, if I dared."

" Why, you dare anything ! " exclaimed Tom.

" Oh, no, I don't.   I splash about a good deal, but
I am a coward, really."

They relapsed into silence.   Presently Tom began,

" It's been awfully dull in town ; nobody to speak
to, except Mrs. Cormack."

" Mrs. Cormack ! " cried Adela.   " I thought you
hated her ? "

“ Well, I’ve thought a little better of her lately.”

“ To think of your making friends with Mrs. Cormack ! ”

“ I haven’t made friends with her. She’s not such a bad woman as you’d think, though.”

“ I think she’s horrible,” said Adela.

Tom gave it up.

“ There was no one else,” he pleaded.

“ Well,” retorted Adela, “ when there is anyone else, you never come near them.”

The grammar was confused, but Adela could not improve it, without being landed in unbearable plainness of speech.

“ Don’t I ? ” he asked. “ Why, I come and see you.”

“ Oh, for twenty minutes once a month ; just to keep the acquaintance open, I suppose. It’s like shutting all the gates on Ascension Day (isn’t it Ascension Day ?), only the other way round, you know.”

“ You so often quarrel with me,” said Tom.

“ What nonsense ! ” said Adela. “ Anyhow, I won’t quarrel here.”

Tom glanced at her. She was looking bright and happy and young. He liked her even better here in Dieppe than in a London drawing-room. Her conversation was not so elaborate, but it was more spontaneous and, to his mind, pleasanter. Moreover, the sea air had put colour in her cheeks and painted her complexion afresh. The thought strayed through Tom's mind that she was looking quite handsome. It was the one good thing that he did not always think about her. He went on studying her till she suddenly turned and caught him.

" Well," she asked, with a laugh and a blush, " do I wear well ? "

" You always talk as if you were seventy," said Tom reprovingly.

Adela laughed merrily. The going of Ruston and the coming of Tom were almost too much good-fortune for one day. And Tom had come in a pleasant mood.

" You don't really like Mrs. Cormack, do you ? " she asked. " She hates me, you know."

" Oh, if I have to choose between you——" said Tom, and stopped.

" You stop at the critical moment."

" Well, Mrs. Cormack isn't here," said Tom.

" So I shall do to pass the time ? "

" Yes," he laughed ; and then they both laughed.

But suddenly Adela's laugh ceased, and she jumped up.

" There's Marjory Valentine ! " she exclaimed.

" What ! Where ? " asked Tom, rising.

" No, stay where you are, I want to speak to her. I'll come back," and, leaving Tom, she sped after Marjory, calling her name.

Marjory looked round and hastened to meet her. She was pale and her eyes heavy for trouble and want of sleep.

"Oh, Adela, I'm so glad to find you! I was going to look for you at the hotel. I must talk to you."

"You shall," said Adela, taking her arm and smiling again.

She did not notice Marjory's looks; she was full of her own tidings.

"I want to ask you whether you think Lady Sem-ingham——" began Marjory, growing red, and in great embarrassment.

"Oh, but hear my news first," cried Adela; "Marjory, he's gone!"

"Who?"

"Why, that man Mr. Ruston."

"Gone?" echoed Marjory in amazement.

To her it seemed incredible that he should be gone—strange perhaps to Adela, but to her in-credible.

"Yes, this morning. He got a letter—something about his Company—and he was off on the spot. And Tom—Mr. Loring (he's come, you know), thinks —that that really was his reason, you know."

Marjory listened with wide-open eyes.

"Oh, Adela!" she said at last with a sort of shudder.

She could have believed it of no other man; she

could hardly believe it of one who now seemed to her
hardly a man.

"Isn't it splendid? And he went off without seeing—without going up to the cliff at all. I never
was so delighted in my life."

Marjory was silent. No delight showed on her
face; the time for that was gone. She did not
understand, and she was thinking of the night's
experience and wondering if Maggie Dennison had
known that he was going. No, she could not have
known.

"But what did you want with me, or with
Bessie?" asked Adela.

Marjory hesitated. The departure of Willie Ruston made a difference. She prayed that it meant an
utter difference. There was a chance; and while
there was a chance her place was in the villa on the
cliff. His going rekindled the spark of hope that
almost had died in the last terrible night.

"I think," she said slowly, "that I'll go straight
back."

"And tell Maggie?" asked Adela with excited
eyes.

"If she doesn't know.'

Adela said nothing; the subject was too perilous.
She even regretted having said so much; but she
pressed her friend's arm approvingly.

"It doesn't matter about Lady Semingham just

now," said Marjory in an absent sort of tone. "It will do later."

"You're not looking well," remarked Adela, who had at last looked at her.

"I had a bad night."

"And how's Maggie?"

The girl paused a moment.

"I haven't seen her this morning. She sent word that she would breakfast in bed. I'll just run up now, Adela."

She walked off rapidly. Adela watched her, feeling uneasy about her. There was a strange constraint about her manner—a hint of something suppressed—and it was easy to see that she was nervous and unhappy. But Adela, making lighter of her old fears in her new-won comfort, saw only in Marjory a grief that is very sad to bear, a sorrow that comes where love—or what is nearly love—meets with indifference.

"She's still thinking about that creature!" said Adela to herself in scorn and in pity. She had quite made up her mind about Willie Ruston now. "I'm awfully sorry for her." Adela, in fact, felt very sympathetic. For the same thing might well happen with love that rested on a worthier object than "that creature, Willie Ruston!"

Meanwhile the creature—could he himself at the moment have quarrelled with the word?—was carried over the waves, till the cliff and the house on it

dipped and died away. The excitement of the message and the start was over; the duty that had been
strong enough to take him away could not yet be
done. A space lay bare—exposed to the thoughts
that fastened on it. Who could have escaped their
assault? Not even Willie Ruston was proof; and his
fellow-voyagers wondered at the man with the frowning brows and fretful restless eyes. It had not been
easy to do, or pleasant to see done, this last sacrifice
to the god of his life. Yet it had been done, with
hardly a hesitation. He paced the deck, saying to
himself, "She'll understand." Would any woman?
If any, then, without doubt, she was the woman.
"Oh, she'll understand," he muttered petulantly,
angry with himself because he would not be convinced. Once, in despair, he tried to tell himself that
this end to it was what people would call ordered for
the best—that it was an escape for him—still more
for her. But his strong, self-penetrating sense pushed
the plea aside—in him it was hypocrisy, the merest
conventionality. He had not even the half-stifled
thanksgiving for respite from a doom still longed for,
which had struggled for utterance in Maggie's sobs.
Yet he had something that might pass for it—a feeling that made even him start in the knowledge of its
degradation. By fate, or accident, or mischance—call
it what he might—there was nothing irrevocable yet.
He could draw back still. Not thanksgiving for sin

averted, but a shamefaced sense of an enforced safety made its way into his mind—till it was thrust aside by anger at the check that had baffled him, and by the longing that was still upon him.

Well, anyhow—for good or evil—willing or unwilling—he was away. And she was alone in the little house on the cliff. His face softened; he ceased to think of himself for a moment; he thought of her, as she would look when he did not come—when he was false to a tryst never made in words, but surely the strongest that had ever bound a man. He clenched his fists as he stood looking from the stern of the boat, muttering again his old plea, " She'll understand ! "

Was there not the railway ?

CHAPTER XIX.

PAST PRAYING FOR.

Mrs. Dennison needed not Marjory to tell her. She had received Willie Ruston's note just as she was about to leave her bedroom. It was scribbled in pencil on half a sheet of notepaper.

"Am called back to England—something wrong about our railway. Very sorry I can't come and say good-bye. I shall run back if I can, but I'm afraid I may be kept in England. Will you write?

"W. R. R."

She read it, and stood as if changed to stone. "Something wrong about our railway!" Surely an all-sufficient reason; the writer had no doubt of that. He might be kept in England; that meant he would be, and the writer seemed to see nothing strange in the fact that he could be. She did not doubt the truth of what the note said. A man lying would have piled Pelion on Ossa, reason on reason, excuse on excuse, protestation on protestation. Besides Willie Ruston did not lie. It was just the truth, the all-sufficient truth. There was something wrong with the railway, so he left her. He would lose a day if he missed the boat, so he left her without a word of farewell. The railway must not suffer for his taking holiday; her suffering was all his holiday should make.

Slowly she tore the note into the smallest of fragments, and the fragments fell at her feet. And his passionate words were still in her ears, his kisses still burnt on her cheek. This was the man whom to sway had been her darling ambition, whom to love was her great sin, whom to know, as in this moment she seemed to know him, her bitter punishment. In her heart she cried to heaven, " Enough, enough!"

The note was his—his to its last line, its last word, its last silence. The man stood there, self-epitomised, callous and careless, unmerciful, unbending, unturning; vowed to his quest, recking of naught else. But —she clung to this, the last plank in her shipwreck— great—one of the few for whom the general must make stepping-stones. She thought she had been one of the few; that torn note told her error. Still, she had held out her hands to ruin for no common clay's sake. But it was too hard—too hard—too hard.

" Will you write? " Was he tender there? Her

bitterness would not grant him even that. He did not want her to slip away. The smallest addition will make the greatest realm greater, and its loss sully the king's majesty. So she must write, as she must think and dream—and remember.

Perhaps he might choose to come again—some day—and she was to be ready!

She went downstairs. In the hall she met her children, and they said something to her; they talked and chattered to her, and, with the surface of her mind, she understood; and she listened and answered and smiled. And all that they had said and she had said went away; and she found them gone, and herself alone. Then she passed to the sitting-room, where was Marjory Valentine, breathless from mounting the path too quickly; and at sight of Marjory's face, she said,

"I've heard from Mr. Ruston. He has been called away," forestalling Marjory's trembling words.

Then she sat down, and there was a long silence. She was conscious of Marjory there, but the girl did not speak, and presently the impression of her, which was very faint, faded altogether away, and Maggie Dennison seemed to herself alone again—thinking, dreaming, and remembering, as she must now think, dream, and remember—remembering the day that was gone, thinking of what this day should have been.

She sat for an hour, still and idle, looking out across the sea, and Marjory sat motionless behind, gazing at her with despair in her eyes. At last the girl could bear it no longer. It was unnatural, unearthly, to sit there like that; it was as though, by an impossibility, a dead soul were clothed with a living breathing body. Marjory rose and came close, and called,

"Maggie, Maggie!"

Her voice was clear and louder than her ordinary tones; she spoke as if trying to force some one to hear.

Maggie Dennison started, looked round, and passed her hand rapidly across her brow.

"Maggie, I—I've not done anything about going."

"Going?" echoed Maggie Dennison. But her mind was clearing now; her brain had been stunned, not killed, and her will drove it to wakefulness and work again. "Going? Oh, I hope not."

"You know, last night——" began Marjory, timidly, flushing, keeping behind Mrs. Dennison's chair. "Last night we—we talked about it, but I thought perhaps now——"

"Oh," interrupted Mrs. Dennison, "never mind last night. For goodness' sake, forget last night. I think we were both mad last night."

Marjory made no answer; and Mrs. Dennison, her hand having swept her brow once again, turned to her with awakened and alert eyes.

"You upset me—and then I upset you. And we both behaved like hysterical creatures. If I told you to go, I was silly; and if you said you wanted to go, you were silly too, Marjory. Of course, you must stop; and do forget that—nonsense—last night."

Her tone was eager and petulant, the colour was returning to her cheeks; she looked alive again.

Marjory leant an arm on the back of the chair, looking down into Maggie Dennison's face.

"I will stay," she said softly, ignoring everything else, and then she swiftly stooped and kissed Maggie's cheek.

Mrs. Dennison shivered and smiled, and, detaining the girl's head, most graciously returned her caress. Mrs. Dennison was forgiving everything; by forgiveness it might be that she could buy of Marjory forgetfulness.

There was a ring at the door. Marjory looked through the window.

"It's Mr. Loring," she said in a whisper.

Maggie Dennison smiled—graciously again.

"It's very kind of him to come so soon," said she.

"Shall I go?"

"Go? No, child—unless you want to. You know him too. And we've no secrets, Tom Loring and I."

Tom Loring had mounted the hill very slowly. The giving of that "piece of his mind" seemed not altogether easy. He might paint poor Harry's forlorn state; Mrs. Dennison would be politely concerned and politely sceptical about it. He might tell her again— as he had told her before—that Willie Ruston was a knave and a villain, and she might laugh or be angry, as her mood was; but she would not believe. Or he might upbraid her for folly or for worse; and this was what he wished to do. Would she listen? Probably—with a smile on her lips and mocking little compliments on his friendly zeal and fatherly anxiety. Or she might flash out on him, and call his charge an insult, and drive him away; and a word from her would turn poor old Harry into his enemy. Decidedly his task was no easy one.

It was a coward's joy that he felt when he found a third person there; but he felt it from the bottom of his heart. Divine delay! Gracious impossibility! How often men adore them! Tom Loring gave thanks, praying silently that Marjory would not withdraw, shook hands as though his were the most ordinary morning call, and began to discuss the scenery of Dieppe, and—as became a newcomer—the incidents of his voyage.

"And while you were all peacefully in your beds, we were groping about outside in that abominable fog," said he.

"How you must have envied us!" smiled Mrs. Dennison, and Marjory found herself smiling in emulous hypocrisy. But her smile was very unsuccessful,

17

and it was well that Tom Loring's eyes were on his hostess.

Then Mrs. Dennison began to talk about Willie Ruston and her own great interest in him, and in the Omofaga Company. She was very good-humoured to Tom Loring, but she did not fail to remind him how unreasonable he had been—was still, wasn't he? The perfection of her manner frightened Marjory and repelled her. Yet it would have seemed an effort of bravery, had it been done with visible struggling. But it betrayed no effort, and therefore made no show of bravery.

"So now," said Maggie Dennison, "since I haven't got Mr. Ruston to exchange sympathy with, I must exchange hostilities with you. It will still be about Omofaga—that's one thing."

Tom had definitely decided to put off his lecture. The old manner he had known and mocked and admired—the "these-are-the-orders" manner—was too strong for him. He believed he was still fond of her. He knew that he wondered at her still. Could it be true what they told him—that she was as a child in the hands of Willie Ruston? He hated to think that, because it must mean that Willie Ruston was—well, not quite an ordinary person—a conclusion Tom loathed to accept.

"And you're going to stay some time with the Seminghams? That'll be very pleasant. And Adela will like to have you so much. Oh, you can convert her! She's a shareholder. And you must have a talk to the old Baron. You've heard of him? But then he believes in Mr. Ruston, as I do, so you'll quarrel with him."

"Perhaps I shall convert him," suggested Tom.

"Oh, no, we thorough believers are past praying for; aren't we, Marjory?"

Marjory started.

"Past praying for?" she echoed.

Her thoughts had strayed from the conversation—back to what she had been bidden to forget; and she spoke not as one who speaks a trivial phrase.

For an instant a gleam of something—anger or fright—shot from Maggie Dennison's eyes. The next, she was playfully, distantly, delicately chaffing Tom about the meaning of his sudden arrival.

"Of course *not*——" she began.

And Tom, interrupting, stopped the "Adela."

"And you stay here too?" he asked, to turn the conversation.

"Why, of course," smiled Mrs. Dennison. "After being here all this time, it would look rather funny if I ran away just when Harry's coming. I think he really would have a right to be aggrieved then." She paused, and added more seriously, "Oh, yes, I shall wait here for Harry."

Then Tom Loring rose and took his leave. Mrs.

Dennison entrusted him with an invitation to the whole of the Seminghams' party to luncheon next day ("if they don't mind squeezing into our little room," she gaily added), and walked with him to the top of the path, waving her hand to him in friendly farewell as he began to descend. And, after he was gone, she stood for a while looking out to sea. Then she turned. Marjory was in the window and saw her face as she turned. In a moment Maggie Dennison saw her looking, and smiled brightly. But the one short instant had been enough. The feelings first numbed, then smothered, had in that second sprung to life, and Marjory shrank back with a little inarticulate cry of pain and horror. Almost as she uttered it, Mrs. Dennison was by her side.

"We'll go out this afternoon," she said. "I think I shall lie down for an hour. We managed to rob ourselves of a good deal of sleep last night. You'd better do the same." She paused, and then she added, "You're a good child, Marjory. You're very kind to me."

There was a quiver in her voice, but it was only that, and it was Marjory, not she, who burst into sobs.

"Hush, hush," whispered Maggie Dennison. "Hush, dear. Don't do that. Why should you do that?" and she stroked the girl's hot cheek, wet with tears. "I'm very tired, Marjory," she went on. "Do

you think you can dry your eyes—your silly eyes—and
help me upstairs? I—I can hardly stand," and, as
she spoke, she swayed and caught at the curtain by
her, and held herself up by it. "No, I can go
alone!" she exclaimed almost fiercely. "Leave me
alone, Marjory, I can walk. I can walk perfectly;"
and she walked steadily across the room, and Marjory
heard her unwavering step mounting the stairs to her
bedroom.

But Marjory did not see her enter her room, stop
for a moment over the scraps of torn paper, still lying
on the floor, stoop and gather them one by one, then
put them in an envelope, and the envelope in her
purse, and then throw herself on the bed in an agony
of dumb pain, with the look on her face that had
come for a moment in the garden and came now, fear-
less of being driven away, lined strong and deep, as
though graven with some sharp tool.

CHAPTER XX.

THE BARON'S CONTRIBUTION.

It may be that the Baron thought he had sucked
the orange of life very dry—at least, when the cold
winds and the fog had done their work, he accepted
without passionate disinclination the hint that he
must soon take his lips from the fruit. He went to
bed and made a codicil to his will, having it executed
and witnessed with every requisite formality. Then
he announced to Lord Semingham, who came to see
him, that, according to his doctor's opinion and his
own, he might manage to breathe a week longer; and
Semingham, looking upon him, fancied, without saying, that the opinion was a sanguine one. This happened five days before Harry Dennison's arrival at
Dieppe.

"I am very fortunate," said the Baron, "to have
found such kind friends for the last stage;" and he
looked from Lady Semingham's flowers to Adela's
grapes. "I could have bought them, of course," he
added. "I've always been able to buy—everything."

The old man smiled as he spoke, and Semingham smiled also.

"This," continued the Baron, "is the third time I have been laid up like this."

"There's luck in odd numbers," observed Semingham.

"But which would be luck?" asked the Baron.

"Ah, there you gravel me," admitted Semingham.

"I came here against orders, because I must needs poke my old nose into this concern of yours——"

"Not of mine."

"Of yours and others. Well, I poked it in—and the frost has caught the end of it."

"I don't take any particular pleasure in the concern myself," said Semingham, "and I wish you'd kept your nose out, and yourself in a more balmy climate."

"My dear Lord, the market is rising."

"I know," smiled Semingham. "Tom Loring can't make out who the fools are who are buying. He said so this morning."

The Baron began to laugh, but a cough choked his mirth.

"He's an honest and an able man, your Loring; but he doesn't see clear in everything. I've been buying, myself."

"Oh, you have?"

"Yes, and someone has been selling—selling largely—or the price would have been driven higher.   It is you, perhaps, my friend?"

"Not a share.   I have the vices of an aristocracy. I am stubborn."

"Who, then?"

"It might be—Dennison."

The Baron nodded.

"But what did you want with 'em, Baron?   Will they pay?"

"Oh, I doubt that.   But I wanted them.   Why should Dennison sell?"

"I suppose he doubts, like you."

"Perhaps it is that."

"Perhaps," said Semingham.

In the course of the next three days they had many conversations; the talks did the Baron no good nor, as his doctor significantly said, any harm; and when he could not talk, Semingham sat by him and told stories.   He spoke too, frequently, of Willie Ruston, and of the Company—that interested the Baron. And at last, on the third day, they began to speak of Maggie Dennison; but neither of them connected the two names in talk.   Indeed Semingham, according to his custom, had rushed at the possibility of ignoring such connection.   Ruston's disappearance had shown him a way; and he embraced the happy chance.   He was always ready to think that any "fuss" was a mistake; and, as he told the Baron, Mrs. Dennison had been in great spirits lately, cheered up, it seemed, by the prospect of her husband's immediate arrival. The Baron smiled to hear him; then he asked,

"Do you think she would come to see me?"

Semingham promised to ask her; and, although the Baron was fit to see nobody the next day—for he had moved swiftly towards his journey's end in those twenty-four hours—yet Mrs. Dennison came and was admitted; and, at sight of the Baron, who lay yellow and gasping, forgot both her acting and, for an instant, the reality which it hid.

"Oh!" she cried before she could stop herself, "how ill you look! Let me make you comfortable!"

The Baron did not deny her. He had something to say to her.

"When does your husband come?" he asked.

"To-morrow," said she briefly.

She did all she could for his comfort, and then sat down by his bedside. He had an interval of some freedom from oppression and his mind was clear and concentrated.

"I want to tell you," he began, "something that I have done." He paused, and added a question, "Ruston does not come back to Dieppe, I suppose?"

"I think not. He is detained on business," she answered, "and he will be more tied when my husband leaves."

" Your husband will not long be concerned in the Omofaga," said he.

She started ; the Baron told her what he had told Semingham.

" He will soon resign his place on the Board, you will see," he ended.

She sat silent.

" He will have nothing more to do with it, you will see ; " and, turning to her, he asked with a sudden spurt of vigour, " Do you know why ? "

" How should I ? " she answered steadily.

" And I—I have done my part too. I have left him some money (she knew that the Baron did not mean her husband) and all the shares I held."

" You've done that ? " she cried, with a sudden light in her eyes.

" You do not want to know why ? "

" Oh, I know you admired him. You told me so."

" Yes, that in part. I did admire him. He was what I have never been. I wish he was here now. I should like to look at that face of his before I die. But it was not for his sake that I left him the money. Why, he could get it without me if he needed it ! You don't ask me why ? "

In his excitement he had painfully pulled himself higher up on his pillows, and his head was on the level with hers now. He looked right into her eyes. She was very pale, but calm and self-controlled.

"I don't know," she said. "Why have you?"

"It will make him independent of your husband," said the Baron.

Mrs. Dennison dropped her eyes and raised them again in a swift, questioning glance.

"Yes, and of you. He need not look to you now."

He paused and added, slowly, punctuating every word,

"You will not be necessary to him now."

Mrs. Dennison met his gaze full and straight; the Baron stretched out his hand.

"Ah, forgive me!" he exclaimed.

"There is nothing to forgive," said she.

"I saw; I knew; I have felt it. Now he will go away; he will not lean on you now. I have set him where he can stand alone."

A smile, half scornful and half sad, came on her face.

"You hate me," said the Baron. "But I am right."

"I was—we were never necessary to him," said she. "Ah, Baron, this is no news you give me. I know him better than that."

He raised himself higher still, panting as he rested on his elbow. His head craned forward towards her as he whispered,

"I'm a dying man. You can tell me."

"If you were a dead man——" she burst out passionately. Then she suddenly recovered herself.

"My dear Baron," she went on, "I'm very glad you've done this for Mr. Ruston."

He sank down on his pillows with a weary sigh.

"Let him alone, let him alone," he moaned. "You thought yourself strong."

"I suppose you mean kindly," she said, speaking very coldly. "Indeed, that you should think of me at all just now shows it. But, Baron, you are disquieting yourself without cause."

"I'm an old man, and a sick man," he pleaded, "and you, my dear——"

"Ah, suppose I have been—whatever you like—indiscreet? Well——?"

She paused, for he made a feebly impatient gesture. Mrs. Dennison kept silence for a moment; then in a low tone she said,

"Baron, why do you speak to a woman about such things, unless you want her to lie to you?"

The Baron, after a moment, gave his answer, that was no answer.

"He is gone," he said.

"Yes, he is gone—to look after his railway."

"It is finished then?" he half asked, half implored, and just caught her low-toned reply.

"Finished? Who for?" Then she suddenly raised her voice, crying, "What is it to you? Why can't I be let alone? How dare you make me talk about it?"

"I have done," said he, and, laying his thin yellow hand in hers, he went on, "If you meet him again—and I think you will—tell him that I longed to see him, as a man who is dying longs for his son. He would be a breath of life to me in this room, where everything seems dead. He is full of life—full as a tiger. And you can tell him——" He stopped a moment and smiled. "You can tell him why I was a buyer of Omofagas. What will he say?"

"What will he say?" she echoed, with wide-opened eyes, that watched the old man's slow-moving lips.

"Will he weep?" asked the Baron.

"In God's name, don't!" she stammered.

"He will say, 'Behold, the Baron von Geltschmidt was a good man—he was of use in the world—may he sleep in peace!' And now—how goes the railway?"

The old man lay silent, with a grim smile on his face. The woman sat by, with lips set tight in an agony of repression. At last she spoke.

"If I'd known you were going to tell me this, I wouldn't have come."

"It's hard, hard, hard, but——"

"Oh, not that. But—I knew it."

She rose to her feet.

"Good-bye," said the Baron. "I shan't see you again. God make it light for you, my dear."

She would not seem to hear him. She smoothed

his pillows and his scanty straggling hair; then she kissed his forehead.

"Good-bye," she said. "I will tell Willie when I see him. I shall see him soon."

The old man moaned softly and miserably.

"It would be better if you lay here," he said.

"Yes, I suppose so," she answered, almost listlessly. "Good-bye."

Suddenly he detained her, catching her hand.

"Do you believe in people meeting again anywhere?" he asked.

"Oh, I suppose so. No, I don't know, I'm sure."

"They've been telling me to have a priest. I call myself a Catholic, you know. What can I say to a priest? I have done nothing but make money. If that is a sin, it's too simple to need confession, and I've done too much of it for absolution. How can I talk to a priest? I shall have no priest."

She did not speak, but let him hold her hand.

"If," he went on, with a little smile, "I'm asked anywhere what I've done, I must say, 'I've made money.' That's all I shall have to say."

She stooped low over him and whispered,

"You can say one more thing, Baron—one little thing. You once tried to save a woman," and she kissed him again and was gone.

Outside the house, she found Semingham waiting for her.

"Oh, I say, Mrs. Dennison," he cried, "Harry's come. He got away a day earlier than he expected. I met him driving up towards your house."

For just a moment she stood aghast. It came upon her with a shock; between a respite of a day and the actual terrible now, there had seemed a gulf.

"Is he there—at the house—now?" she asked. Semingham nodded.

"Will you walk up with me?" she asked eagerly. "I must go directly, you know. He'll be so sorry not to find me there. Do you mind coming? I'm tired."

He offered his arm, and she almost clutched at it, but she walked with nervous quickness.

"He's looking very well," said Semingham. "A bit fagged, and so on, you know, of course, but he'll soon get all right here."

"Yes, yes, very soon," she replied absently, quickening her pace till he had to force his to match it. But, half-way up the hill, she stopped suddenly, breathing rapidly.

"Yes, take a rest, we've been bucketing," said he.

"Did he ask after me?"

"Yes; directly."

"And you said——?"

"Oh, that you were all right, Mrs. Dennison."

"Thanks. Has he seen Mr. Loring?"

"No; but he knew he had come here. He told me so."

" Well, I needn't take you right up, need I ? "

Semingham thought of some jest about not intruding on the sacred scene, but the jest did not come. Somehow he shrank from it. Mrs. Dennison did not.

" We shall want to fall on one another's necks," said she, smiling. " And you'd feel in the way. You hate honest emotions, you know."

He nodded, lifted his hat, and turned. On his way down alone, he stopped once for a moment and exclaimed,

" Good heavens ! And I believe she'd rather meet the devil himself. She is a woman ! "

Mrs. Dennison pursued her way at a gentler pace. Before she came in sight, she heard her children's delighted chatterings, and, a moment later, Harry's hearty tones. His voice brought to her, in fullest force, the thing that was always with her—with her as the cloak that a man hath upon him, and as the girdle that he is always girded withal.

When the children saw her, they ran to her, seizing her hands and dragging her towards Harry. A little way off stood Marjory Valentine, with a nervous smile on her lips. Harry himself stood waiting, and Mrs. Dennison walked up to him and kissed him. Not till that was done did she speak or look him in the face. He returned her kiss, and then, talking rapidly, she made him sit down, and sat herself, and took her little boy on her knee. And she called Marjory, telling her jokingly that she was one of the family.

Harry began to talk of his journey, and they all joined in. Then he grew silent, and the children chattered more about the delights of Dieppe, and how all would be perfect now that father was come. And, under cover of their chatter, Maggie Dennison stole a long covert glance at her husband.

"And Tom's here, father," cried the little boy on her lap exultingly.

"Yes," chimed in Madge, "and Mr. Ruston's gone."

There was a momentary pause; then Mrs. Dennison, in her calmest voice, began to tell her husband of the sickness of the Baron. And over Harry Dennison's face there rested a new look, and she felt it on her as she talked of the Baron. She had seen him before unsatisfied, puzzled, and bewildered by her, but never before with this look on his face. It seemed to her half entreaty and half suspicion. It was plain for everyone to see. He kept his eyes on her, and she knew that Marjory must be reading him as she read him. And under that look she went on talking about the Baron. The look did not frighten her. She did not fear his suspicions, for she believed he would still take her word against all the world—ay, against the plainest proof. But she almost broke under the burden of it; it made her heart sick with pity for him. She longed to cry out, then and there, "It isn't true, Harry, my poor dear, it isn't true." She could tell him that—it would not be all a lie. And when the children went away to prepare for lunch, she did much that very thing; for, with a laughing glance of apology at Marjory, she sat on her husband's knee and kissed him twice on either cheek, whispering,

"I'm so glad you've come, Harry."

And he caught her to him with sudden violence—unlike his usual manner, and looked into her eyes and kissed her. Then they rose, and he turned towards the house.

For a moment Marjory and Mrs. Dennison were alone together. Mrs. Dennison spoke in a loud clear voice—a voice her husband must hear.

"We're shamefully foolish, aren't we, Marjory?"

The girl made no answer, but, as she looked at Maggie Dennison, she burst into a sudden convulsive sob.

"Hush, hush," whispered Maggie eagerly. "My God! if I can, you can!"

So they went in and joined the children at their merry noisy meal.

CHAPTER XXI.

A JOINT IN HIS ARMOUR.

WILLIE RUSTON slept, on the night following his return to London, in the Carlins' house at Hampstead. The all-important question of the railway made a consultation necessary, and Ruston's indisposition to face his solitary rooms caused him to accept gladly the proffered hospitality. The little cramped place was always a refuge and a rest; there he could best rejoice over a victory or forget a temporary defeat. There he fled now, in the turmoil of his mind. The question of the railway had hurried him from Dieppe, but it could not carry away from him the memories of Dieppe. Yet that was the office he had already begun to ask of it—of it and of the quiet busy life at Hampstead, where he lingered till a week stretched to two and to three, spending his days at work in the City, and his evenings, after his romp with the children, in earnest and eager talk and speculation. He regretted bitterly his going to Dieppe. He had done what he condemned; he had raised

up a perpetual reproach and a possible danger. He
was not a man who could dismiss such a thing with a
laugh or a sneer, with a pang of penitence and a
swift reaction to the low levels of morality, with a
regret for imprudence and a prayer against consequences. His nature was too deep, and the influence
he had met too strong, for any of these to be enough.
Yet he had suffered the question of the railway to
drag him away at a moment's notice; and he was
persuaded that he must take his leaving as setting an
end to all that had passed. All that must be put
behind; forgetfulness in thought might be a relief
impossible to attain, a relief that he would be ashamed
of striving to attain; but forgetfulness in act seemed a
duty to be done. In his undeviating reference of everything to his own work in life and his neglect of any
other touchstone, he erected into an obligation what
to another would have been a shameless matter of
course; or, again, to yet another, a source of shamefaced relief. His sins were sin first against himself,
in the second degree only against the participant in
them; his preoccupation with their first quality went
far to blind him to the second.

Yet he was very sorry for Maggie Dennison. Nay,
those words were ludicrously feeble for the meaning
he wanted from them. Acutely conscious of having
done her a wrong, he was vaguely aware that he
might underestimate the wrong, and remembered

uneasily how she had told him that he did not understand, and despaired because he could not understand.
He felt more for her now—much more, it seemed to
him; but the consciousness of failure to put himself
where she stood dogged him, making him afraid
sometimes that he could not realise her sufferings,
sometimes that he was imputing to her fictitious tor-
tures and a sense of ignominy which was not her own.
Searching light, he began to talk to Carlin in general
terms, of course, and by way of chance discourse; and
he ran up against a curious stratum of Puritanism
imbedded amongst the man's elastic principles. The
narrowest and harshest judgment of an erring woman
accompanied the supple trader and witnessed the sur-
viving barbarian in Mr. Carlin; an accidental distant
allusion displayed an equally relentless attitude in his
meek hard-working little wife. Willie Ruston drew
in his feelers, and, aghast at the evil these opinions
stamped as the product of his acts, declared for a
moment that his life must be the only and insufficient
atonement. The moment was a brief one. He dismissed the opinions with a curse, their authors with a
smile, and did not scorn to take for comfort even
Maggie Dennison's own enthusiasm for his work.
That had drawn them together; that must rule and
limit the connection which it had created. An end—
a bound—a peremptory stop (there was still time to
stop) was the thing. She would see that, as he saw it.

God knew (he said to himself) what a wrench it was —for she meant more to him than he had ever conceived a woman could mean; but the wrench must be undergone. He would rather die than wreck his work; and she, he knew, rather die than prove a wrecking siren to him.

Suddenly, across the desponding stubbornness of his resolves, flashed, with a bright white light, the news of the Baron's legacy, accompanying, but, after a hasty regretful thought and a kindly regretful smile, obliterating the fact of the Baron's death. Half the steps upward, he felt, which he had set himself painfully and with impatient labour to cut, were hewn deep and smooth for his feet; he had now but to tread, and lift his foot and tread again. From a paid servant of his Company, powerful only by a secret influence unbased on any substantial foundation, he leapt to the position of a shareholder with a larger stake than any man besides; no intrigue could shake him now, no sudden gust of petulant impatience at the tardiness of results displace him. He had never thought of this motive behind the Baron's large purchases of Omofaga shares; as he thought of it, he had not been himself had he not smiled. And his smile was of the same quality as had burst on his face when first Maggie Dennison dropped the veil and owned his sway.

One day he did not go down to the city, but spent

his time wandering on the heath, mapping out what he would do in the fast-approaching days in Omofaga. The prospects were clearing; he had had two interviews with Lord Detchmore, and the Minister had fallen back from his own objections on to the scruples of his colleagues. It was a promising sign, and Willie was pressing his advantage. The fall in the shares had been checked; Tom Loring wrote no more; and Mrs. Carlin had forgotten to mourn the extinct coal business. He came home, with a buoyant step, at four o'clock, to find Carlin awaiting him with dismayed face. There was the worst of news from Queen Street. Mr. Dennison had written announcing resignation of his place on the Board.

"It's a staggering blow," said Carlin, thrusting his hands into his pockets. "Can't you bring him round? Why is he doing it?"

"Well, what does he say?" asked Ruston, a frown on his brow.

"Oh, some nonsense—pressure of other business or something of that kind. Can't you go and see him, Willie? He's back in town. He writes from Curzon Street."

"I don't know why he does it," said Ruston slowly. "I knew he'd been selling out."

"He hasn't made money at that."

"No. I've made the profit there," said Ruston, with a sudden smile.

"The Baron bought 'em, eh?" laughed Carlin. "You generally come out right side up, Willie. You'll go and see him, though, won't you?"

Yes. He would go. That was the resolution which in a moment he reached. If there were danger, he must face it, if there were calamity, he must know it. He would go and see Harry Dennison.

As he was, on the stroke of half-past four, he jumped into a hansom-cab, and bade the man drive to Curzon Street.

Harry was not at home—nor Mrs. Dennison, added the servant. But both were expected soon.

"I'll wait," said Willie, and he was shown up into the drawing-room.

As the servant opened the door, he said in his low respectful tones,

"Mrs. Cormack is here, sir, waiting for Mrs. Dennison."

A moment later Willie Ruston was overwhelmed in a shrilly enthusiastic greeting. Mrs. Cormack had been in despair from *ennui;* Maggie's delay was endless, and Mr. Ruston was in verity a godsend. Indeed there was every appearance of sincerity in the lady's welcome. She stood and looked at him with an expression of most wicked and mischievous pleasure. The remorse detected by Tom Loring was not visible now; pure delight reigned supreme, and gave free scope to her frivolous fearlessness.

"*Enfin!*" she said. "Behold the villain of the piece!"

He opened his eyes in questioning.

"Oh, you think to deceive me too? Why, I have prophesied it."

"You are," said Willie, standing on the hearth-rug, and gazing at her nervous restless figure, so rich in half-expressed hints too subtle for language, "the most outrageous of women, Mrs. Cormack. Fortunately you have a fling at everybody, and the saints come off as badly as the sinners."

A shrug asserted her opinion of his pretences. He answered,

"I really am so unfortunate as not to have the least idea what you're driving at."

An inarticulate scornful little sound greeted this protest.

"Oh, well, I shall wait till you say something," remarked Willie, with a laugh. "I can't deny villainies wholesale, and I can't argue against Gallic ejaculations."

"You still come here?" she asked, ignoring his rudeness, and coming to close quarters with native audacity.

He looked at her for a moment, and then walked up to her chair, and stood over her. She leant back, gazing up at him with a smile.

"Look here! Don't talk nonsense," he said

brusquely; "even such talk as yours may do harm with fools."

"Fools!" she echoed. "You mean——?"

"More than half the world," he interrupted.

"Including——?" she began again in mockery.

"Some of our acquaintance," he answered, with the glimmer of a smile.

"Ah, I thought you were angry!" she cried, pointing at the smile on his lips.

"I shall be, if you don't hold your tongue."

"You beg me to be silent, Mr. Ruston?"

"I desire you not to chatter about me, Mrs. Cormack."

"Ah, what politeness! I shall say what I please," and she rose and stood facing him defiantly.

"I wish," he said, "that I could tell you what they do to gossiping women in Omofaga. It is so very disagreeable—and appropriate."

"Oh, I don't mind hearing."

"I can believe it, but I mind saying."

She flushed, and her breath came more quickly.

"No doubt you will enforce the treatment—in your own interest," she said.

"You won't be there," replied he, with affected regret.

"Well, here I shall say what I please."

"And who will listen?"

"One man, at least," she cried, in incautious

anger. "Ah, you'd like to beat me, wouldn't you?"

"Why suggest the impossible?" he asked, smiling. "I can't beat every——" He paused, and added with deliberateness, "every vulgar-minded woman in London;" and turning his back on her, he sat down and took up a newspaper that lay on the table.

For full five or six minutes Mrs. Cormack sat silent. Willie Ruston glanced through the leading article, and turned the paper, folding it neatly. There was a letter from a correspondent on the subject of the watersheds of Central South Africa, and he was reading it with attention. He thought that he recognised Tom Loring's hand. The watersheds of Omofaga were not given their due. Ah, and here was that old falsehood about arid wastes round Fort Imperial!

"By Jove, it's too bad!" he exclaimed aloud.

Mrs. Cormack, who had for the last few moments been watching him, first with a frown, then with a half-incredulous, half-amazed smile, burst out into laughter.

"Really, one might as well be offended with a grizzly bear!" she cried.

He put down the paper, and met her gaze.

"How in the world," she went on, "does she—there, I beg your pardon. How does anyone endure you, Mr. Ruston?"

As she spoke, before he could answer, the door

opened, and Harry Dennison came in. He entered with a hesitating step. After greeting Mrs. Cormack, he advanced towards Ruston. The latter held out his hand, and Harry took it. He did not look Ruston in the eyes.

"How are you?" said he. "You want to see me?"

"Well, for a moment, if you can spare the time—on business."

"Is it about my letter to Carlin?"

Ruston nodded. Mrs. Cormack kept a close watch.

"I—I can't alter that," said Harry, in a confused way. "Sir George is so crippled now, so much of the work falls on me; I have really no time."

"You might have left us your name."

"I couldn't do that, could I? Suppose you came to grief?" and he laughed uncomfortably.

Willie Ruston was afflicted by a sense of weakness—a vulnerability new in his experience—forbidding him to be urgent with the renegade. Had Carlin been present, he would have stood astounded at his chief's tonguetiedness. Mrs. Cormack smiled at it, and her smile, caught in a swift glance by Ruston, spurred him to a voluble appeal, that sounded to himself hollow and ineffective. It had no effect on Harry Dennison, who said little, but shook his head with unfailing resolution. Mrs. Cormack could not resist the temptation to offer matters an opportunity of development.

“But what does Maggie say to your desertion?” she asked in an innocently playful way.

Harry seemed nonplussed at the question, and Willie Ruston interposed.

“We needn’t bring Mrs. Dennison into it,” he said, smiling. “It’s a matter of business, and if Dennison has made up his mind——”

He ended with a shrug, and took up his hat.

“I—I think so, Ruston,” stumbled Harry.

“Where is Maggie?” asked Mrs. Cormack curiously. “They told me she would be in soon.”

“I don’t know,” said Harry. “She went out driving. She’s sometimes late in coming back.”

Ruston was shaking hands with Mrs. Cormack, and, when he walked out, Harry followed him. The two men went downstairs in silence. Harry opened the front door. Willie Ruston held out his hand, but Harry did not this time take it. Holding the door-knob, he looked at his visitor with a puzzled entreaty in his eyes, and his visitor suddenly felt sorry for him.

“I hope Mrs. Dennison is well?” said Ruston, after a pause.

“No,” answered Harry, with rough abruptness. “She’s not well. I knew how it would be; I told you. You would go.”

“My dear fellow——”

“You would talk to her about your miserable Company—our Company, if you like. I knew it would do her harm. I told you so."

He was pouring out his incoherent charges and repetitions in a fretful petulance.

"The doctor says her nerves are all wrong; she must be left alone. I see it. She's not herself."

"Then that," said Ruston, "is the real reason why you're severing yourself from us?"

"I don't want her to hear anything more about it; she got absorbed in it. I told you she would, but you wouldn't listen. Tom Loring thought just the same. But you would go."

"Is she ill?"

"Oh, I don't know that she's ill. She's—she's not herself. She's strange."

The note of distress in his voice grew more acute as he went on.

"I'm very sorry," said Willie, baldly. "Give her my best——"

"If you want to see me again about it, I—you'll always know where to find me in the City, won't you?" He shuffled his feet nervously, and twisted the door-knob as he spoke.

"You mean," asked Ruston, slowly, "that I'd better not come here?"

"Well, yes—just now," mumbled Harry; and he added apologetically, "She's seeing very few people just now, you know."

"As you please, of course," said Ruston, shortly. "I daresay you're right. I should like to say, Dennison, that I did not intend——" He suddenly stopped short. There was no need to rush unbidden into more falseness. "Good-bye," he said.

Harry took the offered hand in a limp grasp, but his eyes did not leave the ground. A moment later the door closed, and Ruston was alone outside—knowing that he had been turned out—in however ineffective blundering manner, yet, in fact, turned out—and by Harry Dennison. That Harry knew nothing, he hardly felt as a comfort; that perhaps he suspected hardly as a danger. He was angry and humiliated that such a thing should happen, and that he should be powerless to prevent, and without title to resent, the blow.

Looking up he caught sight dimly in the dim light of a lithe figure and a mocking face. Mrs. Cormack had regained her own house by means of the little gate, and stood leaning over the balcony smiling at him like some disguised fiend in a ballet or opera-bouffe. He heard a tinkling laugh. Had she listened? She was capable of it, and if she had, it might well be that she had caught a word or two. But perhaps his air and attitude were enough to tell the tale. She craned her neck over the parapet, and called to him.

"I hope we shall see you soon again. Of course, you'll be coming to see Maggie soon?"

"Oh, soon, I hope," he answered sturdily, and the low tinkle of laughter rang out again in answer.

Without more, he turned on his heel and walked down the street, a morose frown on his brow.

He had been gone some half-hour when, just before eight o'clock, Mrs. Dennison's victoria drove quickly up to the door. The evening was chilly and she was wearing her furs. Her face rose pale and rigid above them; and as she walked to the house, her steps dragged as though in weariness. She did not go upstairs, but knocked, almost timidly, at the door of her husband's study. Entering in obedience to his call, she found him sitting in his deep leathern arm-chair by the fire. She leant her arm on the back and stared over his head into the fire.

"Anyone been, Harry?" she asked.

He lifted his eyes with a start.

"Is it you, Maggie?" he cried, leaping up and seizing her hand. "Why, how cold you are, dear! Come and sit by the fire."

She did as he bade her.

"Any visitors?" she asked again.

"Ruston," he answered, turning and poking the fire as he did so. "He came to see me about the Company, you know."

"Is he long gone?"

"Yes, some time."

"He was angry, was he?"

"Yes, Maggie. But I stuck to it. I won't have anything more to do with the thing."

His petulance betrayed itself again in his voice. She said nothing, and, after a moment, he asked anxiously,

"Do you mind much? You know the doctor——"

"Oh, the doctor! No, Harry, I don't mind. Do as you like. He can get on without us."

"If you really mind, I'll try——"

"No, no, no," she burst out. "You're quite right. Of course you're right. I don't want you to go on. I'm tired of it too."

"Are you?" he asked, with a face suddenly brightening. "Are you really? Then I'm glad I told Ruston not to come bothering about it here."

Had he been listening, he could have heard the sharp indrawing of her breath.

"What do you mean?" she asked.

"Why, I told him not to come and see you till—till you were stronger."

She shot a terrified glance at him. His expression was merely anxious and, according to its wont when he was in a difficulty, apologetic.

"And he won't be here much longer now," he added, comfortingly.

"No, not much," she forced herself to murmur.

"Won't you go and dress for dinner?" he asked,
19

after a moment. "It's ordered for a quarter-past, and it's more than that now."

"Is it? I'll come directly. You go, and I'll follow you. I shan't be long."

He came near to where she sat.

"Are you feeling better?" he asked.

"Oh, Harry, Harry, I'm well, perfectly well! You and your doctor!" and she broke into an impatient laugh. "You'll persuade me into the grave before you've done."

He looked at her for a moment, and then, shaping his lips to whistle, sounded a few dreary notes and stole out of the room.

She heard the door close, and, sitting up, stretched her arms over her head. Then she sighed for relief at his going. It was much to be alone.

CHAPTER XXII.

A TOAST IN CHAMPAGNE.

"A MONTH to-day!" said Lady Valentine, pausing in her writing (she had just set "Octr. 10th" at the head of her paper) and gazing sorrowfully across the room at Marjory.

Marjory knew well what she meant. The poor woman was counting the days that still lay between her and the departure of her son.

"Now don't, mother," protested Marjory.

"Oh, I know I'm silly. I met Mr. Ruston at the Seminghams' yesterday, and he told me that there wasn't the least danger, and that it was a glorious chance for Walter—just what you said from the first, dear—and that Walter could run over and see me in about eighteen months' time. Oh, but, Marjory, I know it's dangerous!"

Marjory rose and crossed over to where her mother sat.

"You must be a Spartan matron, dear," said she. "You can't keep Walter in leading strings all his life."

“ No; but he might have stayed here, and got on, and gone into Parliament, and so on.” She paused and added, “ Like Evan, you know.”

Marjory coloured—more from self-reproach than embarrassment. She had gone in these last weeks terribly near to forgetting poor Evan’s existence.

“ Evan came in while I was at the Seminghams’. He looked so dull, poor fellow. I—I asked him to dinner, Marjory. He hasn’t been here for a long while. We haven’t seen nearly as much of him since we knew Mr. Ruston. I don’t think they like one another.”

“ You know why he hasn’t come here,” said Marjory softly.

“ He spent a week with me while you were at Dieppe. He seemed to like to hear about you.”

A smile of sad patience appeared on Marjory’s face.

“ Oh, my dear, you are such a bad hinter,” she half laughed, half moaned.

“ Poor Evan! I’m very sorry for him; but I can’t help it, can I ? ”

“ It would have been so nice.”

“ And you used to be such a mercenary creature ! ”

“ Ah, well, my dear, I want to keep one of my children with me. But, if it can’t be, it can’t.”

Marjory bent down and whispered in her mother’s ear, “ I’m not going to Omofaga, dear.”

"Well, I used to be half afraid of it," admitted Lady Valentine (she forgot that she had half hoped it also); "but you never seem to be interested in him now. Do you mind Evan coming to dinner?"

"Oh, no," said Marjory.

Since her return from Dieppe she had seemed to "mind" nothing. Relaxation of the strain under which her days passed there had left her numbed. She was conscious only of a passionate shrinking from the sight or company of the two people who had there filled her life. To meet them again forced her back in thought to that dreary mysterious night with its unsolved riddle, that she feared seeking to answer.

Her mother had called on Maggie Dennison, and came back with a flow of kindly lamentations over Maggie's white cheeks and listless weary air. Her brother was constantly with Ruston, and tried to persuade her to join parties of which he was to be one. She fenced with both of them, escaping on one plea and another; and Maggie's acquiescence in her absence, no less than Ruston's failure to make a chance of meeting her, strengthened her resolve to remain aloof.

Young Sir Walter also came to dinner that night; he was very gay and chatty, full of Omofaga and his fast-approaching expedition. He greeted Evan Haselden with a manner that claimed at least equality; nay, he lectured him a little on the ignorant interference of a stay-at-home House of Commons with the work of the men on the spot, in South Africa and elsewhere; people on this side would not give a man a free hand, he complained, and exhorted Evan to take no part in such ill-advised meddling.

Hence he was led on to the topic he was never now far away from—Willie Ruston—and he reproached his mother and sister for their want of attention to the hero.

This was the first gleam of light for poor Evan Haselden, for it told him that Willie Ruston was not, as he had feared, a successful rival. He rejoiced at Lady Valentine's hinted dislike of Ruston, and anxiously studied Marjory's face in hope of detecting a like disposition. But his vanity led him to return Walter's lecture, and he added an innuendo concerning the unscrupulousness of adventurers who cloaked money-making under specious pretences. Walter flared up in a moment, and the dinner ended in something like a dispute between the two young men.

" Well, Dennison's found him out, anyhow," said Evan bitterly. " He's cut the whole concern."

" We can do without Dennison," said young Sir Walter scornfully.

When the meal was finished, young Sir Walter, treating his friend without ceremony, carelessly pleaded an engagement, and went out. Lady Valentine, interpreting Evan's glances, and hoping against hope, seized the chance of leaving him alone with her daughter. Marjory watched the manœuvre without thwarting it. Her heart was more dead to Evan than it had ever been. Her experiences at Dieppe had aged her mind, and she found him less capable of stirring any feeling in her than even in the days when she had half made a hero out of Willie Ruston.

She waited for his words in resignation; and he, acute enough to mark her moods, began as a man begins who rushes on anticipated defeat. What is unintelligible seems most irresistible, and he knew not at what point to attack her indifference. He saw the change in her; he could have dated its beginning. The cause he found somehow in Ruston, but yet it was clear to him that she did not think of Ruston as a suitor—almost clear that she heard his name and thought of him with repulsion—and that the attraction he had once exercised over her was gone.

The weary talk wore to its close, ending with angry petulance on his side, and, at last, on hers with a grief that was half anger. He could not believe in her decision, unless there were one who had displaced him; and, seeing none save Ruston, in spite of his own convictions, he broke at last into a demand to be told whether she thought of him. Marjory started in horror, crying, " No, no," and, for all Evan's preoccupation, her vehemence amazed him.

" Oh, you've found him out too, perhaps," he

sneered. " You've found him out by now. All the same, it was his fault that you didn't care for me before."

" Evan," she implored, " do, pray, not talk like that. There's not a man in the whole world that I would not have for my husband rather than him."

" Now," he repeated; " but I'm speaking of before."

Half angry again at that he should allow himself such an insinuation, she yet liked him too well, and felt too unhappy to be insincere.

" Well," she said with a troubled smile, " if you like, I've found him out."

" Then, Marjory," cried Evan, in a spasm of reviving hope, " if that fellow's out of the way——"

But she would not hear him, and he flung himself out of the house with a rudeness that his love pardoned.

She heard him go, in aching sorrow that he, who felt few things deeply, should feel this one so deeply. Then, following the calls of society, which are followed in spite of most troubles, she, pale-faced and sad, and her mother, almost weeping in motherly distress, dressed themselves to go to a party. Lady Semingham was at home that night.

At the party all was gay and bright. Lady Semingham was chattering to Mr. Otto Heather. Semingham was trying to make Mr. Foster Belford understand the story of the Baron and Willie Ruston, Lord Detchmore, who had come in from a public dinner, was conspicuous in his blue riband, and was listening to Adela Ferrars with a smile on his face. Marjory sat down in a corner, hoping to escape introductions, and, when an old friend carried her mother off to eat an ice, she kept her place. Presently she heard cried, "Mrs. Dennison," and Maggie came in with her usual grace. It seemed as though the last few months were blotted out, and they were all again at that first party at Mrs. Dennison's where Willie Ruston had made his *entrée*. The illusion was not to lack confirmation, for, a moment later, Ruston himself was announced, and the sound of his name made Adela turn her head for one swift moment from her distinguished companion.

"Ah!" said Lord Detchmore, "then I must go. If I talk to him any more I'm a lost man."

"There's Mr. Loring in the corner—no, not that corner; that's Marjory Valentine. He will take your side."

"Why are they all in corners?" asked Detchmore.

"They don't want to be trodden on," said Adela, with a grimace. "You'd better take one too."

"There's Mrs. Dennison in a third corner. Shall I take that one, or should I get trodden on there?"

Adela looked up swiftly. His remark hinted at gossip afloat.

"Take one for yourself," she began, with an uneasy laugh. But the laugh suddenly became genuine for the very absurdity of the thing. "We'll go and join Mr. Loring, shall we?" she proposed.

Lord Detchmore acquiesced, and they walked over to where Tom stood. On their way, to their consternation, they encountered Willie Ruston.

"Now we're in for it," breathed Detchmore in low tones. But Ruston, with a bow, passed on, going straight as an arrow towards where Maggie Dennison sat. Lord Detchmore raised his eyebrows, Adela shut her fan with a click, Tom Loring, when they reached him, was frowning. Away across the room sat Marjory alone.

"Good heavens! he let me alone!" exclaimed Lord Detchmore.

"Perhaps I was your shield," said Adela. "He doesn't like me."

"Nor you, Loring, I expect?"

Presently Lord Detchmore moved away, leaving Adela and Tom together. They had been together a good deal lately, and their tones showed the intimacy of friendship.

"That man," said Adela quickly, "suspects something. He's a terrible old gossip, although he is a great statesman, of course. Can't you prevent them talking there together?"

"No," said Tom composedly, "I can't; she'd send me away if I went."

"Then I shall go. Why isn't Harry here?"

"He wouldn't come. I've been dining with him at the club."

"He ought to have come."

"I don't believe it would have made any difference."

Adela looked at him for a moment; then she walked swiftly across the room to Maggie Dennison, and held out her hand.

"Maggie, I haven't had a talk with you for ever so long. How do you do, Mr. Ruston?"

Ruston shook hands but did not move. He stood silently through two or three moments of Adela's forced chatter. Mrs. Dennison was sitting on a small couch, which would just hold two people; but she sat in the middle of it, and did not offer to make room for Adela. When Adela paused for want of anything to say, there was silence. She looked from the one to the other. Ruston smiled the smile that always exasperated her on his face—the smile of possession she called it in an attempt at definition.

"Look at Marjory!" said Mrs. Dennison. "How solitary she looks! Poor girl! Do go and talk to her, Adela."

"I came to talk to you," said Adela, in fiery temper.

"Well, I'll come and talk to you both directly," said Maggie.

"We're talking business," added Willie Ruston, still smiling.

"Oh, if you don't want me!" cried Adela, and she turned away, declaring in her heart that she had made the last effort of friendship.

With her going went Ruston's smile. He bent his head, and said in a low voice,

"You are the only woman whom I could have left like that, and the only one whom I could have found it hard to leave. Was it very hard for you?"

"It was just the truth for me," she answered.

"Of course you were angry and hurt. I was afraid you would be," he said.

She looked at him with a curious smile.

"But then," he continued, "you saw how I was placed. Do you think I didn't suffer in going? I've never had such a wrench in my life. Won't you forgive me, Maggie?"

"Forgive! What's the use of talking like that? What's the use of my 'forgiving' you for being what you are?"

"You talk as if you'd found me out in something."

She turned to him, saying very low,

"And haven't you found me out, too? We are face to face now, Willie."

He did not fully understand her. Half in justification, half in apology, he said doggedly,

" I simply had to go."

" Yes, you simply had to go. There was the railway. Oh, what's the use of talking about it?"

" I was afraid you meant to have nothing more to do with me."

" Or you wished it?" she asked quickly.

He started. She had discerned the thoughts that came into his mind in his solitary walks.

" Don't be afraid. I've wished it," she added.

There was a pause; then he, not denying her charge, whispered,

" I can't wish it now—not when I'm with you."

" To have nothing more to do with you! Ah, Willie, I have nothing to do with anything but you."

A swift glance from him told her that her appeal touched him.

" What else is left me? Can I live as I am living?"

" What are we to do?" he asked. " We shall see one another sometimes now. I can't come to your house, you know. But sometimes——"

" At a party—here and there! And the rest of the time I must live at—at home! Home!"

He bent to her, whispering,

" We must arrange——"

" No, no," she replied, passionately. " Don't you see?"

" What?" he asked, puzzled.

"Oh, you don't understand! It's not that. It's not that I can't live without you."

"I never said that," he interposed quickly.

"And yet I suppose it is that. But it's something more. Willie, I can't live with him."

"Does he suspect?" he asked in an eager whisper.

"I don't know. I really don't know. It's worse if he doesn't. Oh, if you knew what I feel when he looks at me and asks——"

"Asks what?"

"Nothing—nothing in words; but, Willie, everything, everything. I shall go mad, if I stay. And then don't you see——?" She stopped, going on again a moment later. "I've borne it till I could see you. But I can't go on bearing it."

He glanced at her.

"We can't talk about it here," he said. "Everybody will see how agitated you are."

For answer she schooled her face to rigidity, and her hands to motionlessness.

"You must talk about it—here and now," she said. "It's the only time I've seen you since—Dieppe. What are you going to do, Willie?"

He looked round. Then, with a smile, he offered his arm.

"I must take you to have something," he said. "Come, we must walk through the room."

She rose and took his arm. Bowing and smiling,

she turned to greet her acquaintances. She stopped to speak to Lord Detchmore, and exchanged a word with her host.

"Yes. What are you going to do?" she asked again, aloud.

They had reached the room where the *buffet* stood. Mrs. Dennison, after a few words to Lady Valentine, who was still there, sat down on a chair a little remote from the crowd. Ruston brought her a cup of coffee, and stood in front of her, with the half-conscious intention of shielding her from notice. She drank the coffee hastily; its heat brought a slight glow to her face.

"You're going as you planned?" she asked.

He answered in low, dry tones, emptied of all emotion.

"Yes," said he, "I'm going."

She stretched out her hand towards him imploringly.

"Willie, you must take me with you," she said.

He looked down with startled face.

"My God, Maggie!" he exclaimed.

"I can't stay here. I can't stay with him."

Her lips quivered; he took her cup from her (he feared that she would let it fall), and set it on the table. Behind them he heard merry voices; Semingham's was loud among them. The voices were coming near them.

"I must think," he whispered. "We can't talk now. I must see you again."

"Where?" she asked helplessly.

"Carlin's. Come up to-morrow. I can arrange it. For heaven's sake, begin to talk about something."

She looked up in his face.

"I could stand here and tell it to the room," she said, "sooner than live as I live now."

He had no time to answer. Semingham's arm was on his shoulder. Lord Detchmore stood by his side.

"I want," said Semingham, "to introduce Lord Detchmore to you, Mrs. Dennison. It's not at all disinterested of me. You must persuade him — you know what about."

"No, no," laughed the Minister, "I mustn't be talked to; it's highly improper, and I distrust my virtue."

"I'll be bound now that you were talking about Omofaga this very minute," pursued Semingham.

"Of course we were," said Ruston.

"You're a great enthusiast, Mrs. Dennison," smiled Detchmore. "You ought to go out, you know. Can't you persuade your husband to lend you to the expedition?"

Ruston could have killed the man for his *malapropos* jesting. Maggie Dennison seemed unable to answer it. Semingham broke in lightly,

“It would be a fine chance for proving the quality—and the equality—of women,” said he. “I always told Mrs. Dennison that she ought to be Queen of Omófaga.”

“And I hope,” said Detchmore, with a significant smile, “that there’ll soon be a railway to take you there.”

Even at that moment, the light of triumph came suddenly gleaming into Ruston’s eyes. He looked at Detchmore, who laughed and nodded.

“I think so. I think I shall be able to manage it,” he said.

“That’s an end to all our troubles,” said Semingham. “Come, we’ll drink to it.”

He signed to a waiter, who brought champagne. Lord Detchmore gallantly pressed a glass on Mrs. Dennison. She shook her head, but took it.

“Long life to Omofaga, and death to its enemies!” cried Semingham in burlesque heroics, and, with a laugh—that was, as his laughs so often were, as much at himself as at the rest of the world—he made a mock obeisance to Willie Ruston, adding, “*Moriamur pro rege nostro!*” and draining the glass.

Maggie Dennison’s eyes sparkled. Behind the mockery in Semingham’s jest, behind the only half make-believe homage which Detchmore’s humorous glance at Ruston showed, she saw the reality of deference, the acknowledgment of power in the man she loved. For a brief moment she tasted the troubled joy which she had paid so high to win. For a moment her eyes rested on Willie Ruston as a woman's eyes rest on a man who is the world's as well as hers, but also hers as he is not the world's. She sipped the champagne, echoing in her low rich voice, so that the men but just caught the words, "*Moriamur pro rege nostro*," and gave the glass into Ruston's hand.

A sudden seriousness fell upon them. Detchmore glanced at Semingham, and thence, curiously, at Willie Ruston, whose face was pale and marked with a deep-lined frown. Mrs. Dennison had sunk back in her chair, and her heart rose and fell in agitated breathings. Then Willie Ruston spoke in cool deliberate tones.

"The King there was a Queen," he said. "You've drunk to the wrong person, Semingham. I'll drink it right," and, bowing to Maggie Dennison, he drained his glass. Looking up, he found Detchmore's eyes on him in overpowering wonder.

"If I tell you a story, Lord Detchmore," said he, "you'll understand," and, yielding his place by Maggie Dennison, he took Detchmore with him, and they walked away in talk.

It was an hour later when Lord Detchmore took leave of his host.

"Well, did you hear the story?" asked Semingham.

"Yes; I heard it," said Detchmore, "about the telegram, wasn't it?"

"Yes, and of course, you see, it explains the toast."

"That sounds like a question, Semingham."

"Oh, no. The note of interrogation was—a printer's error."

"It's a remarkable story."

"It really is," said Semingham.

"And—is it the whole story?"

"Well, isn't it enough to justify the toast?"

"It—and she—are enough," said Detchmore. "But, Semingham——"

Lord Semingham, however, took him by the arm, walked him into the hall, got his hat and coat for him, helped him on with them, and wished him good-night. Detchmore submitted without resistance. Just at the last, however, as he fitted his hat on his head, he said,

"You're unusually explicit, Semingham. He goes to Omofaga soon, don't he?"

"Yes, thank God," said Semingham, almost cheerfully.

CHAPTER XXIII.

THE CUTTING OF THE KNOT.

" You can manage it for me ?" asked Willie Ruston.

" I suppose I can," answered Carlin; " but it's rather queer, isn't it, Willie ? "

" I don't know whether it's queer or not; but I must talk to her for half-an-hour."

" Why not at Curzon Street ? "

Ruston laughed a short little laugh.

" Do you really want the reason stated ? " he inquired.

Carlin shook his head gloomily, but he attempted no remonstrance.   He confined himself to saying,

" I hope the deuce you're not getting yourself into a mess ! "

" She'll be here about five.   You must be here, you know, and you must leave me with her.   Look here, Carlin, I only want a word with her."

" But my wife——"

" Send your wife somewhere—to the theatre with

the children, or somewhere. Mind you're here to receive her."

He issued his orders and walked away. He hated making arrangements of this sort, but there was (he told himself) no help for it. Anything was better than talking to Maggie Dennison before the world in a drawing-room. And it was for the last time. Removed from her presence, he felt clear about that. The knot must be cut; the thing must be finished. His approaching departure made a natural and inevitable end to it; and her mad suggestion of coming with him shewed in its real enormity as he mused on it in his solitary thoughts. For a moment she had carried him away. The picture of her pale eloquent face, and the gleam of her eager eyes had almost led him to self-betrayal; the idea of her in such a mood beside him in his work and his triumphs had seemed for the moment irresistible. She could double his strength and make joy of his toil. But it could not be so ; and for it to be so, if it could be, he must stand revealed as a traitor to his friend, and be banned for an outlaw by his acquaintance. He had been a traitor, of course, but he need not persist. They—she and he— must not stereotype a passing madness, nor refuse the rescue chance had given them. There was time to draw back, to set matters right again—at least, to trammel up the consequence of wrong.

When she came, and Carlin, frowning perplexedly,

had, with awkward excuses, taken himself away, he said all this to her in stumbling speech. From the exaltation of the evening before they fell pitiably. They had soared then in vaulting imagination over the bristling barriers; to-day they could rise to no such height. Reality pressed hard upon them, crushing their romance into crime, their passion to the vulgarity of an everyday intrigue. This secret backstairs meeting seemed to stamp all that passed at it with its own degrading sign; their high-wrought defiance of the world and the right dwindled before their eyes to a mean and sly evasiveness. So felt Willie Ruston; and Maggie Dennison sat silent while he painted for her what he felt. She did not interrupt him; now and again a shiver or a quick motion shewed that she heard him. At last he had said his say, and stood, leaning against the mantelpiece, looking down on her. Then, without glancing up, she asked,

"And what's to become of me, Willie?"

The sudden simple question revealed him to himself. Put in plain English, his rigmarole meant, "Go your way and I'll go mine." What he had said might be right—might be best—might be duty—might be religion—might be anything you would.. But a man may forfeit the right to do right.

"Of you?" he stammered.

"I can't live as I am," she said.

He began to pace up and down the room. She

sat almost listlessly in her chair. There was an air of helplessness about her. But she was slowly thinking over what he had said and realising its purport.

"You mean we're never to meet again?" she asked.

"Not that!" he cried, with a sudden heat that amazed himself. "Not that, Maggie. Why that?"

"Why that?" she repeated in wondering tones. "What else do you mean? You don't mean we should go on like this?"

He did not dare to answer either way. The one was now impossible—had swiftly, as he looked at her, come to seem impossible; the other was to treat her as not even he could treat her. She was not of the stuff to live a life like that.

There was silence while he waged with himself that strange preposterous struggle, where evil seemed good, and good a treachery not to be committed; wherein his brain seemed to invite to meanness, and his passion, for once, to point the better way.

"I wish to God we had never——" he began; but her despairing eyes stifled the feeble useless sentence on his lips.

At last he came near to her; the lines were deep on his forehead, and his mouth quivered under a forced smile. He laid his hand on her shoulder. She looked up questioningly.

"You know what you're asking?" he said.

She nodded her head.

"Then so be it," said he; and he went again and leant against the mantelpiece.

He felt that he had paid a debt with his life, but knew not whether the payment were too high.

It seemed to him long before she spoke—long enough for him to repeat again to himself what he had done—how that he, of all men, had made a burden that would break his shoulders, and had fettered his limbs for all his life's race—yet to be glad, too, that he had not shrunk from carrying what he had made, and had escaped coupling the craven with his other part.

"What do you mean?" she asked at last; and there was surprise in her tone.

"It shall be as you wish," he answered. "We'll go through with it together."

Though he was giving what she asked, she seemed hardly to understand.

"I can't let you go," he said; "and I suppose you can't let me go."

"But—but what'll happen?"

"God knows," said he. "We shall be a long way off, anyhow."

"In Omofaga, Willie?"

"Yes."

After a pause she rose and moved a step towards him.

"Why are you doing it?" she asked, searching his eyes with hers. "Is it just because I ask? Because you're sorry for me?"

She was standing near him, and he looked on her face. Then he sprang forward, catching her hands.

"It's because you're more to me than I ever thought any woman could be."

She let her hands lie in his.

"But you came here," she said, "meaning to send me away."

"I was a fool," he said, grimly, between his teeth.

She drew her hands away, and then whispered,

"And, Willie—Harry?"

Again he had nothing to answer. She stood looking at him with a wistful longing for a word of comfort. He gave none. She passed her hand across her eyes, and burst into sudden sobs.

"How miserable I am!" she sobbed. "I wish I was dead!"

He made as though to take her hand again, but she shrank, and he fell back. With one hand over her eyes, she felt her way back to her chair.

For five minutes or more she sat crying. Ruston did not move. He had nothing wherewith to console her, and he dared not touch her. Then she looked up.

"If I were dead?" she said.

"Hush! hush! You'd break my heart," he answered in low tones.
swered in low tones.

In the midst of her weeping, for an instant she smiled.

"Ah, Willie, Willie!" she said; and he knew that she read him through and through, so that he was ashamed to protest again.

She did not believe in that from him.

Presently her sobs ceased, and she crushed her handkerchief into a ball in her hand.

"Well, Maggie?" said he in hard even tones.

She rose again to her feet and came to him.

"Kiss me, Willie," she said; "I'm going back home."

He took her in his arms and kissed her. She released herself, and gazed long in his face.

"Why?" he asked. "You can't bear it; you know you can't. Come with me, Maggie. I don't understand you."

"No; I don't understand myself. I came here meaning to go with you. I came here thinking I could never bear to go back. Ah, you don't know what it is to live there now. But I must go back. Ah, how I hate it!"

She laid her hand on his arm.

"Think—if I came with you! Think, Willie!"

"Yes," he said, as though it had been wrung from him, "I know. But come all the same, Maggie," and with a sudden gust of passion he began to beseech her, declaring that he could not live without her.

“No, no,” she cried; “it’s not true, Willie, or you’re not the man I loved. Go on, dear; go on. I shall hear about you. I shall watch you.”

“But you’ll be here—with him,” he muttered in grim anger.

“Ah, Willie, are you still—still jealous? Even now?”

A silence fell between them.

“You shall come,” he said at last. “What do I care for him or the rest of them? I care for nothing but you.”

“I will not come, Willie. I dare not come. Willie, in a week—in a day—Willie, my dear, in an hour you will be glad that I would not come.”

As she spoke, her voice grew louder. The words sounded like a sentence on him.

“Is that why?” he asked, regarding her with moody eyes.

She hesitated before she answered, in bewildered despair.

“Yes. I don’t know. In part it is. And I daren’t think of Harry. Let me think, Willie, that it’s a little bit because of Harry and the children. I know I can’t expect you to believe it, but it is a little, though it’s more because of you.”

“Of me?—for my sake, do you mean?”

“No; not altogether for your sake; because of you.”

"And, Maggie, if he suspects?"

"He won't suspect," she said. "He would take my word against the world."

"They suspect—some of them—that woman Mrs. Cormack. And—does Marjory?"

"It is nothing. He won't believe. Marjory will not say a word."

"You'll persuade him that there was nothing——?"

"Yes; I'll persuade him," she answered.

She began to pull a glove on to her hand.

"I must go," she said. "It's nearly an hour since I came."

He took a step towards her.

"You won't come, Maggie?" he urged, and there was still eagerness in his voice.

"Not again, Willie. I can't stand it again. Good-bye. I've given you everything, Willie. And you'll think of me now and then?"

He was unmanned. He could not answer her, but turned towards the wall and covered his face with his hand.

"I shan't think of you like that," she said, a note of wondering reproach in her voice. "I shall think of you conquering. I like the hard look that they blame you for. Well, you'll have it soon again, Willie."

She moved towards the door. He did not turn.

She waited an instant looking at him. A smile was on her lips, and a tear trickled down her cheeks.

"It's like shutting the door on life, Willie," she said.

He sprang forward, but she raised her hand to stay him.

"No. It is—settled," said she; and she opened the door of the room and walked out into the little entrance-hall.

It was a wet evening, and the rain pattered on the roof of the projecting porch. They stood there a moment, till her cabman, who had taken refuge in the lee of the garden wall, brought his vehicle up to the door. They heard a step creak behind them in the hall, and then recede. Carlin was treading on tip-toe away.

Maggie Dennison put out her hand and met Ruston's. She pressed his hand with strength more than her own, and she said, very low,

"I am dying now—this way—for my king, Willie," and she stepped out into the rain, and climbed into the cab.

"Back to where you brought me from," she called to the man, and leaning forward, where the cab lamps caught her face, so that it gleamed like the face of some marble statue, she looked on Willie Ruston. Her lips moved, but he heard no word. The wheels turned and the lamps flashed, and she was carried away.

Willie started forward a step or two, then ran to the gate and, leaning on it, watched the red lights as they fled away; and long after they were gone, he stood there, bareheaded, in the drenching rain. He did not think; he still saw her, still heard her voice, and watched her broad low brow. She still stood before him, not the fairest of women, but the woman who was for him. And the rumble of retreating wheels sounded again in his ears. She was gone.

How long he stood he did not know. Presently he felt an arm passed through his, and he was led back to the house.

Old Carlin took him through the hall into his own little study, where a bright fire blazed, and gave him brandy, which he drank, and helped him off with his wet coat, and put a cricketing jacket on him, and pushed him into an arm-chair, and hunted for a pair of slippers for him.

All this while neither spoke; and at last Carlin, his tasks done, stood and warmed himself at the fire, looking steadily in front of him, and never at his friend.

"You dear old fool," said Willie Ruston.

"Ah, well, well, you mustn't take cold. If you were laid up now, what the deuce would become of Omofaga?"

His small, sharp, shrewd eyes blinked as he spoke, and he glanced at Willie Ruston as he named Omofaga.

Willie sprang to his feet with an oath.

"My God!" he cried, "why do you do this for me? Who'll do anything for her?"

Carlin blinked again, keeping his gaze aloof. Then he held out his hand, and Willie seized it, saying,

" I'm—I'm precious hard hit, old man."

The other nodded and, as Willie sank back in his chair, stole quietly out of the room, shutting the door close behind him.

Willie Ruston drew his chair nearer the fire, and spread out his hands to the blaze. And as the heat warmed his frame, the stupor of his mind passed, and he saw some of what was true—a glimpse of his naked self thrown up against the light of the love that others found for him. And he turned away his eyes, for it seemed to him that he could not look long and endure to live. And he groaned that he had won love and made for himself so mighty an accuser of debts that it lay not in him to pay. For even then, while he cursed himself, and cursed the nature that would not be changed in him; even while the words of his love were in his ears, and her presence near with him; even while life seemed naught for the emptiness her going made, and himself nothing but longing for her; even then, behind regret, behind remorse, behind agony, behind self-contempt and self-disgust, lay hidden, and deeper hidden as he thrust it down, the knowledge that he was glad—glad that his life was his own again, to lead and make and shape; wherein to take and hold, to play and win, to fasten on what was his, and to beat down his enemies before his face. That no man could rob him of, and the woman who could would not. So, as Maggie Dennison had said, in the passing of an hour he was glad; and in the passing of a week he had learnt to look in the face of the gladness which he had and loathed.

CHAPTER XXIV.

THE RETURN OF A FRIEND.

ABOUT a week later, Tom Loring sat at work in
his rooms. The table was strewn with books of blue
and of less alarming colours. Tom was smoking a
short pipe, and when he paused for a fresh idea, the
smoke welled out of his mouth, aye, and out of his
nose, thick and fast. For a while he wrote busily;
then a dash of his pen proclaimed a finished task, and
he lay back in the luxury of accomplishment. Presently he pushed back his chair, knocked out his pipe,
refilled it, and stretched himself on the sofa. After
the day's work came the day's dream; and the day's
dream dwelt on the coming of the evening hour, when
Tom was to take tea with Adela Ferrars at half-past
five. When he had an appointment like that, it
coloured his whole day, and made his hard labour
pass lightly. Also it helped him to forget what there
was in his own life and his friends' to trouble him;
and he nursed with quiet patience a love that did not
expect, that hardly hoped for, any issue. As he had

21 (317)

been content to be Harry Dennison's secretary, so he seemed satisfied to be an undeclared lover; finding enough for his modesty in what most men would have felt only a spur to urge them to press further.

He was roused by a step on the stair. A moment later, Harry Dennison burst into the room. Tom had seen him a few days before, uneasy, troubled, apologetic, talking of Maggie's strange indisposition—she was terribly out of sorts, he had said, and appeared to find all company and all talk irksome. He had spoken with a meek compassion that exasperated Tom—an unconsciousness of any hardship laid on him. Tom sat up, glad to console him for an hour; glad, perhaps, of any company that would trick an hour into the past. But to-day Harry's step was light; there was a smile on his lips, a gleam of hope in his eyes; he rushed to Tom, seized his hand, and, before he sat down or took off his hat, blurted out,

"Tom, old boy, she wants you to come back."

Tom started.

"What?" he cried, "Mrs. Dennison wants——"

"Yes," Harry went on, "she sent for me to-day, and told me that she saw how I missed you, and that she was sorry that she had—well—sorry for all the trouble, you know. Then she said, 'I wonder if Tom (she called you Tom) bears malice. Tell him Omofaga is quite gone, and I want him to come back, and if he'll come here, I'll go on my knees to him.'"

Harry stopped, smiling joyfully at his wonderful news. Tom wore a doubtful look.

"I can't tell you," said Harry, "what it means to me. It's not only your coming, old chap, though, heaven knows, I'm gladder of that than I've been of anything for months—but you see what it means, Tom? It means—why, it means that we're to be as we were before that fellow came. Tom, she spoke to me more as she used to-day."

His voice faltered; he spoke as an innocent loyal man might of a pardon from some loved capricious Sovereign. He had not understood the disfavour—he had dimly discerned inexplicable anger. Now it was past, and the sun shone again. Tom found himself saying,

"I wish there were more fellows in the world like you, Harry."

Harry's eyes opened in momentary astonishment at the irrelevance, but he was too full of his news and his request to stay for wonder.

"You'll come, Tom?" he asked. "You won't refuse her?" "Could any one refuse her anything?" was what his tone said. "We want you, Tom," he went on. "Hang it, I've had no one to speak to lately but that Cormack woman. I hate that woman. She's always hinting something—some lie or other, you know."

"Don't be too hard on little Mrs. Cormack," said Tom.

He remembered certain words which had shown a soft spot in Mrs. Cormack's heart. Harry did not know that she had grieved to hear him pacing up and down.

"You'll come, Tom? I know, of course, that you've a right to be angry, and to say you won't, and all that. But I know you won't do it. She's not well, Tom; and I—I can't always understand her. You used to understand her, Tom. She used to like your chaff, you know."

Tom would not enter on that. He pressed Harry's hand, answering,

"Of course, I'll come."

"Bring all this with you," cried Harry. "I shan't take up your time. You must stick to your own work as much as you like. When'll you come, Tom?"

"Why, to-morrow," said Tom Loring.

"Not now?"

"I might, if you like," smiled Tom.

"That's right, old chap. You can send round for your things. Bring a bag, and come to-night. Your room's there for you. I told them to keep it ready. Damn it, Tom, I thought things would come straight some day, and I kept it ready."

Had things come straight? Tom did not know.

"I say," pursued Harry, "I met Ruston to-day. He was very kind about my cutting the Omofaga. I wonder if I've been unjust to him!"

Then Tom smiled.

"I shouldn't bother about that, if I were you," said he.

"Well, he's not a thin-skinned chap, is he?" asked Harry, with relief.

"I should fancy not," said Tom.

"You see, he's off in a fortnight, and I thought we ought to part friends. So I told him—well, I said, you know, that when he came back, we should be glad to see him."

Tom began to laugh.

"You're getting quite a diplomatist, Harry," he said.

When Harry bustled away, his high spirits raised higher still by Tom's ready assent, Tom put on the garb of society, and took a cab to Adela Ferrars'.

"She'll be very pleased about this," thought Tom, as he went along. "It's good news to take her."

But whatever else Tom Loring knew, it is certain that he was not infallible on the subject of women and their feelings. He recognised the fact (having indeed suspected it many times before) when Adela, on the telling of his tidings, flashed out in petulance,

"She's sent for you back?" she asked; and Tom nodded.

"And you're going?" was the next quick question.

"Well, I could hardly refuse, could I?"

" No; I suppose not—at least not if you're Maggie Dennison's dog, for her to drive away with a stick and whistle back at her pleasure."

Tom had been drinking tea. He set down the cup, and feebly stroked his thigh with his hand; and he glanced at Adela (who was rattling the tea things) with deprecatory surprise.

" I hadn't thought of it like that," he ventured to remark.

" Oh, of course, you hadn't. Maggie sends you away—you go. Maggie sends a footman (well, then, Harry) for you—and back you go. And I suppose you'll say you're very sorry, won't you? and you'll promise you won't do it again, won't you ? "

" I don't think I shall be asked to do that," said Tom, speaking seriously, but showing a slight offence in his manner.

" But if she tells you to?" asked Adela scornfully.

" I didn't think you'd take it like this. Why shouldn't I go back ? "

" Oh, go back ! Go back and fetch and carry for Maggie, and write Harry's speeches till the end of the chapter. Oh, yes, go back."

Tom was puzzled.

" Has anything upset you to-day?" he asked.

" Has anything upset me !" echoed Adela, throwing her eyes up to the ceiling.

Tom finished his tea in a nervous gulp.

"I don't see why I shouldn't go back," he said.

"Well, I'm telling you to go back," said Adela. "Go back till she's had enough of you again—and then be turned out again."

Tom's face grew crimson.

"At least," he said slowly, "she has never spoken to me like that."

Adela had left the table and taken an arm-chair near the fire. Her back was to the door and her face towards Tom; she held a fire-screen between her and him, letting the blaze burn her face. But Tom, being unobservant, paid no attention to the position of the fire-screen. With a look of pain on his face, he took up his hat and rose to his feet. The meeting had been very different from what he had hoped.

"When do you go?" she asked brusquely.

"To-night. I'm just going back to my rooms for a bag, and then I shall go. I'm sorry you should— I'm sorry you don't think I'm doing right."

"It doesn't matter two straws what I think," said Adela behind the screen.

"Aye, but it does to me," said Tom.

She made no answer, and he stood for a moment, looking uneasily at the intruding fire-screen.

"Well, good-bye," he said.

"Good-bye."

"I shall see you soon, I hope."

“ If Maggie will let you come.”

“ I don’t know,” said Tom, “ what pleasure you find in that. It seems to me that as a gentleman—to say nothing of my being their friend—I must go back.”

She made no retort to this, and he moved a step towards the door. Then he turned and glanced at her. She had dropped the screen and her eyes were fixed on the fire. He sighed, frowned, shrugged his shoulders, turned, and made for the door again. In another second he would have been gone, but Adela cried softly,

_“ Mr. Loring.”

“ Yes,” he answered, coming to a halt.

“ Stay where you are a minute. Will you stay there a minute ? ”

“ An hour if you like,” said Tom.

“ I just want to say that—that—You’re coming nearer !—I want you to stay just where you are.”

Tom halted. He had, in fact, been coming slowly towards her.

“ I suppose,” said Adela, in quite an indifferent tone, “ that you’ll settle down with the Dennisons again ? ”

“ I don’t know. Yes ; I suppose so.”

“ Do you,” said Adela, sinking far into the recesses of the arm-chair, and holding up the screen again, “ like being there better than anywhere else ? I suppose Maggie is very charming ? ”

" You know just what she is."

" I'm sure I don't.   I'm a woman."

There was a long pause.   Tom felt absurd, standing there in the middle of the room.   Suddenly Adela leapt to her feet.

" Oh, go away!   Yes, you're right to go back.   Oh, yes, you're quite right.   Good-bye, Mr. Loring."

For a moment longer Tom stood still; then he moved, not towards the door, but towards Adela. When he spoke to her it was in a husky voice.   There were no sweet seducing tones in his voice.

" There's only one place in the world I really care to be," he said.

She did not speak.

" Harry and Mrs. Dennison are my friends," he said, " and as long as my time's my own, I'll give it to them.   But you don't suppose I go there for happiness ? "

" I don't suppose you ever did anything for happiness," said Adela, as though she were advancing a heinous charge.   " Really, nothing makes me so impatient as an unselfish man."

Tom smiled, but his smile was still a nervous one. Nevertheless he felt less absurd.   A distant presage of triumph stole into his mind.

" Don't you want me to go ? " he asked.

" You may go wherever you like," said she.

Tom came still nearer.   Adela held out her hand

and said "good-bye." Tom took the hand and held it.

"You see," he said, "I didn't think I had anywhere else to go. I did know a charming lady who was very witty and—very rich——!"

"I—I'll put some more in Omofaga and lose it. Oh, you are stupid, Tom! I really thought I should have to ask you myself, Tom. I'd have done it sooner than let you go."

It was not, happily, in the end necessary, and Adela said with a sigh,

"I believe that I've something to thank Mr. Ruston for, after all."

"What's that?"

"Why, he made me resolved to marry the man who of all the world was most unlike him."

"Then I've something to thank him for too."

"Tom," she said, "I don't know what I said to you. I—I was jealous of Maggie Dennison."

It was later by an hour when Tom Loring took his way, not to his rooms for a bag, but straight to Curzon Street. Adela had consented not to wait ("In one's eleventh season one does not want to wait," she said), and Tom considered that it was now hardly worth while to move. So he broke into Harry Dennison's study with a radiant face, crying,

"Harry, I'm not coming to you after all, old fellow."

Harry started up in dismay, but a short explanation turned his sorrow into rejoicing. Again and again he shook Tom's hand, telling him that the man who won a good wife won the greatest treasure earth could offer—and (he added) "by Jove, Tom, I believe the best chance of heaven too," and Tom gripped Harry's hand and cleared his own throat. Then they both felt very much ashamed, and, by way of forgetting this deplorable outburst of emotion (which Tom felt was quite un-English, and smacked indeed of Mrs. Cormack), agreed to go upstairs and announce the news to Maggie.

"She'll be delighted," said Harry.

Tom followed him upstairs to the drawing-room. Mrs. Dennison was sitting by the fire, doing nothing. But she sprang up when they came in, and advanced to meet Tom. He also felt like an ill-used subject as she gave him her hand and said,

"How forgiving you are, Tom!"

He looked in her face, and found her smiling under sad eyes. And he muttered some confused words about "all that" not mattering "tuppence." And indeed Mrs. Dennison seemed content to take the same view, for she smiled again and said,

"Ah, well, there's an end of it, anyhow."

Then Harry, who had been wondering why Tom delayed his tidings, burst out with them, and Tom added lamely,

" Yes, it's true, Mrs. Dennison.   So you see I can't come."

She laughed.

" I must accept your excuse," she said, and added a few kind words. " As for Adela," she went on, " she's never been to see me lately, but for your sake I'll be humble and go and see her to-morrow."

Harry, as though suddenly remembering, exclaimed that he must tell the children; in fact, he had an idea that a man liked to talk about his engagement to a woman alone, and plumed himself on getting out of the room with some dexterity. So Tom and Maggie Dennison were left for a little while together.

At first they talked of Adela, but it was on Tom's mind to say something else, and at last he contrived to give it utterance.

" I can't tell you," he said, looking away from her, " how glad I was to get your message. This—this trouble—has been horrible.   I know I behaved like a sulky fool.   I was quite wrong.   It's awfully good of you to forget it."

" Don't talk like that," she said in a low, slow voice.   " How do you think Harry's looking?"

" Oh, better than I have seen him for a long time.   But you're not looking very blooming, Mrs. Dennison."

She leant forward.

"Do you think he's happy, or is he worrying? He talks to you, you know."

"I think he's happier than he's been for months."

She lay back with a sigh.

"I hope so," she said.

"And you?" he asked, timidly yet urgently.

It seemed useless to pretend complete ignorance, yet impossible to assert any knowledge.

"Oh, why talk about me? Talk about Adela."

"I love Adela," he said gravely, "as I've never loved any other woman. But when I was a young man and came here, you were very kind to me. And I—no, I'll go on now—I looked up to you, and thought you the—the grandest woman I knew; and to us young men you were a sort of queen. Well, I haven't changed, Mrs. Dennison. I still think all that, and, if you ever want a friend to help you, or—or a servant to serve you, why, you can call on me."

She sat silent while he spoke, gazing at the ground in front of her. Tom grew bolder.

"There was one thing I came to Dieppe to do, but I hadn't the courage there. I wanted to tell you that Harry—that Harry was worthy of your love. I thought—well, I've gone further than I thought I could. You know; you must forgive me. If there's one thing in all the world that makes me feel all I ever felt for you, and more, it's to see him happy again, and you here trying to make him. Because I know that, in a way, it's difficult."

" Do you know? " she asked.

" Yes, I know. And, because I know, I tell you that you're a wife any man might thank God for."

Mrs. Dennison laughed; and Tom started at the jarring sound. Yet it was not a sound of mirth.

" You had temptations most of us haven't—yes, and a nature most of us haven't. And here you are. So,"—he rose from his chair and took her hand that drooped beside her, and bent his head and kissed it— " though I love Adela with all my heart, still I kiss your hand as your true and grateful servant, as I used to be in old days."

Tom stopped; he had said his say, and his voice had grown tremulous in the saying. Yet he had done it; he had told her what he felt; and he prayed that it might comfort her in the trouble that had lined her forehead and made her eyes sad.

Mrs. Dennison did not glance at him. For a moment she sat quite silent. Then she said,

" Thanks, Tom," and pressed his hand.

Then she suddenly sat up in her chair and held her hand out before her, and whispered to him words that he hardly heard.

" If you knew," she said, " you wouldn't kiss it; you'd spit on it."

Tom stood, silently, suddenly, wretchedly conscious

that he did not know what he ought to do. Then he blurted out,

" You'll stay with him ?"

" Yes, I shall stay with him," she said, glancing up; and Tom seemed to see in her eyes the picture of the long future that her words meant. And he went away with his joy eclipsed.

CHAPTER XXV.

THE MOVING CAR.

IN the month of June two years later, Lord Semingham sat on the terrace outside the drawing-room windows of his country house. By him sat Adela Loring, and Tom was to be seen a hundred yards away, smoking a pipe, and talking to Harry Dennison. Suddenly Semingham, who had been reading the newspaper, broke into a laugh.

"Listen to this," said he. "It is true that the vote for the Omofaga railway was carried, but a majority of ten is not a glorious victory, and there can be little doubt that the prestige of the Government will suffer considerably by such a narrow escape from defeat, and by Lord Detchmore's ill-advised championship of Mr. Ruston's speculative schemes. Why is the British Government to pull the chestnuts out of the fire for Mr. Ruston? That is what we ask."

Lord Semingham paused and added,

"They may well ask. I don't know. Do you?"

"Yesterday," observed Adela, "I received a communication from you in your official capacity. It was not a pleasant letter, Lord Semingham."

"I daresay not, madam," said Semingham.

"You told me that the Board regretted to say that, owing to unforeseen hindrances, the work in Omofaga had not advanced as rapidly as had been hoped, and that for the present it was considered advisable to devote all profits to the development of the Company's territory. You added however, that you had the utmost confidence in Mr. Ruston's zeal and ability, and in the ultimate success of the Company."

"Yes; that was the circular," said Semingham. "That is, in fact, for some time likely to be the circular."

They both laughed; then both grew grave, and sat silent side by side.

The drawing-room window was thrown open, and Lady Semingham looked out. She held a letter in her hand.

"Oh, fancy, Adela!" she cried. "Such a terrible thing has happened. I've had a letter from Marjory Valentine—she's in awful grief, poor child."

"Why, what about?" cried Adela.

"Poor young Walter Valentine has died of fever in Omofaga. He caught it at Fort Imperial, and he was dead in a week. Poor Lady Valentine! Isn't it sad?"

Adela and Semingham looked at one another. A

22

moment ago they had jested on the sacrifices demanded by Omofaga; Semingham had seen in the division on the vote for the railway a delightful extravagant burlesque on a larger stage of the fatefulness which he had whimsically read into Willie Ruston's darling scheme. Adela had fallen into his mood, adducing the circular as her evidence. They were taken at their word in grim earnest. Omofaga claimed real tears, as though in conscious malice it had set itself to outplay them at their sport.

"You don't say anything, Alfred," complained little Lady Semingham from the window.

"What is there to say?" asked he, spreading out his hands.

"The only son of his mother, and she is a widow," whispered Adela, gazing away over the sunny meadows.

Bessie Semingham looked at the pair for an instant, vaguely dissatisfied with their want of demonstrativeness. There seemed, as Alfred said, very little to say; it was so sad that there ought to have been more to say. But she could think of nothing herself, so, in her pretty little lisp, she repeated,

"How sad for poor Lady Valentine!" and slowly shut the window.

"He was a bright boy, with the makings of a man in him," said Semingham.

Adela nodded, and for a long while neither spoke

again. Then Semingham, with the air of a man who seeks relief from sad thoughts which cannot alter sadder facts, asked,

"Where are the Dennisons?"

"She went for a walk by herself, but I think she's come back and gone a stroll with Tom and Harry." As she spoke, she looked up and caught a puzzled look in Semingham's eye. "Yes," she went on in quick understanding. "I don't quite understand her either."

"But what do you think?" he asked, in his insatiable curiosity that no other feeling could altogether master.

"I don't want to think about it," said Adela. "But, yes, I'll tell you, if you like. She isn't happy."

"No. I could tell you that," said he.

"But Harry is happy. Lord Semingham, when I see her with him—her sweetness and kindness to him —I wonder."

This time it was Semingham who nodded silent assent.

"And," said Adela, with a glance of what seemed like defiance, "I pray."

"You're a good woman, Adela," said he.

"He sees no change in her, or he sees a change that makes him love her more. Surely, surely, some day, Lord Semingham——?"

She broke off, leaving her hope unexpressed, but a faint smile on her face told of it.

"It may be—some day," he said, as though he hardly hoped. Then, with one of his quick retreats, he took refuge in asking, "Are you happy with your husband, Adela? I hope to goodness you are."

"Perfectly," she answered, with a bright passing smile.

"But you get no dividends," he suggested, raising his brows.

"No; no dividends," said she. "No more do you."

"No; but we shall."

"I suppose we shall."

"He'll pull us through."

"I wish he'd never been born," cried Adela.

"Perhaps. Since he has, I shall keep my eye on him."

From the shrubbery at the side of the lawn, Maggie Dennison came out. She was leaning on her husband's arm, and Tom Loring walked with them. A minute later they had heard from Adela the news of the ending of young Sir Walter's life and hopes.

"Good God!" cried Harry Dennison in grief.

They sat down and began to talk sadly of the lost boy. Only Maggie Dennison said nothing. Her eyes were fixed on the sky, and she seemed hardly to hear. Yet Adela, stealing a glance at her, saw her clenched hand quiver.

"Do you remember," asked Semingham, "how at Dieppe Bessie would have it that the little red crosses were tombstones? She was quite pleased with the idea."

"Yes; and how horrified the old Baron was," said Adela.

"Both he and Walter gone!" mused Harry Dennison.

"Well, the omen is fulfilled now," said Tom Loring. "Ruston need not fear for himself."

Harry Dennison turned a sudden uneasy glance upon his wife. She looked up and met it with a calm sad smile.

"He was a brave boy," she said. "Mr. Ruston will be very sorry." She rose and laid her hand on her husband's arm. "Come, Harry," she said, "we'll walk again."

He rose and gave her his arm. She paused, glancing from one to the other of the group.

"You mustn't think he won't be sorry," she said pleadingly.

Then she pressed her husband's arm and walked away with him. They passed again into the fringing shrubbery and were lost to view. Tom Loring did not go with them this time, but sat down by his wife's side. For a while no one spoke. Then Adela said softly,

"She knows him better than we do. I suppose

he will be sorry. Will he be sorry for Marjory too?"

"If he thinks of her," said Semingham.

"Yes—if he thinks of her."

Semingham lit a cigarette and watched the smoke curl skywards.

"Some of us are bruised," said he, "and some of us are broken."

"Not beyond cure?" Adela beseeched, touching his arm.

"God knows," said he with a shrug.

"Not beyond cure?" she said again, insisting.

"I hope not, my dear," said Tom Loring gently.

"Bruised or broken—bruised or broken!" mused Semingham, watching his smoke-rings. "But the car moves on, eh, Adela?"

"Yes, the car moves on," said she.

"And I don't know," said Tom Loring, "that I'd care to be the god who sits in it."

.   .   .   .

While Maggie Dennison walked with Harry in the shrubbery, and the group on the terrace talked of the god in the car, on the other side of the world a man sat looking out of a window under a new-risen sun. Presently his eyes dropped, and they fell on a wooden cross that stood below the window. A cheap wreath of artificial flowers decked it—a wreath one of Ruston's company had carried over seas from the grave of his dead wife, and had brought out of his treasures to honour young Sir Walter's grave; because he and they all had loved the boy. And, as Maggie Dennison had said, Ruston also was sorry. His eyes dwelt on the cross, while he seemed to hear again Walter's merry laugh and confident ringing tones, and to see his brave, lithe figure as he sprang on his horse and cantered ahead of the party, eager for the road, or the sport, aye, or the fight. For a moment Willie Ruston's head fell, then he got up—the cross had sent his thoughts back to the far-off land he had left. He walked across the little square room to an iron-bound box; unlocking it, he searched amid a pile of papers and found a woman's letter. He began to read it, but, when he had read but half, he laid it gently down again among the papers and closed and locked the box. His face was white and set, his eyes gleamed as if in anger. Suddenly he muttered to himself,

" I loved that boy. I never thought of it killing him."

And on thought of the boy came another, and for an instant the stern mouth quivered, and he half-turned towards the box again. Then he jerked his head, muttering again; yet his face was softer, till a heavy frown grew upon it, and he pressed his hand for the shortest moment to his eyes.

It was over—over, though it was to come again. Treading heavily on the floor—there was no lightness left in his step—he reached the door, and found a dozen mounted men waiting for him, and a horse held for him. He looked round on the men; they were fine fellows, tall and stalwart, ready for anything. Slowly a smile broke on his face, an unmirthful smile, that lasted but till he had said,

"Well, boys, we must teach these fellows a little lesson to-day."

His followers laughed and joked, but none joined him where he rode at their head. The chief was a man to follow, not to ride with, they said, half in liking, half in dislike, wholly in trust and deference. Yet in old days he had been good to ride with too.

The car was moving on. Maybe Tom Loring was not very wrong, when he said that he would not care to be the man who sat in it.

THE END.

APPLETONS' TOWN AND COUNTRY LIBRARY.

PUBLISHED SEMIMONTHLY.

1. *The Steel Hammer.* By Louis Ulbach.
2. *Eve.* A Novel. By S. Baring-Gould.
3. *For Fifteen Years.* A Sequel to The Steel Hammer. By Louis Ulbach.
4. *A Counsel of Perfection.* A Novel. By Lucas Malet.
5. *The Deemster.* A Romance. By Hall Caine.
6. *A Virginia Inheritance.* By Edmund Pendleton.
7. *Ninette:* An Idyll of Provence. By the author of Véra.
8. *"The Right Honourable."* By Justin McCarthy and Mrs. Campbell-Praed.
9. *The Silence of Dean Maitland.* By Maxwell Gray.
10. *Mrs. Lorimer:* A Study in Black and White. By Lucas Malet.
11. *The Elect Lady.* By George MacDonald.
12. *The Mystery of the "Ocean Star."* By W. Clark Russell.
13. *Aristocracy.* A Novel.
14. *A Recoiling Vengeance.* By Frank Barrett. With Illustrations.
15. *The Secret of Fontaine-la-Croix.* By Margaret Field.
16. *The Master of Rathkelly.* By Hawley Smart.
17. *Donovan:* A Modern Englishman. By Edna Lyall.
18. *This Mortal Coil.* By Grant Allen.
19. *A Fair Emigrant.* By Rosa Mulholland.
20. *The Apostate.* By Ernest Daudet.
21. *Raleigh Westgate;* or, Epimenides in Maine. By Helen Kendrick Johnson.
22. *Arius the Libyan:* A Romance of the Primitive Church.
23. *Constance,* and *Calbot's Rival.* By Julian Hawthorne.
24. *We Two.* By Edna Lyall.
25. *A Dreamer of Dreams.* By the author of Thoth.
26. *The Ladies' Gallery.* By Justin McCarthy and Mrs. Campbell-Praed.
27. *The Reproach of Annesley.* By Maxwell Gray.
28. *Near to Happiness.*
29. *In the Wire-Grass.* By Louis Pendleton.
30. *Lace.* A Berlin Romance. By Paul Lindau.
31. *American Coin.* A Novel. By the author of Aristocracy.
32. *Won by Waiting.* By Edna Lyall.
33. *The Story of Helen Davenant.* By Violet Fane.
34. *The Light of Her Countenance.* By H. H. Boyesen.
35. *Mistress Beatrice Cope.* By M. E. Le Clerc.
36. *The Knight-Errant.* By Edna Lyall.
37. *In the Golden Days.* By Edna Lyall.
38. *Giraldi;* or, The Curse of Love. By Ross George Dering.
39. *A Hardy Norseman.* By Edna Lyall.
40. *The Romance of Jenny Harlowe,* and *Sketches of Maritime Life.* By W. Clark Russell.
41. *Passion's Slave.* By Richard Ashe-King.
42. *The Awakening of Mary Fenwick.* By Beatrice Whitby.
43. *Countess Loreley.* Translated from the German of Rudolf Menger.
44. *Blind Love.* By Wilkie Collins.
45. *The Dean's Daughter.* By Sophie F. F. Veitch.
46. *Countess Irene.* A Romance of Austrian Life. By J. Fogerty.
47. *Robert Browning's Principal Shorter Poems.*
48. *Frozen Hearts.* By G. Webb Appleton.
49. *Djambek the Georgian.* By A. G. von Suttner.
50. *The Craze of Christian Engelhart.* By Henry Faulkner Darnell.
51. *Lal.* By William A. Hammond, M. D.
52. *Aline.* A Novel. By Henry Gréville.
53. *Joost Avelingh.* A Dutch Story. By Maarten Maartens.
54. *Katy of Catoctin.* By George Alfred Townsend.
55. *Throckmorton.* A Novel. By Molly Elliot Seawell.
56. *Expatriation.* By the author of Aristocracy.
57. *Geoffrey Hampstead.* By T. S. Jarvis.

121. *From the Fire Rivers.* By Mrs. F. A. STEEL.
122. *An Innocent Impostor, and other Stories.* By MAXWELL GRAY.
123. *Ideala.* By SARAH GRAND.
124. *A Comedy of Masks.* By ERNEST DOWSON and ARTHUR MOORE.
125. *Relics.* By FRANCES MACNAB.
126. *Dodo: A Detail of the Day.* By E. F. BENSON.
127. *A Woman of Forty.* By ESMÈ STUART.
128. *Diana Tempest.* By MARY CHOLMONDELEY.
129. *The Recipe for Diamonds.* By C. J. CUTCLIFFE HYNE.
130. *Christina Chard.* By Mrs. CAMPBELL-PRAED.
131. *A Gray Eye or So.* By FRANK FRANKFORT MOORE.
132. *Earlscourt.* By ALEXANDER ALLARDYCE.
133. *A Marriage Ceremony.* By ADA CAMBRIDGE.
134. *A Ward in Chancery.* By Mrs. ALEXANDER.
135. *Lot 13.* By DOROTHEA GERARD.
136. *Our Manifold Nature.* By SARAH GRAND.
137. *A Costly Freak.* By MAXWELL GRAY.
138. *A Beginner.* By RHODA BROUGHTON.
139. *A Yellow Aster.* By Mrs. MANNINGTON CAFFYN ("IOTA").
140. *The Rubicon.* By E. F. BENSON.
141. *The Trespasser.* By GILBERT PARKER.
142. *The Rich Miss Riddell.* By DOROTHEA GERARD.
143. *Mary Fenwick's Daughter.* By BEATRICE WHITBY.
144. *Red Diamonds.* By JUSTIN McCARTHY.
145. *A Daughter of Music.* By G. COLMORE.
146. *Outlaw and Lawmaker.* By Mrs. CAMPBELL-PRAED.
147. *Dr. Janet of Harley Street.* By ARABELLA KENEALY.
148. *George Mandeville's Husband.* By C. E. RAIMOND.
149. *Vashti and Esther.*
150. *Timar's Two Worlds.* By M. JOKAI.
151. *A Victim of Good Luck.* By W. E. NORRIS.
152. *The Trail of the Sword.* By GILBERT PARKER.

Each, 12mo. Paper, 50 cents ; cloth, 75 cents and $1.00.

GEORG EBERS'S ROMANCES.

CLEOPATRA. Translated from the German by MARY J. SAFFORD. 2 volumes.

A THORNY PATH. (PER ASPERA.) Translated by CLARA BELL. 2 volumes.

AN EGYPTIAN PRINCESS. Translated by ELEANOR GROVE. 2 volumes.

UARDA. Translated by CLARA BELL. 2 volumes.

HOMO SUM. Translated by CLARA BELL. 1 volume.

THE SISTERS. Translated by CLARA BELL. 1 volume.

A QUESTION. Translated by MARY J. SAFFORD. 1 volume.

THE EMPEROR. Translated by CLARA BELL. 2 volumes.

THE BURGOMASTER'S WIFE. Translated by MARY J. SAFFORD. 1 volume.

A WORD, ONLY A WORD. Translated by MARY J. SAFFORD. 1 volume.

SERAPIS. Translated by CLARA BELL. 1 volume.

THE BRIDE OF THE NILE. Translated by CLARA BELL. 2 volumes.

MARGERY. (GRED.) Translated by CLARA BELL. 2 volumes.

JOSHUA. Translated by MARY J. SAFFORD. 1 volume.

THE ELIXIR, AND OTHER TALES. Translated by Mrs. EDWARD H. BELL. With Portrait of the Author. 1 volume.

Each of the above, 16mo, paper cover, 40 cents per volume ; cloth, 75 cents. Set of 22 volumes, cloth, in box, $16.50.

Also, 12mo edition of the above (except "A Question," "The Elixir," "Cleopatra," and "A Thorny Path "), in 8 volumes, cloth, $1.00 each.

New York: D. APPLETON & CO., Publishers, 72 Fifth Avenue.

*T*HE MANXMAN. By HALL CAINE, author of "The Deemster," "Capt'n Davy's Honeymoon," "The Scapegoat," etc. 12mo. Cloth, $1.50.

" Within the last few years there have come to the front in England, as writers of fiction, Barrie, Stevenson, Crockett, Weyman, and Hall Caine—the last, if we may judge by his latest work, the greatest."—*Boston Advertiser.*

" The most powerful story that has been written in the present generation."—*Edinburgh Scotsman.*

" It is difficult not to speak with what may seem indiscriminate praise of Mr. Hall Caine's new work."—*London Daily News.*

" The book, as a whole, is on a rare level of excellence—a level which we venture to predict will always be rare."—*London Chronicle.*

" A story of marvelously dramatic intensity, and in its ethical meaning has a force comparable only to Hawthorne's 'Scarlet Letter.'"—*Boston Beacon.*

" We agree with those who hold 'The Manxman' to be the best of Mr. Hall Caine's stories, and one of the best stories of the year."—*The Critic.*

" A singularly powerful and picturesque piece of work, extraordinarily dramatic. . . . Taken altogether, 'The Manxman' can not fail to enhance Mr. Hall Caine's reputation. It is a most powerful book."—*London Standard.*

" The story will assuredly rank with Mr. Caine's best work, and will obtain immediate favor with the lovers of strong and pure romance."—*London Globe.*

" The story that will absorb thousands of readers, and add rare laurels to the reputation of its author. . . . A work such as only a great story-teller could imagine. . . . A really great novel."—*Liverpool Post.*

" A book the construction and execution of which very few living European novelists could excel. The fullness of the texture in this last novel, the brilliancy of the successive episodes, the gravity and intensity of the sentiment, the art with which the ever-deepening central tragedy is relieved by what is picturesque and what is comic—all this has only to be seriously considered to be highly appreciated. 'The Manxman' is a contribution to literature, and the most fastidious critic would give in exchange for it a wilderness of that deciduous trash which our publishers call fiction."— EDMUND GOSSE, *in St. James's Gazette.*

" A work of rare merit and striking originality. . . . Indubitably the finest book that Mr Hall Caine has yet produced. It is a noble contribution to the enrichment of English fiction and the advancement of its author's fame."—*London Academy.*

" It will be read and reread, and take its place in the literary inheritance of the English-speaking nations, like George Eliot's great books."—*The Queen.*

" 'The Manxman,' we may say at once, confirms the author's claim to rank among the first novelists of the day. . . . The story is constructed and worked out with consummate skill, and, though intensely tragic, it is lightened by some charming descriptions of scenery and local customs. The characters, even the minor ones, are closely studied and finely executed, and show a deep experience and knowledge of human nature, in its lighter as well as darker aspects, such as only a master hand could faithfully have drawn."—*London Literary World.*

" In truth it is Mr. Caine's masterpiece, and congratulations are pouring in upon him from right and left. . . . The story had only been issued a few hours when Mr. Gladstone wrote to the Isle of Man to express his admiration for the new success."—*London correspondence of the New York Critic.*

New York: D. APPLETON & CO., 72 Fifth Avenue.